She arrived at dawn

Jesse watched the woman walk out of the mist and darkness. She was young, tall, and slender almost to the point of thinness, dressed like a teenager in faded jeans and running shoes, a cotton windbreaker zipped up to her chin against the raw autumn air. Her face was pale and angular, bare of makeup, her eyes shadowed and sad. It was an elegant face, compelling, with strong cheekbones and a delicately chiseled jawline.

She glanced toward the trees where he stood, and her eyes caught his attention. They were large, with a thick fringe of lashes and a hint of a slant. There was something familiar about those eyes.

Jesse straightened, staring at her. The sense of familiarity would not leave him. Did he know this woman?

Dear Reader,

Spellbinders! That's what we're striving for. The editors at Silhouette are determined to capture your imagination and win your heart with every single book we publish. Each month, six Special Editions are chosen with *you* in mind.

Our authors are our inspiration. Writers such as Nora Roberts, Tracy Sinclair, Kathleen Eagle, Carole Halston and Linda Howard—to name but a few—are masters at creating endearing characters and heartrending love stories. Their characters are everyday people—just like you and me—whose lives have been touched by love, whose dream and desire suddenly comes true!

So find a cozy, quiet place to read, and create your own special moment with a Silhouette Special Edition.

Sincerely,

Rosalind Noonan
Senior Editor
SILHOUETTE BOOKS

LUCY HAMILTON
An Unexpected Pleasure

Silhouette Special Edition

Published by Silhouette Books New York

America's Publisher of Contemporary Romance

SILHOUETTE BOOKS
300 East 42nd St., New York, N.Y. 10017

ISBN: 0-373-09337-3

First Silhouette Books printing October 1986

America's Publisher of Contemporary Romance

Printed in the U.S.A.

Books by Lucy Hamilton

Silhouette Special Edition

A Woman's Place #18
All's Fair #92
Shooting Star #172
The Bitter with the Sweet #206
An Unexpected Pleasure #337

Silhouette Intimate Moments

Agent Provocateur #126

LUCY HAMILTON

is happily married and the mother of a young daughter. She writes in her spare time, and she says she looks forward to "translating a lifelong affection for books into a new career."

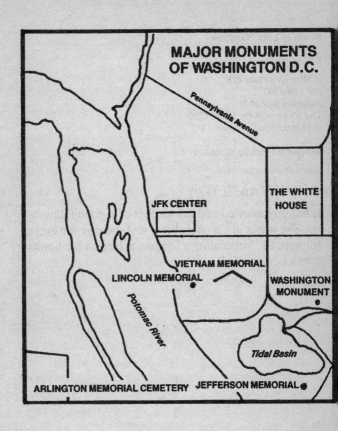

MAJOR MONUMENTS OF WASHINGTON D.C.

Pennsylvania Avenue

JFK CENTER

THE WHITE HOUSE

VIETNAM MEMORIAL

LINCOLN MEMORIAL

WASHINGTON MONUMENT

Potomac River

Tidal Basin

ARLINGTON MEMORIAL CEMETERY

JEFFERSON MEMORIAL

Chapter One

She came at dawn.

A wet night lightened sluggishly toward a gray and gloomy day, but Washington, D.C., still slept. The air was cold, and the low, sullen sky drizzled intermittently on the city, promising heavier rain to come. The globes of the streetlamps seemed to float in the air, glowing misty golden in the drab half-light of the growing day. They cast a russet gleam on her hair as she passed beneath them and shone wetly on the fallen leaves of October beneath her feet.

Jesse watched the woman walk out of the mist and darkness. She was young, tall, and slender almost to the point of thinness, dressed like a teenager in faded jeans and running shoes, with a cotton windbreaker zipped up to her chin against the raw autumn air. Her face was pale and angular, bare of makeup, her eyes shadowed and sad.

It was an elegant face, not pretty, but compelling, with strong cheekbones and a delicately chiseled jawline.

She glanced toward the trees where he stood, and her eyes caught his attention. They were large and slightly elongated, with a thick fringe of lashes and the hint of a slant. There was something familiar about those eyes, but Jesse couldn't pin down the reason for it. He straightened, staring at her. He couldn't see the color of her eyes and suddenly wished quite powerfully that he could.

That odd sense of familiarity persisted, and he squinted slightly, trying to see. Her nose was not small, but narrow and aristocratic...and very slightly crooked. Even across the distance separating them, he could see and recognize a small bump on the bridge of that arrogant nose. He wondered how she'd broken it. Her auburn hair was thick and wavy; misted and curling in the dampness, it tumbled in careless waves onto her shoulders. A coppery strand blew across her eyes, and she pushed it absently away.

She could have been any age from fifteen to thirty, but Jesse realized that his initial impression of her as teenaged had been mistaken. At first glance she looked like an underfed urchin, but there was something in the confident set of her shoulders, the smooth rhythm of her walk, that spoke of an unexpected maturity. Jesse shook the damp hair back from his forehead and watched her.

Few people visited the Vietnam Veterans' Memorial at that early hour. Perhaps, like Jesse himself, she had deliberately chosen to come at this time of relative solitude. She walked slowly along the gleaming black wall, past a photograph, a much-read and tattered letter, a posy of handpicked flowers left by other visitors.

He leaned his shoulder against a tree trunk, hands shoved deep into the pockets of his trench coat. She came to a halt some fifteen yards from him. He could see the rigid tension in her back as she stood there, too still, arms at her sides. She stood very stiff and erect, almost at attention, facing the wall from a distance of six or seven feet.

Jesse could hear the quiet patter of rain on the leaves above his head. Behind him, men's voices shattered the dawn silence. Annoyed at an intrusion into the contemplative silence, he turned his head to look. There were four of them approaching the wall, their voices beery and overloud, the sound carrying on the cold, still air.

"Drink a toast to old Charley!"

"Best friend a guy ever had!"

"Ol' Charley!"

They straggled to a halt on the other side of the wide, flattened V of polished black stone. The beery banter died away as they faced the wall. By unspoken consent they had formed up in a ragged line, four ordinary men hovering on the brink of middle age, their hair thinning, their belts straining around budding paunches.

One hand snapped up in a sharply formal salute, then another, and another. An imperceptible stiffening straightened their spines, the half-remembered echo of boot camp and parade grounds. The salutes held for several long seconds, then snapped down in unison. They turned and walked slowly, silently away, lost in memories twenty years old.

When Jesse looked at the woman again, she still stood motionless, staring at the wall before her. The rain was gaining strength, a steady shower that wet her hair and soaked into the shoulders of her thin jacket. Jesse didn't think she was even aware of it.

As he watched she took one halting step toward the wall, then three more, until she stood a pace away from the neatly carved columns of names. Once, twice, her right hand lifted toward the wall, then fell back to her side. The third time she raised her arm slowly until her fingertips were a scant inch from the polished stone. Jesse could see the tremor that shook her as she forced herself to reach across that last inch of space.

He knew how hard it was for her to make that last move. He could feel the effort it cost her to touch the cold stone, its glossy surface broken by the slight roughness of the lettering. He'd felt that same hesitance the first time he'd seen the wall, the same reluctance to touch it and feel the cold, smooth finality of it. He was well aware that it was possible to know something with your brain for years, yet never accept the terrible truth with your heart.

This was a place where people accepted the truth.

The name she touched was at the level of her shoulder. She ran her fingertips lightly across it, then traced the letters more slowly, one by one. Her right palm covered the name in a caressing movement while she lifted her left hand to her mouth, her knuckles pressed against her lips.

Jesse squinted, trying to focus more sharply on her. The sense of familiarity would not leave him. Did he know this woman? Had he known her sometime in the past?

The rain was falling steadily, soaking her jacket so the blue darkened to black, flattening her hair to her head. Heedless, she stared at that name while the rain mingled with her tears.

Jesse spun away from the sight, gazing blindly through the trees at the Reflecting Pool, its surface dimpling with rain. Her grief was raw and new in spite of the years; to watch was intrusive, an invasion.

Behind him Constitution Avenue was beginning to fill with workday traffic, but the honking of horns and squealing of brakes were muffled by the trees. He shivered and flipped up the collar of his trench coat, then glanced at the woman again. She still hadn't moved, and he felt a pang of concern for her. She wasn't dressed for this weather, and if she didn't dry off and get warm pretty soon she was going to be ill. She looked as if she could use a good meal, too, and also as if she couldn't afford many of those.

Jesse took a step toward her, then hesitated. This woman was a stranger to him, in spite of that odd sense of familiarity. He was torn between a desire to help and a reluctance to interfere. The desire to help won out.

He made his steps deliberately noisy on the sidewalk as he approached her, but she didn't notice him. Jesse paused two steps away.

The feeling of familiarity was stronger than ever as he studied her profile. He knew this woman. Somehow, from somewhere, he knew her. He searched his memory for a clue. The tears slid down her cheeks, and she scrubbed them absently away with the heel of her hand. He saw a sprinkling of freckles across her cheekbones and the bridge of her nose.

And suddenly he knew who she was. Jesse shrugged out of his trench coat and stepped closer.

"Cate?"

She turned toward him, but her gaze was blank. Her reddened eyes were wide and empty, her cheeks shining wet with tears and rain. She looked at him, but Jesse knew she didn't really see him.

"Cate? It is Cate Benton, isn't it?" Looking at her now, he could see the skinny, red-haired little girl in this slender woman with auburn waves.

"What...?" Her voice was raw and hoarse. She shook her head, blinked, and focused on his face. "Who are...?'' She frowned and concentrated on him; then her eyes widened. ''Is that you, Jesse? Jesse MacLeod?''

He smiled. ''It's me, all right.''

''I can't believe it.'' She reached out for his hand, not quite able to believe he was real. He must be, though, for his hand was warm and solid in hers. When he opened his arms to her, she walked into them without hesitation, linking her hands behind his waist and clinging to him as he embraced her.

For a long moment, they simply held each other, Jesse's cheek against Cate's wet hair, her face in his shoulder. He could feel the years sliding away as he held her. She was as slim and fine-boned as she had been as a child, though they'd called her skinny then.

When he released her, his arms felt empty. Her hair smelled of rain and flowers, and the fragrance lingered in his nostrils.

He kept her hands in his. ''Cate Benton, I can't believe it's actually you.''

''Me either.'' She shook her head again, trying to clear it. ''I can't... I'm sorry, Jesse, I can't seem to make sense.'' She scrubbed the tears away and sniffed hard. ''It's not Cate Benton anymore, though; it's Cate Drummond.'' She touched his cheek lightly, ran her fingers over his jacket sleeve. ''I just can't believe it's you! I never imagined—''

''Neither did I.'' He looked her up and down with a small smile. ''I can tell it's you, though. You never did take care of yourself.''

''What do you mean I don't...?''

He grinned at her with the familiarity of lifelong friendship. ''You're standing out here in the rain and getting soaked.''

She looked down at herself, surprised to see how wet she actually was. "Oh! I didn't realize." She brushed ineffectively at her soggy jacket. "I didn't mean to get all wet out here, but it's the first time I've been able to come here and see..."

She turned back to the wall and reached out to touch it again. Jesse read the name beneath her fingers. "Bradley J. Drummond." He looked from the name to Cate's face.

"Brad Drummond? Mike's friend Brad?" He remembered Brad well. Jesse's brother, Mike, was five years younger than he was. Mike and Brad and Cate, a year younger than the two boys, had been inseparable as children, the terrible trio of the neighborhood.

He remembered the three of them well, the two boys with little redheaded Caitlin following them. It seemed they'd always been trotting at his heels. Though he'd called them pests and despaired of ever being left alone, Jesse had been secretly flattered by their hero worship.

He remembered Cate as a fearless child, reckless and quick-tempered, an adventurer. Brad had been quieter, with a keen intelligence and steady courage hidden beneath his solemn demeanor. Jesse's brother Mike had been their hit man. Cate had concocted the pranks that got them into trouble, Mike had executed their tricks and Brad had been the one who got them out of trouble.

"Brad?" Jesse repeated, not wanting to believe what his eyes told him. "He...?"

Cate nodded. "We'd been married for two months when he left. He was only in Asia for seven weeks."

"You and Brad. That's why your name's different, of course." Jesse shook his head. "I just can't believe you were old enough to be married."

"It was right after I finished high school. I was almost eighteen, and Brad was nineteen." She smiled at his muttered exclamation of disbelief, a sad little smile. "We were in love, Jesse. Age didn't matter to us." She shook her head. "It feels like a million years ago. I thought I was so mature then, so grown-up. I didn't know what grown-up was."

Cate caressed the letters one last time, then turned away, jamming her hands in her jacket pockets. Jesse draped his coat around her shoulders.

"Come with me, Cate, and let me buy you a cup of coffee. You need to dry off and get warm."

"Coffee sounds good." She gave him a wan smile. "At the moment it even sounds better than those ice-cream bars you used to give me."

Absently she pulled his coat more closely around her, welcoming its warmth. Jesse could feel her shivering. He didn't know if it was from the cold or emotional shock, but he felt another stab of concern.

"Funny you would remember the ice-cream bars." He took her elbow to urge her along. "Come on, Cate. You need to get warm."

"Yeah, I know." She glanced at the wall, then nodded and let him lead her away. Jesse laid an arm lightly around her shoulders and led her toward Constitution Avenue.

"Did you leave your car somewhere around here?"

She shook her head. "I came on the bus. I didn't drive. Parking around here is impossible."

"You're telling me?" He laughed quietly. "How'd you get here? Walk?"

"Do you mind walking a little?"

"No." Her teeth were chattering. "I don't mind."

Jesse pulled her closer to his side. "There's a coffee shop near George Washington U. I go there a lot. The food's good, and it's not far to walk."

She was shivering harder now, and Jesse felt an upsurge of the same protective concern he'd felt when she fell off her bike and broke her nose. She'd been eight years old at the time and unwilling to admit her pain. She didn't want to admit how bad she felt now, either, but if he was any judge, and he assuredly was, she was well on her way to a nasty case of the flu.

The coffee shop was small and bright and noisy, its steamy atmosphere redolent with the aromas of coffee and bacon and morning rain. Cate followed Jesse to a booth near the back and huddled into the corner of the seat, shivering despite the warmth. She felt hollow inside, empty and echoing and a little disoriented, as if she were waking from a dream. She could tell that she was developing a fever.

"Keep that coat around you," Jesse commanded when she started to take it off. "You're halfway to pneumonia already, from the looks of it."

"Thanks." Too cold for pride, she huddled into it. "I could get awfully fond of this coat. It's a lot colder than I thought it would be this morning."

He smiled. "And I thought you liked the cold! You're probably the only kid in Columbus, Ohio, who put snowballs in the deep freeze so you could have snowball fights in July."

Cate smiled weakly. "That was snow. This is rain. Somehow the precipitation isn't as much fun when it's liquid."

"It's harder to throw, too."

Cate shook her head at him in disbelief. "I can't believe you'd remember those snowballs. You remember a lot of things, don't you?"

"Yeah. Like when you broke into my ice-cream truck and ate so much you made yourself sick. You threw up all over my fudge pops."

"Jesse! I want you forget stuff like that. That's embarrassing!"

"But memorable," he said, grinning. "Anyway, how could I forget all that stuff? You and Brad and Mike were always underfoot." He looked down, tracing the faded pattern on the pink Formica tabletop. "How old were you when I went away to college, Cate?"

"I was twelve." She looked across the table at him, her eyes grave. She reached carefully out to touch the narrow leather band that slashed starkly across his forehead and cheek. "What happened to your eye, Jesse? Was it the war?"

He touched the black leather patch that covered his left eye. "Mmm-hmm. I wouldn't have been surprised if you hadn't recognized me."

"You're still the Jesse I remember. An eye patch can't change that."

It was no more than the truth. The eye patch didn't detract from his looks, and Jesse's looks had always been exceptional. Six feet tall, with a rangy build that hinted at unsuspected strength, he was broad shouldered and narrow hipped, moving with athletic grace. His face was square, with deep-set eyes beneath level brows and lean cheeks, scored by deep lines. It was a harder face than the face she remembered, though, almost severe until he smiled.

"I never knew that you were hurt. I'm sorry, Jesse."

He shook his head sharply, almost angrily. "Don't be! This—" he touched the eye patch "—it's nothing. Your loss... I'm sorry, Cate. I didn't realize you and Brad..."

"You were already in Vietnam. I wouldn't expect you to know about it."

"Even so..."

"Hi, Dr. Jesse! Good to see ya." The waitress who greeted him was about forty, tall and angular with a plain, cheerful face. "What'll you have, kids?" She carried an order pad in one hand, a coffeepot in the other.

Jesse turned over their cups. "We'll have some coffee to start with, Angie, thanks." He grinned. "It's cold out there."

"You need a woman to take care of you, Jesse." She didn't seem to hear his derisive snort as she poured the coffee, put the pot on the table and turned her gap-toothed smile on Cate. "Do you take cream, miss?"

Cate smiled up at her. "No, thank you." She curled her fingers around the thick china cup, savoring the warmth. "This is all I need."

"We'll have breakfast, too, Angie," Jesse corrected. "The special for both of us."

"I'm not very hungry," Cate protested, but Jesse shook his head.

"You need breakfast. The special, Angie."

"You listen to the doc, sweetie," Angie concurred with a nod. "He knows what he's talking about." Scribbling on her pad, she strode away.

That was the second time she'd referred to him as a doctor, Cate realized. She grimaced wryly at Jesse. "You're just as bossy as you ever were, aren't you?"

He smiled in calm agreement, and Cate caught her breath. It was a gentle smile, but there was a hint of something else beneath it, something deep and dangerous. There was, she realized, more than a hint of danger about the man behind the expensively tailored veneer, something enticing and risky. She'd known that Jesse was considered a lady-killer in high school, but at the time, Cate had been too young to appreciate his appeal. Now she could clearly see both the appeal and the danger. He reminded her of a pirate, a very civilized pirate.

Cate began to realize that if he meant for her to eat breakfast, she was going to eat it, hungry or not.

"You're a pretty smooth operator, aren't you, Jesse? Or should that be Dr. MacLeod?"

"Yeah."

"You're actually a doctor?" She tipped her head to the side, studying him, trying to see the Jesse she remembered as a doctor. "What kind are you? What's your specialty?"

"Peds. Pediatrics."

She thought about that for a moment, then nodded. "Yes, I can see you with kids. You must like kids, since you let me live beyond the age of nine. I have trouble seeing you as a doctor, though. When did you decide on that?"

"When I got home from Asia. I still had a year of college to finish, and after that I went to medical school in Cleveland, at Case Western. I did my residency here in D.C., and I just stayed."

"Why medicine, though?" The Jesse she'd known had been an indifferent student. "I don't remember science being your long suit in school. I don't remember *school* being your long suit, for that matter."

"I was a medic in the marines. By the time I came home I knew what I wanted to do. What about you, Cate? What do you do?"

She was prevented from replying by the arrival of her breakfast. She gawked at the overflowing platter in front of her, then looked up disbelievingly at Jesse.

"You don't seriously expect me to eat all this?" *This* was two eggs, surrounded by crisp bacon, hash browns, sliced tomatoes, two large corn muffins with butter and jam, and a huge glass of orange juice. "This isn't a meal, Jesse, it's a whole buffet!"

He paused in buttering a muffin. "Everyone should start the day with a good breakfast," he told her seriously. "And you'd better eat up, or you'll hurt Angie's feelings. She's very proud of the food she serves."

Cate took a bite of her muffin. It was delicious. "Mmm. She has reason to be proud."

His mouth full, he nodded. "Eat."

She ate. Between bites she looked quizzically across the table at him. "How did you recognize me, Jesse? You haven't seen me in at least ten years."

He grinned, with a wickedly amused glint in his eye. "It's more like fifteen years, but I knew who you were. Do you really think I could forget the skinniest redhead in Columbus? You haven't changed much at all."

"Have too," she retorted around a mouthful of potatoes.

"Oh, yeah? How?"

"I got my braces off when I was fifteen." She swallowed and gave him a toothy grin.

"Lovely teeth" was his solemn assessment. "Your orthodontist should be proud of his work."

"It was Dr. Murchison. I know you remember *him*."

"The Annihilator?" Jesse shuddered. "The memories haunt me still." He waved his fork at her plate. "Eat up, Cate."

She lifted another forkful of eggs, but her stomach suddenly rebelled. She set them down untasted. "I'm sorry, Jesse, but I can't eat any more." She looked at her plate, then quickly closed her eyes as her stomach lurched. A spasm of shivering racked her, and she clenched her teeth and pulled Jesse's coat more closely around her.

Jesse reached across the table and laid his palm on her cheek. Cate stiffened when he touched her, startled by the quick rush of pleasure she felt. Jesse shook his head in gentle reproof and held her face between his hands.

"Hold still a minute. I think you have a fever." He touched her cheek, then her forehead, with cool, gentle fingers, and shook his head. "You sure do, little Cate. About 101, I'd say."

"I'm not little," she protested with the last of her strength, then abandoned pretense and dropped her face wearily into her hands, weak and shaky and nauseous. "And I can tell when I have a fever. Oh boy, Jesse, I feel crummy."

"I'll bet you do." He pushed back his plate and stood. "I'm going to take you home and plop you into bed."

"You're not tucking me in, Jesse MacLeod." She closed her eyes wearily.

"Just try and stop me. I tucked you in when you were six, and I can do it again."

There was still a little fight left in her. She raised her head to scowl blearily at him. "You *tried* to tuck me in, you mean. I bit you."

And she had, too, incensed at the idea that she, a very dignified and mature six-year-old, needed to be tucked in. Jesse remembered the incident ruefully.

"Try that this time, Cate, and I'll bite you back."

Chapter Two

"Come on, Cate, wake up."

The voice was deep and insistent, a rumble beneath her ear. Unwilling to wake, she squeezed her eyes shut and burrowed her face deeper into something warm and scratchy-woolly.

"Cate, come on!"

The voice was exasperated. Strong hands lifted her away from the woolly-warm something she had nestled against.

"Wake up so you can tell me where your door is, will you?"

He was obviously going to keep yelling at her until she opened her eyes, so Cate did so reluctantly. She blinked in confusion at the burled-walnut dashboard of an expensive car, then squinted out through the windshield at her familiar Georgetown street. She turned to look up into a face she'd known all her life, the familiar features seen through a glass that aged and distorted them.

It was Jesse's face, of course, just as it was Jesse's chest she was cuddled against, as she had as a child. She wasn't a child anymore, though, was she? Heat washed into her cheeks, and she slid quickly into her own seat, sitting very stiff and erect. The cool, dignified effect she sought was spoiled by a shattering sneeze.

Jesse pressed a snowy handkerchief into her hand. There was the suspicion of a chuckle in his voice. "Just tell me where your door is so I can park the car, okay?"

"It's around the corner, at the side of the building."

Sniffling, she pointed him in the right direction. Jesse turned into the narrow, cobbled side street and wedged his low-slung sports car into a barely adequate space directly in front of her door. He killed the engine and regarded her discreet brass number plate with amused exasperation.

Her apartment was on the second floor, above an art gallery, in an old, narrow brick building. It sat smugly on the corner of a block of old, narrow brick buildings housing other art galleries, exclusive little shops and small exotic restaurants. It was a newly fashionable district, not low-rent. A wrought-iron gate at street level opened onto a steep flight of stairs. Her door was on the second floor.

"If you have sense enough to find a place like this to live, Cate, how come you don't have sense enough to dress for the weather?"

Cate scrubbed at her pink nose with the handkerchief, then favored Jesse with a frosty gaze. "I told you, it's colder than I thought it was going to be," she informed him in a haughty croak. "And anyway, I never get sick."

"That's what they all say." He slid out of the car, then bent to grin at her. "And they all get sick, sooner or later."

Cate pushed her door open as he walked around the car, but when she tried to climb out she found she had no strength. She pushed herself to her feet and clung dizzily to the door, unable to go farther. Muttering under his breath about overly independent idiots, Jesse wrapped a strong arm around her waist and dragged her briskly up the stairs and into her apartment. Independent or not, Cate was grateful for his strength. She seemed to have none of her own.

It was blissfully warm and dry inside, and Cate was content to let Jesse remove his raincoat for her and deposit her in a deep wing chair. He hung the damp coat on an antique brass hall tree and looked around him, assessing, approving, and a touch amused. The apartment was furnished with a pleasing mixture of antiques and modern pieces, some good, some just appealing, with touches of dime-store whimsy. The living room was comfortably cluttered with books, prints and framed photographs, and an interesting mélange of knick-knacks. A second look showed Jesse that some of the knickknacks were cheap and bright, while a few were recognizable as good-to-excellent art. Standing beside a gaudy "souvenir of Washington" ashtray, a chinese porcelain horse caught his eye. The mixture reminded him of Cate, good taste with a sense of humor.

Cate rolled her head back against the soft chintz to look up at him. "Do you approve?" she asked dryly.

"Very much." He shrugged out of his tweed jacket. "It's nice to know you grew up to have good taste, Cate." He peeled her soggy windbreaker off her and dropped her back into the chair, where she slumped limply against the cushions. "Don't go anywhere, okay?" He strode out of the room.

"Where would I go?" she muttered to the empty room.

She had no intention of moving. It was all she could do to keep from sliding out of the chair and onto the floor. Her head was swimming, every muscle in her body ached, and spasmodic shivers racked her. She wanted nothing more than to crawl into bed and turn her electric blanket up to high.

"Here." Jesse strode back into the room and tossed a towel into her lap. He draped another over her head and perched on the arm of her chair to begin briskly rubbing her hair dry.

"I can do that," she protested, reaching up for the towel.

He pushed her hands away. "Quit trying to be tough, Cate; you're just getting in my way. You didn't have sense enough to come in out of the rain and now you're going to have to pay for it. Just sit there and relax."

Cate would have liked to argue, if only for the sake of her pride, but that wish died quickly under his gentle touch. There was something so comforting, so intimate and caring, about the simple gesture that her protest died unspoken.

Jesse moved the towel in rhythmic circles over her scalp, from her forehead to her nape, soothing and comforting, relaxing her into a warm, sleepy lassitude. After a few minutes he pulled her closer to him, leaning her against his leg. Cate abandoned any pretense of resistance. She laid her cheek on his hard thigh and went limp, her senses filled with the warm scent of him—spicy cologne, hospital antiseptic, and man.

She was utterly safe, because Jesse was taking care of her. She hadn't consciously thought about him in years, yet here he was, at the moment when she needed someone, taking care of her as he had when she was a child. She felt as secure and protected now as she had then. When he took the towel away she gave a sleepy murmur of protest.

"Come on, Cate." He pulled her out of the chair. "You can't go to sleep just yet."

He steered her down the hall, past her big kitchen and tiny dining room to the bathroom. Vast and Victorian, the bath had escaped renovation, retaining both its charm and its eccentricity. A wrought-iron boudoir chair stood beside a massive claw-foot tub, and Jesse set her on the chair. He twisted the porcelain taps to send a steaming torrent into the tub, then knelt in front of her and pulled off her soggy shoes.

Cate huddled on the stool and shivered. "How did you find the bathroom?"

He tossed the shoes aside and threw her an amused glance as he began on her socks. "I looked. I figured it had to be around here somewhere." The socks dispensed with, he pulled her thin sweater off and began unbuttoning her flannel shirt. That brought her out of her torpor.

"I can—" She was racked by a coughing spell. "I can do the rest." She swatted ineffectually at his hands.

"You'd collapse in the middle of it." He calmly finished undoing her shirt. "I'm a doctor, remember?" With a rather clinical detachment he stripped it off her. "And besides that I baby-sat you when you were six. I've already seen it all. Stand up."

She stood, wobbling, and he unbuckled her belt. His fingers brushed lightly over the sensitive skin of her stomach as he unsnapped the waistband of her jeans and slid the zipper down. Her shiver wasn't from the cold.

Oh, yes, there was a dangerous edge to this new Jesse. Even in her weakened state she could recognize it. Quick and light, his hands brushed her hips, thighs, knees as he stripped the jeans from her legs. He dropped them atop the pile of her discarded clothes and pulled a bath sheet off the rail to swaddle her warmly.

Though she was naked except for a gossamer bra and wispy panties, he didn't even seem to see her. Cate would have been horrified and infuriated if he'd made a pass at her. Naturally she was hurt and irritated by his evident detachment. She might still have been a bony six-year-old for all the notice he took of her.

It didn't seem fair. She was aware of him, strong and gentle and utterly male, but he seemed completely impervious to her.

He bent over the tub to test the water temperature and Cate watched helplessly, unable to look away. Muscles bunched and flexed as he moved, stretching the silky cotton shirt and soft flannel trousers. Cate felt an unfamiliar stirring low in her stomach.

She clenched her muscles against the sensation. She shouldn't think of him that way. He was treating her like a little sister; she should think of him as a big brother. That was the way things had always been between them.

"Jesse?" she asked abruptly.

"Hmm?" He adjusted the flow of water.

"Are you a good doctor?"

He grinned over his shoulder at her. "The very best. Why would you even ask?"

"Oh, come on! I'm serious."

"Hey, I'm so good I know exactly what's wrong with you. You have the same kind of virus I see in kids every day."

"Poor kids," Cate mumbled. "I hope *they* don't feel this rotten."

"These bugs always hit adults the hardest." He took a jar of bath crystals from a shelf and sniffed the contents, then added a generous dollop to the water. They burst into foam, filling the room with a spicy scent. With a satisfied nod Jesse turned off the water and stood.

"Can you do the rest?"

She nodded firmly. "I'll do it. You don't need to play baby-sitter any more."

"Aw, shucks! And I was just getting used to it...."

"Jesse!" she squeaked, her face flaming.

"I'm going, I'm going." He walked to the doorway, then paused. "I know you're just too tough for words, but yell if you need help, okay?"

"I will, I will, I promise!" she agreed.

She would have agreed to anything to get him out of the bathroom. She eased herself into the tub, sighing with relief. Jesse was right about the bath; it was exactly what she needed. It warmed and soothed her achy body. She slid down into the deep tub, submerging herself until she was half floating in the steaming water. Resting her head on the rim, she lifted one leg and watched the bubbles stream down it and plop onto the water.

She wasn't exactly voluptuous, was she? Skinny was more accurate, or even scrawny, with ribs that showed and boyishly narrow hips. Her breasts were high and as small as a girl's. She stared at them accusingly, then slid back beneath the water. No wonder he'd treated her like a child. On the other hand, she had to admit that could be for the best....

Warm and drowsy, she was drifting toward sleep when Jesse knocked on the door.

"Time to come out of there!" he called, startling her. "Do you need any help?"

"No!" she squeaked, and sat up quickly, sending a fragrant wave slopping over the side of the tub. The sudden movement made her dizzy. "No!" she repeated, more firmly this time. "I'll be right out."

"You'll need this." The door opened a few inches and Jesse's shirt-sleeved arm appeared, dropped a flannel nightgown on the towel rack and vanished. "Don't take long."

Cate didn't. She was well aware that Jesse was not above coming back to dress her himself. She rubbed herself quickly dry, shivering all the time, and dragged on the gown and her heavy robe, which hung behind the door. Warmly wrapped in layers of flannel and wool, she padded across the hall to her bedroom. Jesse was waiting for her there with aspirin and tea.

"Get in," he ordered, and held back the bedclothes for her. "You look like the dog's lunch."

"I don't feel *that* good."

"I'm not surprised."

Shivering, feverish and miserable, she crawled into bed and let him tuck the covers around her. If he thought of her as a child she might as well let him treat her like one. And he wasn't dangerous at all, she thought sleepily; he was gentle and caring, someone she could lean on.

She blinked groggily at him. "How come you can spend all this time treating me like a sick kid? Don't you have to go to work or something?"

"I was at the hospital all night. They won't look for me again until tomorrow morning. Here." He handed her the aspirin, and she looked at them quizzically.

"Don't I get something more exotic than aspirin? High-powered antibiotics or something?"

"The only thing that'll do your virus any good at all is plain old aspirin. Take 'em."

She obediently swallowed the tablets, then collapsed against the pillows. She let her eyes fall closed for a moment, then looked up at him. The room was dim, the drawn curtains closing out the gray day. The small bedside lamp cast a golden circle of light that didn't reach Jesse, who was seated on the end of the mattress. She couldn't read his expression.

"Jesse?"

He had to turn his head to look at her, because his left side, with the blind eye, was toward her. "Hmm?"

"Why are you doing all this for me? You don't have to."

"Sure I do." He grinned, teasing. "*Somebody* has to take care of you."

Cate shook her head. "I'm not a kid anymore, Jesse. Believe it or not, I'm all grown up. You've done too much for me already." She reached out to him, and he took her hand. "Thank you for everything, Jesse. I'll be fine." It was a fairly blunt dismissal, but she was suddenly, overwhelmingly tired, too tired to be polite. Jesse just smiled.

"I'll see that you are, Cate."

"Whatever." She closed her eyes and relaxed beneath the bedclothes. "G'night, Jesse. Or good morning." Her brain wasn't capable of further effort. Jesse clasped her limp hand in his for a moment, then lifted it to brush his lips lightly over her palm. She was asleep before he left the room.

Cate awakened to the dim light of late afternoon filtering through the curtains. She felt a little better. The worst of the aching and fever had abated, leaving her weak and thirsty. Her throat was parched and dry from the fever, and she badly wanted a drink. She lay and listened to the silence for several minutes, gathering her strength.

Jesse had apparently taken her rather impolite suggestion and gone on his way after tucking her in. Already the morning's events seemed fuzzy and unreal, like a film seen long ago. He had cared for her just the way he had when she was little. It had been nice. She could probably have gotten herself home and into bed on her own, but it would have been much more difficult. It had been nice to have him here.

And now that he'd gone she was lonely.

Resolutely she pushed the feeling away. She'd been alone for ten years without allowing herself to be lonely. She'd even managed to face that wall, after avoiding the ordeal for weeks.

When Cate closed her eyes she could see Brad's name, neatly cut into the black stone. Somehow the sight of that wall, that name, had hurt more than standing by the grave in the Ohio cemetery. It made the tragedy of the past real again, almost unbearably real. Closing her eyes, Cate gave herself up to the memories for a moment, then emptied her mind, letting them slide away.

She came back to the present, to her darkening bedroom and her thirst. Her mouth was dry and stale, her throat parched, and she *had* to have a drink. Carefully, since even cautious movement made the room sway and dip around her, she sat up and swung her legs off the bed. Her feet met the floor with a small thud, and to her dismay she felt the solid pine planks rock beneath the braided rug. She clutched her bedpost until the room steadied, then aimed herself at the door. The bathroom was just across the hall; surely she could make it that far.

She made it as far as her doorway before the lurching floor and her unsteady knees defeated her. She staggered as the room began to revolve, grabbed for the door frame, missed it and fell heavily to the floor.

She lay there with the wind knocked out of her, disgusted with her own weakness, and was astonished to hear the heavy pounding of running footsteps. She rolled onto her side and looked up to see Jesse hurtling toward her from the living room, his face dark and furious. He looked dangerous.

"What in God's name happened to you?" He flung himself to one knee beside her and dragged her up into his arms, her face against his chest. "What are you doing out here, anyway?" he demanded roughly.

Cate let her head loll back and stared blearily up at him. "I was trying to get a drink of water," she croaked.

"Why the hell didn't you call me to help?"

He was furious with her, but Cate was beginning to get angry, too, as her redhead's temper took over.

"Why should I?" she snapped. "I didn't know you were here."

"You idiot!" His arm tightened around her, shaking her. "Of course I'm here. Anyway, I left a glass of water on your nightstand."

"Well, how was I supposed to know that?" She glared at him for a moment; then her chin began to quiver. "I didn't mean to fall," she wailed, and as the tears welled over she buried her face in her hands.

"Oh, Cate." Jesse pulled her close, cradling her against his chest. "I shouldn't yell at you when you don't feel good." He stroked her hair soothingly. "Come on, sweetheart, I'm sorry." He cupped her chin in his palm and lifted her face away from his shirtfront. "I'm sorry, Catie," he murmured, and bent to kiss her mouth.

It was a gentle kiss, a tender kiss of comfort and consolation, but it had the oddest effect on Cate. Her lips moved beneath his, tentatively at first, then searching, seeking. She could feel a little tremor pass through him; then he responded. The tip of his tongue touched her upper lip, withdrew, then traced lightly across it, a gossamer touch, burning hot.

Cate began to shiver as desire washed through her. She was at the edge of a precipice, and she could either retreat or jump into the unknown. If she retreated Jesse would make no attempt to bring her back, but if she jumped... She shivered again, then with a little moan parted her lips to accept the kiss and threw herself over the edge.

And then she was dissolving, melting from the inside out, drowning in his kiss, and a volatile brew of surprise, sheer physical delight and something approaching fear. Without the support of his arms she would have collapsed in a heap. Her nightgown was chaste flannel, high necked and ankle length, but his hands burned through it as if it wasn't there. His fingers might have been caressing her naked skin, scorching and strong and gentle and arousing.

Arousing. She'd almost forgotten what that felt like, the melting inside, the thundering heart and shaky breathing and the pure, pure pleasure of it. She'd shut that part of herself away for so long that the delight was almost frightening. Oh, yes, Jesse was a dangerous man, and the danger was far more seductive and enticing than she had guessed. Primitive panic flared as quickly as desire had.

"No!" With the last scrap of her strength she wrenched her lips away from his. Shaking, she hid her face against his chest, fighting for strength, for control.

"Cate?" His voice was gentle, though she could feel his heart thundering beneath her cheek. "Are you all right?"

She nodded mutely into his shirtfront. He tried to lift her face to look at her, but she pulled away from his hand, burrowing into him.

His chest lifted and fell in a deep breath, and the heavy beat of his heart began to slow. "Do you still want a drink of water?" he asked the top of her head. She nodded again. "Okay, we'll go get it."

He hauled her to her feet and steadied her with one hand while he bent and picked up her robe. Taking great care to touch her as little as possible, he helped her into it, wrapping it closed across her breasts and high at her throat and tying the belt firmly. Cate knew her shyness amused him, but she couldn't bring herself to look up and meet his eyes. She couldn't help the fact that her face was scarlet, either.

Head down, eyes averted, she let Jesse lead her to the kitchen and seat her at the table. She stared at her hands until a steaming bowl of chicken noodle soup was shoved under her nose. A cup of tea followed the soup, and Cate glanced up to see Jesse smiling across the kitchen at her. Quickly she looked down again.

"Soup and tea?" she inquired of her bowl. "I didn't know you cooked."

"I cook quite well, actually, but not in this kitchen." He shook his head in gentle reproof as he ladled out another bowl of soup. "All I could find was a jar of mustard, a pickle jar with no pickles left in it and five different kinds of dry-mix soup. I'm amazed that your milk isn't curdled."

"I haven't been doing a lot of cooking lately," she replied loftily, and concentrated on tasting her soup.

"Have you been doing any eating? You look like you could use a few good meals."

Cate glanced at him, her eyes wounded, then dropped her head. "Thanks!" she snapped. "I know I'm skinny; you don't have to rub it in." Her voice wobbled on the edge of tears, and she bit her lip hard.

"Hey." Jesse reached out to catch her hand in his. "Don't get upset, Cate, please. It was just a joke." He took her chin in his fingers and turned her face to his. "It was a joke, Cate, that's all." His face was gentle, his smile kind.

"I know," she said. "But I can't..." Her voice broke.

"Oh, Cate, I'm sorry. I shouldn't tease you when you don't feel good." He stroked her cheek lightly, then took his hand away. "Just eat your soup. You need the fluids and salts."

"Okay, Doc." She gave him a watery smile and sipped her tea.

Jesse smiled gently at her then bent over his own bowl. She couldn't know what that smile meant to him. And she'd be better off not knowing what the kiss had meant. He'd seen the fear in her eyes, and though he didn't understand it, he didn't want to frighten her anymore. She couldn't look him in the face without blushing, her hands were trembling, she could barely speak...and all because he'd given in to feelings he hadn't even known he was experiencing.

He'd been concerned about her, worried that she wasn't taking care of herself. He'd been delighted to realize that the woman he found at the wall was little Cate Benton. He hadn't realized that she was Cate Drummond, a widow now, and he hadn't realized how badly he wanted her.

He still hadn't quite integrated his memories with this tall, graceful woman. She was a woman, little Cate was a woman now. Well, of course she was; it was just that he still had to get used to the idea.

On the other hand, Jesse thought, she had to get used to the idea of him as an overworked, underpaid pediatrician with only one eye and plenty of scars, both visible and invisible. He was no great bargain, he had to admit it. He rather thought that he would adjust to the new Cate more easily than she would adjust to him.

She wasn't adjusting well at the moment. When he slid his chair back she jumped as if she'd been stung. Jesse sighed heavily and dropped his elbows onto the table again. He spoke quietly.

"Please relax, Cate. *Please*. I can't stand for you to be afraid of me."

"Oh, Jesse..." Her voice was low and unhappy. "It's not that. I don't think I could be afraid of you."

"Well, you're a long way from being relaxed with me, aren't you?" He shook his head. "Cate, what did I do to scare you this way?"

She stared at him, her eyes wide and confused. "You know—"

"No, Cate, I don't."

"You..." She gulped. "You kissed me!"

He regarded her gravely for a moment. "Yes, I did. There's nothing so terrible about that, is there?" Cate had to look away from his level gaze after a moment. "Cate, you scared me half to death! I heard you fall, and I didn't know what had happened. You could have been seriously hurt, all for nothing more than a drink of water, so I yelled at you and made you cry. I wanted to comfort you. So I kissed you."

"To comfort me."

"To comfort you."

Cate looked down again. "That wasn't a comforting kiss."

"It was a little...more than I bargained for," Jesse said carefully. "You pack quite a punch, lady."

She looked up to see a smile tugging at his lips and couldn't quite suppress a chuckle. She tilted her head to the side, unconsciously flirtatious. "Did it ever occur to you that I might be too sick to be kissed?"

"Nope." He folded his arms across his chest and met her gaze with a smile, waiting for the next volley.

"Serve you right if you catch my virus."

"I'll take my chances."

Cate flushed at the gleam in his good eye. She wasn't as ready as he was to admit what that kiss had done to her.

He sobered. "Don't worry, Cate. I won't push you into anything you don't want. Now that we've found each other again after all this time, we can't just walk away from each other, though."

"You're right." She sighed. "I'm sorry, Jesse." She surprised them both by taking his hand in hers. Jesse turned his hand over and clasped her fingers. "I don't seem to be very sensible tonight."

"You don't feel good tonight, that's all." He rose, keeping her hand in his and drawing her to her feet. "And it's time for you to go back to bed." He pulled her against his side, supporting her with an arm around her waist. Cate smiled tiredly up at him.

"Are you gonna tuck me in again?" She didn't think she would mind at all...this time.

Jesse's grin was wicked. "That's the plan."

Chapter Three

"G'night, Jesse."

"Good night, Cate."

Jesse pressed the light switch as he returned Cate's mumbled good-night. Dim light from the hallway slanted across the room. It glinted on Cate's hair, tumbled on the pillow as she buried her face and drifted into sleep. Already he could hear her breathing deepen and slow. He half stepped back into the room, then caught himself.

He wanted to go back to her bedside and kiss her cheek again, as he had when he tucked her snugly beneath her patchwork quilt. That would accomplish little more than to rouse her from the sleep she needed so badly. That it would also satisfy something deep within him could not be allowed to matter.

"Good night, Cate," he whispered, and walked quietly back to the living room.

He had located her linen closet that afternoon, and now he took out a pillow and two blankets to make up a bed for himself on the sofa. It might not be the most comfortable bed available, but he would put up with a little discomfort in order to be near Cate. Her fever was returning; her cheek had burned hot against his lips. He wouldn't leave her alone while she was so ill.

The dream came to Cate out of a deep, heavy sleep. She was walking through a cold, foggy night, hurrying. The air was clammy on her face, dank and unpleasant with the odor of mold and wet leaves. She didn't want to go forward into the darkness, but she was compelled by some force she didn't understand. She was afraid; she could taste the fear, bitter and brassy in her throat. She couldn't turn back, though, and walked on into the swirling, blinding murk.

Someone was there, up ahead, calling to her from the darkness, calling her name. She quickened her pace, half running, slipping and stumbling on the wet grass. A sense of urgency was growing in her, pressing her on, and as the unseen being called to her again she suddenly realized why.

It wasn't just "someone" ahead of her; it was Brad, calling to her from the Memorial. He was there, she knew he was, just on the other side of the wall. She ran forward, plunging out of the mist. He was there, smiling at her, beckoning to her, whole and happy and young, so very young.

She could see him, and she ran toward him, eager to touch him, hold him, talk to him, and tell him all the things she never got to say.

She sprinted toward him, toward the wall, and crashed into the unyielding stone. Cold and solid and gleaming black, it stood implacably between them, barring any contact. Behind that impersonal barrier Brad was still beyond her reach.

"Brad!" Cate screamed his name again and again, but she couldn't reach him. He was moving away from her, drawn smoothly back into the darkness, still smiling, still beckoning. Sobbing in frustration and fury, she clawed at the wall with her fingernails, beat at it with her fists, frantic to reach him.

He drifted farther and farther away, back into the dark regions, smiling unseeingly at her. He was still beckoning to her from the distance when strong hands grasped her shoulders and pulled her roughly away from the wall.

Trapped within her nightmare, she fought the hands that were pulling her away from Brad. The grasp on her shoulders tightened, shaking her.

"Cate, wake up! Come on, sweetheart, wake up!" Jesse's voice in her ears and his arms around her finally brought her to wakefulness. "Cate, Cate, it's all right," he murmured over and over. She blinked at him, then burst into tears. "It's all right, Cate. It was only a dream."

He reassured her, murmuring soft words of comfort as she wept out her grief and fright, stroking her shoulders and back, holding her close and rocking her gently until her sobs quieted and her trembling eased.

When Cate raised her face from his naked shoulder to scrub at the tears on her cheeks, he stroked them away for her, then loosened his hold on her so he could look at her.

"You had a nightmare, Cate. Are you all right now?"

"Uh-huh." She sniffed. "I'm sorry to be so stupid...."

"It's not stupid. Everyone has bad dreams. There's nothing stupid about that."

Cate nodded again, but was prevented from replying by a spasm of coughing. Jesse held her until it was over, then stood and lifted her to her feet beside him. Cate shivered as the air struck her skin. Her fever had burned and then broken as she slept, leaving her nightgown clammy and damp, her hair matted to her scalp.

"Come on, sweetheart, you need to get changed."

Teeth chattering, she let him lead her to the bathroom and seat her on the dressing stool again. She huddled there while he turned on the radiant wall heater and took a clean gown from the cupboard. The heater coils began to glow, filling the room with warmth, and Jesse turned back to Cate, the gown in his hand.

"Stand up." He pulled her to her feet and began unbuttoning the neck of her sweat-damp gown.

"Jesse, what are you doing?"

"Getting you out of this nightgown." He began to pull it off her.

"No!" Cate clamped her arms against her sides, anchoring the gown. "I can do it myself."

"Maybe so." Jesse patiently took her hands and raised them, then quickly divested her of the garment. "But you're weak, and it'll be a lot easier, not to mention quicker, if I do it." He tossed the gown away and pushed her down on the stool, draping a bath sheet around her for warmth. "You'll feel better if you're clean." He turned to the sink and began soaping a washcloth. "It'll only take a minute to give you a quick wash."

Even as Cate's foggy brain was beginning to understand what that meant, he was turning back to her with the soapy cloth. He extracted her right arm from the towel and began to wash her hand. The warm cloth slid in soapy circles over her palm and wrist and forearm, past the sensitive hollow of her elbow and up to her shoulder.

He dropped the soapy cloth in the sink and took another to rinse away the soap.

Quick and neat, he washed her other arm, then loosened the towel. His hand smoothed the length of her back, from the fine bones of her shoulders to the satiny curves below her waist. His touch was light and soothing, and Cate's skin sprang to life beneath it, heating and tingling. When he opened the towel and touched the cloth to her throat she shivered, her muscles weak and lax, her skin exquisitely sensitive.

She watched his hand, lean and brown and strong, stroking the cloth over her breasts. Her breathing was shallow and shaky, her heartbeat racing as her body helplessly answered his touch. When he took the cloth away her swollen breasts and taut nipples betrayed her arousal.

Jesse said nothing, but Cate clutched the towel across her chest, hiding her body from him as she looked away to hide what must show in her eyes. He quickly washed and dried her legs, then dropped the fresh nightgown over her head, pulling it well down over her hips before taking the towel from beneath it.

Cate was grateful for his consideration, but painfully aware that Jesse knew what she'd been feeling. She was mortified, but not even her embarrassment could prevent her from watching his body hungrily as he hung up the towel he'd used.

He had been asleep, and wore only his flannel trousers, hastily pulled on when her screams woke him. She couldn't keep herself from watching the shift and play of the strong muscles beneath his skin. His shoulders were wide and powerfully muscled, his waist lean and narrow. There was a scar on his back, a white line that began at his side, just above his low-riding waistband, and slanted upward and inward to within an inch of his spine.

Cate shuddered. She didn't know what had caused that injury, she didn't think she wanted to know, but the scar was so close to his spine.... Jesse turned and caught her watching him, saw the expression on her face.

"What is it, Cate?"

She shook her head, mute.

"Come on, what's wrong? You look as if you'd seen a ghost."

"It's just...that scar...on your back," she said awkwardly.

He shrugged. "I have scars all over me, I'm afraid. I'm sorry they upset you; I know they're pretty ugly."

"It's not that!" she protested quickly. "It's not that at all! It's just that you were hurt...." Her voice trailed away, and Jesse dropped to one knee before her, taking her by the shoulders.

"That was a long time ago, Cate. The old wounds don't hurt anymore." He grinned wryly. "At least the ones that show don't."

Cate looked into his face and nodded. She knew all too well that invisible wounds could be far more painful than visible ones.

"Where's your hairbrush?" he asked, interrupting her thoughts.

"In the medicine cabinet." She pointed, and he took out the brush. "Why do you want that?"

"I'm going to brush your hair out, and then you're going back to bed. You look wrung out."

Cate wasn't flattered by his description, but she had to admit she was feeling weaker by the minute. She half thought Jesse's hair-brushing might be another sensuous experience, but she was wrong. She didn't know if she'd been afraid or eager, but she did feel a pang of disappointment when he merely brushed her hair quickly, then lifted her to her feet.

This time he didn't even kiss her, just pulled the covers up to her chin and brushed her cheek lightly with his fingertip as he left. She stared into the darkness, vaguely hurt, and annoyed with herself for it. She could hear his quiet footsteps, then the rustle of blankets and the soft creak of the sofa as he lay down. She almost imagined she could hear the quiet rhythm of his breathing. Cate turned on her side, getting comfortable, and tried to breathe in sync with Jesse.

She was drifting into sleep when the first teasings of the nightmare began again. She could feel the cold and the dampness on her face; she heard Brad calling to her and knew she could never reach him. . . .

She sat up with a jerk, her heart pounding violently in her chest. Through the thundering of her blood in her ears she could hear Jesse running to her.

He whipped around the door frame and crossed the room in two long strides to wrap her in his arms. This time she didn't hesitate to take the comfort he offered, but buried her head in his shoulder, emptying her mind of the dream.

"I'm sorry," she said when she could. Her voice wobbled.

"What for?"

"For being so stupid. I woke you up again."

"You had another nightmare," Jesse replied with gentle reproof. "I'm sure you planned that just to wake me up." His lips curved in a lopsided grin, and he brushed a fingertip over her cheek. "You were crying, Cate. I doubt that you do that for effect."

"I never cry!" she muttered, turning her face away and scowling at the quilt. "Hardly ever, anyway." She sniffed, blinking away the tears, and then yawned hugely. "I'm so tired... but I don't want to go to sleep again."

"You've got to sleep."

"The dream... it'll come back." She yawned again, fighting her exhaustion.

"Go to sleep, Cate." He loosened his arms and laid her back on the pillow, letting his hands slide lightly down her arms. As his hands left hers, though, Cate started, grabbing for him.

"No!" There was a high thread of panic in her voice. "Please, don't go!"

"But you have to sleep...."

"Don't go," she begged groggily. "I'll sleep if you're here." She pulled him closer. "Just lie down here and sleep."

Reluctantly Jesse relented. He might have continued to argue, but he could see it would be fruitless. Though he didn't know how he could sleep cuddled up to Cate, she clearly wasn't going to be able to sleep alone.

With a rueful sigh he slid onto the bed beside her, stretching himself out on top of the quilt. She nestled against him, then roused again.

"You can't sleep on top of the covers, Jesse. You'll freeze! Here." She lifted the bedclothes for him, then tucked them around him when he was underneath.

"Now will you go to sleep?" he asked in quiet desperation.

"Mmm." She curled against him, fitting her body to his. "This is nice." She breathed deeply, relaxing into comfort, while Jesse tensed, fighting the demands of his clamoring body. "Jesse?" she said suddenly.

"What is it, Cate?" he asked, exasperated.

"Isn't this nice?" She squirmed closer, her thighs brushing his, the soft curves of her derriere pressing his stomach.

Jesse laughed softly, a laugh that was nearly a groan. "Yes, it's nice, Cate. Now, go to *sleep*."

"Mmm." She sighed deeply, shifting to rest her head against his shoulder. He could tell that she'd slipped into sleep when her breathing deepened and slowed, becoming quiet and regular.

"Yes," he whispered against her hair. "It's nice." Jesse kissed her hair lightly and tried to relax, willing himself to sleep.

Beep-beep-beep-beep!
The shrill alarm jerked Cate violently from a deep and dreamless sleep. Heart pounding, she rolled over to flail at her alarm clock on the nightstand. She meant to flail at the clock, that is, but she rolled sharply up against something warm and solid and muscular.

Jesse grunted as her elbow thumped into his midsection. He just managed to catch her hand before she could decapitate him as she swung for the clock.

"Hold it!" He pulled her arm down. "Stop it, Cate" You're going to knock me out."

"I—" She jerked her hand free and clapped it over her mouth, staring at him with wide, shocked eyes.

Jesse could see the realization dawn—she'd spent the night with him in her bed—and then the shock and embarrassment. The alarm on his wristwatch beeped piercingly on.

"Cate?" he said gently.

She stared at him with stricken eyes.

"If you get off my arm I can shut my watch off."

Cate's eyes widened even farther; then with a gasp she rolled away and huddled on the far side of the bed. Jesse pressed a button on his watch and the beeping ceased, leaving in its place a reverberating silence. Jesse touched her shoulder, and she stiffened at the light contact.

"Did you sleep well?" he asked politely.

Cate rolled over to face him again, trying to keep her gaze riveted on his face. She wanted to avoid looking at the broad chest with its dusting of dark hair, at the muscular arms and strong shoulders. All she could think of was being held in those arms all night, of being cradled against that chest.

"Cate?" Jesse prompted after a few seconds.

"What?" Her voice was sharp with nerves.

"Did you sleep all right?"

"Oh! Oh, yes, I did."

"No more dreams?"

"Hm-mm." She shook her head.

"Good," he said, smiling. "Sleep was what you needed. Now I've got a favor to ask you. I have to get to the hospital, so if you don't mind I'll claim the bathroom first."

"I—I don't mind." Cate would have said practically anything to get him out of the room and gain herself some time alone.

"Thanks, sweetheart." He leaned over and kissed her burning cheek, then tossed back the bedclothes and rolled out of bed. He stood and stretched luxuriously, arms over his head, back arched.

Helplessly Cate followed his movements. His skin was stretched over the bone and muscle beneath it like tanned satin, smooth and gleaming with a soft luster. Dark hair trailed in a narrow line from the broad patch across his upper chest to disappear into the waistband of his slacks.

The gray flannel rode low on his hips, clinging to his hipbones before molding to his thigh muscles.

Cate realized where her thoughts were going and jerked her eyes back to his face. He was smiling at her, and she could feel her face burn even hotter than before. He knew what she'd been thinking. And he knew she knew he knew. Cate was about as embarrassed as it was possible for one woman to be.

Jesse took pity on her and walked to the door.

"I'll be out of your way in a few minutes." He paused. "Do you have a razor?"

"Medicine cabinet. Second shelf."

"Thanks!" Then he was gone.

Cate listened for the closing of the bathroom door, then flopped back on her pillow, pressing her hands to her scalding cheeks. Now that she was wide awake, in full command of all her faculties, she remembered everything that had gone on last night. She didn't know how she was going to face Jesse to say goodbye.

Of course she wouldn't be able to face him at all if she didn't get some clothes on. In a sudden flurry she erupted from the bed and sprinted to her closet to riffle frantically through the garments there.

A little while later, washed and combed and dressed, Cate hesitated outside the kitchen door. Her heart was pounding, her palms clammy. She didn't want to face Jesse. She wondered how often he awakened with a woman in his arms. He'd been blasé about it, but she was afraid she just wasn't capable of matching that casual attitude. If she couldn't match it, though, at least she could pretend she did. She drew a deep breath, wiped her damp palms down the legs of her jeans and pushed open the swinging door.

Jesse stood at the stove, wearing yesterday's slightly rumpled clothes, with a dish towel tucked in at his waist and the aroma of sizzling bacon rising around him. Cate felt her stomach protest hungrily. He must have gone out to buy food. She knew that all she'd had on hand was four poppy-seed bagels and a dab of elderly cream cheese.

Jesse glanced over his shoulder at the sound of the door. "Do you want two eggs or just one, Cate?" He turned back to his bacon, forking one slice onto a plate and rearranging the others.

"Just one." If Cate had expected a probing discussion of last night's sleeping arrangements she was going to be disappointed. She stood in the middle of the kitchen for a minute, unsure of what to do. "Shall I make toast?"

"Yeah, thanks. I'll have whole wheat."

Cate opened the refrigerator and studied the interior for a moment before she took out the bread and butter. She dropped two slices into the toaster and opened cabinet doors. Cans and packages were neatly stacked there.

"How much do I owe you for the groceries, Jesse?"

"Don't worry about it." He shrugged and broke an egg into the skillet. "How do you want your egg?"

"Over light. Jesse, listen to me, please. I can pay for my food. I may not always dress like a fashion plate, but I'm not poor."

"And you can remember what poor feels like, can't you?" Jesse looked around, and their gazes held the memories they shared.

Cate's eyes widened. "That's why you always gave me free ice-cream bars. You said they were damaged and you couldn't sell them, but that wasn't true was it?" Her tone was almost accusing.

"Your mother worked hard, harder than she should have had to, my mom always said. She could barely pay for the necessities. She didn't have money to give you for things like ice-cream bars."

"So you gave me the ice cream instead."

"Yeah."

Cate scowled. "I never guessed that—"

"You weren't *supposed* to guess, Cate. That was the point. Would you have accepted them if you knew?"

"You know I wouldn't have. I don't even like the idea of it now."

"Well, don't offer to pay me back for them after all this time," he said quickly. He turned from the stove, spatula in hand, frowning. "I mean it. I'll let you pay me back for the food, because you're right, you can afford to pay for your own groceries. I'm not even *discussing* those ice-cream bars, though." He glared at her as the egg in the skillet behind him sputtered and smoked. "Well?" he demanded. "Do you have anything to say about it?"

Cate's nerves began to ease; Jesse was funny when he was being stern.

She gave him a limpid gaze. "Yeah, I have something to say."

"What?"

"Your egg is burning."

"My—"

He whirled around and swore, snatching the skillet off the flame. The egg, which had been "over light" several minutes before, was now cooked to a solid rubbery blob. Muttering under his breath, Jesse scraped it into the garbage and took another from the carton. Cate caught his eye as he straightened and closed the refrigerator door, and his scowl deepened.

"And don't you even think about laughing, Caitlin Drummond, or you'll get that hockey puck for breakfast!"

"Not even a grin, I promise." With an effort she kept her face straight. Hands raised in innocent protest, she turned away, concentrating on the toast. By the time it popped up Jesse had two plates of perfect bacon and eggs on the table.

Cate couldn't think of anything intelligent to say, and Jesse seemed disinclined to talk. They ate in silence for several minutes, Cate's tension returning as she wondered when, or if, he would mention the things that hovered and hummed in the thick silence between them.

"You must be feeling better." The remark startled Cate out of her reverie.

"I am. My fever's gone; that makes the difference."

"That's good. As long as your fever doesn't climb again you shouldn't have any more nightmares."

Cate's gaze dropped to her plate. She stared in apparent fascination at the remnants of her breakfast while the quick, betraying blood rushed to her cheeks.

"That's good," she managed after a pause that lasted a few seconds too long.

"Cate." Jesse reached across the table to lift her chin so he could look into her face. "Don't be embarrassed, please. There's no reason for it."

She pulled her chin free. "That's easy for you to say."

Jesse watched her averted face. "It's the truth. You had a nightmare and you needed comfort. There's nothing wrong in that, Cate."

"Maybe not," she retorted, "but it's humiliating, and I wish it had never happened!" She shoved her chair back from the table with a screech and stood, clattering her dishes together to carry them to the sink. Her hands full of china, she spun around too quickly and her coffee cup slid off the pile. She watched it tumble toward the sink, grabbed for it too late, and flinched as it shattered against the white porcelain.

"Ohhh!" She stared at the shards of china and pressed a hand to her mouth as quick tears spilled down her cheeks. Jesse took the other dishes from her hands and set them carefully on the counter.

"Was it an antique cup, Cate? Or an heirloom?" He took her shoulders and turned her away from the sink, his gaze gentle and concerned. "Don't cry. We can check the antique shops and find one to replace it." He pulled her into his arms, stroking her hair. "Cate, don't cry, please. It's only a cup."

"I know it's only a cup! It's not even an antique or anything; it's just a cheap set of china I got a few years ago." She shoved herself roughly out of his arms, taking a couple of staggering steps away to lean heavily on the counter. "It's not the cup—"

Jesse followed to rest a hand lightly on her shoulder. "I know it's not the cup," he said gently. "I understand." His fingers moved against her shoulder, lightly caressing the delicate skin of her neck. With a gentle pressure he brought her around to face him. "I do understand." He lifted her face and brushed a tear from her cheek. "I wish I could stay here with you, but they'll be looking for me at the hospital in half an hour. You take care of yourself today. Drink a lot of fluids and eat a decent dinner." He waited until she nodded, then smiled. "That's good. I'll see you, Cate."

He bent to quickly kiss her lips, then was out of the kitchen in three strides. A moment later Cate heard the front door close behind him.

The quiet thump and click seemed to echo through the suddenly silent apartment. The kitchen, in fact the whole apartment, had felt crowded to Cate a moment before, but now the rooms seemed hollow and echoing with emptiness. She continued to lean against the tile countertop for several long minutes, then pushed herself away to begin the task of cleaning up.

Chapter Four

I'll see you,'" Cate grumbled under her breath as she loaded film into a camera. "'See you,' he says. See me when? This time next year? Phooey!"

She closed the back of the camera with an irritated snap and shoved it back on its shelf, then paced agitatedly across to the studio window and stared down at the narrow street below. The midday sun was warm even for Washington in October; it baked the cobbles and glowed on the bright russets and golds of fallen leaves.

Below her window three little girls jumped rope, chanting a nonsense rhyme that began, "Down in the valley where the green grass grows." A black cat, fat and sleek, drowsed atop a brick wall across the street, indifferent to a dog snuffling at the fascinatingly feline scent on the bricks below. A young couple, college age, strolled along the block, arms around each other, murmuring lovers' secrets.

It was a perfectly beautiful autumn day, and everyone seemed to be outside, enjoying themselves. Everyone except Cate. Cate was inside, cleaning lenses and loading cameras and fuming.

She had waited two long days for Jesse to make good on his promise to "See you." She had expected him to telephone or stop by to check on her. She'd spent two days leaping for the phone when it rang and sprinting to the door to greet the UPS man with her order of photo-print paper. The UPS man had been startled by the fervor of her greeting, but she had heard nothing at all from Jesse.

As her embarrassment at pulling him into her bed had faded, her desire to see Jesse again had grown. Her emotions had run the gamut from longing to impatience to disappointment to anger to worry and back to an impatient longing.

Her bout with the flu was only a memory now, and she felt perfectly fine...physically. She was thoroughly on edge, pacing her apartment, fidgety, unable to settle down to work. She looked outside again. The lovers had disappeared around the corner, and the dog had gone in search of easier prey, but the girls still jumped and giggled, and the cat still lazed in the sun.

Cate whirled away from the window. She would go nuts if she stayed inside another minute! Moving with brisk purpose, she picked a camera and two lenses off the shelf and stowed them in a padded bag, along with several rolls of film and some filters. She would go for a walk and photograph anything that caught her eye. It might not be photography with any concrete purpose, but at least she'd be out in the fresh air, getting some exercise.

And she wouldn't be stewing about why in the world Jesse hadn't at least telephoned to make sure she wasn't suffering a relapse.

Camera bag in hand, she swung open the coat closet in the front hall. Her battered leather jacket had been pushed to one side of the rail, and when she pulled it off the hanger something fell to the floor with a soft plop. She tucked the jacket under her arm and stooped to see what had fallen.

She reached past her waterproof boots and under her coats, and pulled out a pair of gloves. Men's gloves. Of supple suede, dark brown, thinly lined. They were Jesse's gloves, of course. She turned them in her hands, caressing the soft leather with her fingertips. The weather had been so warm that Jesse probably hadn't noticed that his gloves were gone.

She drew them through her fingers, then folded them neatly. He might not have missed them yet, but he'd need them when the weather turned cold again. She ought to return them, or at least call to tell him where they were. She didn't even have to speak to Jesse himself; she could call his office. After his departure she had found a business card propped on her living room telephone. His office number was printed on the front and, scrawled on the back, his home number and "Call me anytime, J."

She hadn't had the nerve to do that yet, but now she had the excuse of the gloves. She had to let him know where they were; she couldn't leave him gloveless in the coming cold weather. She turned toward the phone, then hesitated. What would she say to him?

"Jesse, I've got your gloves" would do for a start, she told herself, disgusted with her own timidity. She plucked the card off her bulletin board and punched the digits of his office number before she could chicken out.

It rang once. "Dr. MacLeod's office," said a mellifluous female voice. "How may I help you?"

"Is...uh... Could I speak to Jes...to Dr. MacLeod, please?"

Cate could have kicked herself for stammering like a schoolgirl. The receptionist didn't seem to notice anything amiss.

"Dr. MacLeod is out of the office right now. Did you want to make an appointment?"

"No. No, thank you. I'm not a patient of Dr. MacLeod's; I'm a friend of his."

"Would you like to leave a message?" the woman offered helpfully. "He should be in later this afternoon."

"All...all right. My name is Cate Drummond, and I have a pair of his gloves to return to him. Actually, I was just going out. I could bring them by the office and leave them with you, if you can tell me how to get there."

"There's no need to do that. Dr. MacLeod is at the hospital this afternoon. You can find him there."

"Oh, but I—"

"He'll be in the pediatrics pavilion. His office is on the sixth floor. Sooner or later he'll turn up there."

"But—"

Once again her protest was ignored. "I'll leave a message at the hospital so he'll know to expect you, Miss Drummond." Cate heard a beep on the line. "The other line is ringing. I'll leave that message at the hospital. Thank you for calling." With a click, she hung up.

Cate stared at the receiver for a moment, then carefully cradled it. That decision was out of her hands. Jesse would get the message, and if she didn't turn up with his gloves she would look like a cowardly idiot.

There was a little flutter of nerves in her stomach, but she ignored it. She was anxious to see Jesse. After all, she'd just been complaining about not seeing him. This was her chance.

In spite of her brave thoughts she carried her camera on her walk to the hospital. She used it, too, pausing to photograph some children playing, a squirrel crossing the street via a telephone wire and the rococo facade of the old hospital building. Holding the camera in her hands like a sophisticated security blanket, she entered the hospital and asked directions to the pediatrics pavilion.

The corridors were chilly and tile-walled, with that faint, indefinable smell that was unmistakably hospital. All around her people were hurrying down the halls, moving with brisk purpose. Cate hesitated to stop any of them to ask directions—they all looked so *busy*, probably on errands of life and death.

Instead she wandered on her own through a seemingly endless green-tiled labyrinth, following confusing and sometimes contradictory directional signs until at last she stood outside a set of wide doors labeled Pediatrics.

She hesitated in the middle of the wide hallway, uncertain what to do next. Three nurses emerged, laughing together as they walked past her. A young man in white, laden with bottles of some clear liquid, hurried into the ward. He pushed the door wide, and Cate could see a group of men and women standing in the middle of the hall.

There were perhaps ten of them, dressed in green surgical clothing or white lab coats over street clothes. One man, standing with his back to her, caught her eye.

He wasn't the tallest man there, but Cate would have recognized that easy, erect carriage anywhere, the bearing of the conquering pirate. As she watched he pushed back his lab coat and thrust his hands into the pockets of his flannel slacks, rocking back on his heels as he listened to one of the other men.

The young man in white hurried past them on his errand, and the door swung closed again, cutting off her view. Cate didn't allow herself time to hesitate, but stepped quickly forward, catching the door and pushing it open again before it stopped swinging.

She strode toward the group with the same purposeful air she had watched everyone else using. She might be shaking inside, but she was darned if she'd let it show. Jesse was laughing at something a lanky, balding man had said and didn't hear her approach.

"Jesse?" She touched his arm lightly, and he looked around to see who was there.

"Cate!" He broke into a broad grin and pulled her close to his side with an arm around her shoulders. The casually possessive gesture startled her, implying an intimacy his cohorts were quick to notice. He didn't stop with the hug, but bent and brushed his lips lightly over her cheek, then studied her face. "You look a lot better. How do you feel?"

"Fine. I feel fine." Somehow she managed to speak normally, despite the shaking in her chest. "That flu, or whatever it was, went away just as quickly as it hit me."

"You're sure?" He laid his hand along her cheek for a moment, checking for fever.

"I'm sure, really." Cate smiled, ignoring the chaos his touch was creating inside her. "I'm absolutely fine. I was fine the day before yesterday."

"Then why are you here?" He caught himself and grimaced at his misstatement. "I didn't mean that the way it sounded. I'm glad you decided to come see this place."

"Actually, I came to bring you these." She pulled the gloves from her pocket and presented them to him.

"And the camera?"

"I was on my way out to take some pictures when I found your gloves. Your receptionist said you were over here, so I just aimed my walk in this direction."

"Which takes the wind right out of my sails," he said dryly. "And my ego." He grinned. "Thank you for returning the gloves, Cate. I guess they fell out of my coat pocket. I'd never have noticed they were gone until some cold morning when I really needed them and they weren't there." His gratitude was sincere, and for a minute Cate just stood there grinning foolishly up at him.

"Aren't you going to introduce us, Jesse?"

If the lanky man Jesse had been laughing with hadn't interrupted her reverie Cate might have stood there all day, content just to look at Jesse.

"Only if I have to." Jesse slipped Cate's hand into his and drew her into the circle. "Cate, this pushy fellow is David Gold, pediatric cardiologist. David, meet Cate Drummond, a childhood friend I've just rediscovered." The lanky Dr. Gold took Cate's hand and shook it firmly.

"Delighted to meet you, Miss Drummond," he began, grinning. "I can see why Jesse's so reluctant to share you."

"Thank you," she said, blushing. "And call me Cate, please, Dr. Gold."

"Not Dr. Gold. David."

He released her hand, and Jesse presented her to the others. Cate knew she would forget most of the names and the faces they belonged with, but she remembered a couple. Maggie Oswald was in her late thirties, a pretty pediatrician with ash-blond hair and hazel eyes, and a Jim Somebody was an intern, a gentle-eyed bear of a man in his late twenties, with curly black hair and a thick beard. The rest, doctors and nurses and a respiratory therapist with an unpronounceable Slavic name, were a blur to her. She smiled and shook hands and hoped she'd manage to remember some of them.

After the introductions were made they slowly drifted away, leaving her alone with Jesse. Cate had felt their curious glances and wondered if they were interested in every woman Jesse was acquainted with, or just her. As Jesse led her toward his office she glanced back to see several pairs of eyes still trained on her.

She and Jesse walked around a corner and out of sight, and she sighed with relief.

"Whew! I feel like I've just been under a microscope! Are they that interested in all your woman friends?"

"They've never met any of my other woman friends. You'd better get used to the idea of being a hot topic of conversation."

"A hot topic, huh?" Cate retorted. "They're all very nice, but I feel like a lab specimen."

"Don't worry about it. Even the most interesting specimens lose their appeal after a while."

Cate cast a sidelong look at him. "I don't know if that was reassuring or an insult, Jesse."

He gave her a too-innocent smile. "Reassuring, of course. I wouldn't dream of insulting you, my dear." He stopped by a door and unlocked it. "Here's my cubbyhole." He ushered her inside and closed the door.

Cate looked around the office, windowless walls lined with bookshelves, bookshelves crammed with an extremely untidy mélange of books, journals, papers and knickknacks. His desk, a scratched and dented metal reject from some other office, was similarly heaped with academic jetsam, as well as a cheap ceramic mug proclaiming him the "World's Greatest Doctor," a truly lovely antique brass barometer and a plastic paper-weight containing a garish rendition of the Las Vegas Strip, which snowed when shaken.

She wondered what this eclectic clutter said about the man who kept it on his desk. Cate's fingers itched to lift her camera, to capture the contrast between the almost overwhelmingly cluttered office and the elegant man. She could take pictures of him here, pictures that would capture the emotion and action of his days. She wanted to take out her camera right then, but she knew what his response would be. She would have to lead up to it slowly, get Jesse used to the idea, but she was determined that she *would* take pictures of him.

In the meantime she would study him, looking for the aspects of his personality and character that she wanted to illustrate. She surveyed the eight-by-eight office again.

"I'm really glad you found my gloves," he was saying as he walked around the desk to rummage in a drawer. "I'm sorry about the gossip, though."

"The gossip?"

"Where do you think curiosity leads?" He looked up from the drawer and grinned.

"It leads to gossip," she concluded with weary resignation. She plucked a messy stack of medical journals off the only extra chair in the tiny room, set them on the floor and seated herself. "Terrific."

"Can't be helped." He shoved the drawer closed and sat down. "I'm not supposed to know," he said, giving her a conspiratorial grin, "but there's been a totally un-justifiable amount of discussion around this hospital about the state of my love life. I've kept my professional and social lives strictly separate, but discretion just seems to have fanned the flames. Now you walk innocently over here with my gloves and smack into the middle of all the speculation.''

Cate rolled her eyes. "Good timing is my middle name!"

Jesse laughed. "Don't worry, Cate, you'll be old news in a few days.''

"Now *that's* an insult!" she replied, laughing. "And don't try to tell me it isn't!"

"It was meant to be reassuring," he retorted with a wounded stare. He leaned back and waved a hand at their surroundings. "How do you like my office?"

"Lovely place," she told him politely, and he snorted in derision.

"If you like the insides of garbage dumpsters." He looked around and winced. "I'm not being persecuted, though. All the offices are like this. Except Maggie Oswald's. Somehow she managed to finagle the office at the end of the hall, and it has a window. She has some kind of plant growing on the sill.''

"Could you grow a plant in here?"

"Mushrooms, maybe," he suggested. "Don't they grow in the dark?"

"I think so. In caves or something." Cate shrugged. "I've never paid too much attention to where they come from.''

"Me either. I pay more attention to them when they're sautéed," Jesse said, drawing the words out with voluptuous relish, "and poured all over a nice, rare steak."

"Stop it!" she commanded. "I didn't have lunch and you're making me hungry.''

"I'm hungry, too. Why don't we go have dinner?"

Cate looked at her watch, then, quizzically, at Jesse. "It's only three-thirty."

"Yeah. You're hungry, I'm hungry, and just think— we won't have to wait for a table."

"Jesse, I only came over here to bring your gloves back," she protested.

She was nervous at the idea of sharing a meal with him. It had taken all her resolve simply to bring his gloves to him in person; she wasn't sure she was up to sharing a meal tête-à-tête.

"So?" Jesse shrugged off her protest. "Let me repay you for the favor with dinner."

He didn't wait for her to agree, but stood and shrugged off his lab coat, tossing it at an already overburdened bamboo coatrack. It hit, stuck for a moment, then slithered off. Jesse plucked it off the floor and draped it over one of the bamboo curlicues, then retrieved a tweed sport coat from beneath several other garments and pulled it on.

"Jesse, I'm not dressed for dinner in a restaurant." She spread her hands, and Jesse gave her jeans, sweater and leather jacket a quick study.

"Quit worrying about trivialities. You look fine."

"I'm dragging a big, clunky camera bag around!"

"So pretend it's a new style of purse. Nobody will even notice." Walking around the desk, he reached for Cate's hand. "Come on. I know the perfect place."

"A place where we can go dressed like this and get steak at three-thirty in the afternoon?" She let him push her out the door. "Sounds wonderful." Her tone was dry.

He paused in the process of locking the door to grin down at her. "If you think I'm talking about Chopped Steak à la Ronald, you're wrong. This is the real thing." His voice dropped to a seductive murmur. "Thick, tender aged beef, broiled to perfection, topped with—"

Cate shook her head. "You aren't going to let up until I agree to have dinner with you, are you?"

"Nope." He was hiding a grin. The dimple at the left corner of his mouth betrayed him. Cate had to drag her gaze away from the dimple, from his lips, then drag her mind away from thoughts of kissing that dimple and those lips.

She looked down, hiding her face from his too-perceptive gaze, making a business of rearranging the contents of her camera bag until she had her expression under control.

"Okay." She looked up and grinned. "If I can't win I'll give in gracefully." She fell into step with him. "I'm warning you, though—this had better be a good steak!"

Jesse laughed.

If the aromas in the air were any indication, Bobby's Steak House served very good steaks indeed, but the atmosphere was something Cate hadn't expected. Despite its prosaic name the restaurant was a place for romantic dinners for two. The tables were separated and screened by lush banks of potted greenery, the lights, even at four in the afternoon, were so low as to be nearly non-existent, and the banquette they were seated on was plush, comfortable and curved, so that she and Jesse were seated too close together for Cate's peace of mind.

Jesse didn't seem to notice anything unusual. He draped an arm along the banquette behind her and sat back to peruse the menu in comfort.

"What'll you have, Cate?"

"Ahh." She pulled herself together to glance at the menu. "The filet, I think. Medium." She didn't think she could make sense of the printed words, but filet mignon was always safe.

"Sounds good." Jesse turned to the hovering waiter and ordered Cate's filet, a porterhouse for himself and a bottle of red wine. He handed the menus to the waiter and sat back again, his arm still behind Cate's shoulders, his fingers brushing her neck. She stiffened in spite of herself, and he looked at her curiously.

"What's the matter, Cate? Is the seat uncomfortable?"

"No, no, it's fine." Her voice was breathy and unsteady.

"Then what is it? You're as nervous as a cat. Do I scare you that much?"

Cate edged away from him even as she shook her head in quick denial. "You don't scare me, Jesse...."

"Then what's wrong? You're about to jump out of your skin."

"It's just this place." She waved a hand at their dim surroundings.

"What's the matter with it?" Jesse looked around and saw nothing amiss.

"It's just... it's so dark, and private... and romantic!" she blurted.

Jesse just stared for a moment. "And you're uncomfortable because it's dark and private and romantic in here?" he asked incredulously.

Cate nodded in mute embarrassment. After a very long moment Jesse sat back, letting his breath hiss out between his teeth. With exaggerated care he removed his arm from her shoulders.

"I wonder," he said with quietly stinging sarcasm, "if you'd prefer a drive-up hamburger after all." He gave her a look of intense exasperation. "I brought you here because the food's good, Cate. They broil the best steak I've had in D.C., and it's never noisy." He favored her with a last fulminating glance and stared gloomily at the thin lemon slice floating in his water glass.

The silence hung thickly between them.

"I'm being an idiot, aren't I?" Cate said at last to the tablecloth.

"You certainly are," Jesse agreed. "But if you eat every bite of your steak I'll think about forgiving you."

Cate slanted him a wary, sidelong glance. He was smiling, and she lifted her face to smile sheepishly back. "I'm—"

"Your steak, madam." She was interrupted by the waiter, and the rest of her apology was forgotten with the first whiff of a mouth-watering aroma. Plump and perfect, topped with sautéed mushrooms and a dollop of herbed butter, the steak sizzled gently on a steel platter, surrounded by julienned vegetables and a baked potato, and accompanied by sauces and a basket of bread.

Embarrassment was forgotten in the upsurge of hunger. Cate ate in rapt silence for several minutes, perfectly willing to concentrate on the food rather than waste time making light conversation.

"Well, what's the verdict?" Jesse asked.

She looked at her nearly empty plate. "The evidence speaks for itself, doesn't it? I didn't mean to make a pig of myself, but I did."

"You ate a good meal with a healthy appetite, and that's nothing to apologize for. I hope you aren't one of those women who feel it's unfeminine to eat a decent meal."

"Are you kidding?" she scoffed. "You know me better than that. But are you one of those men who think women shouldn't have hearty appetites?"

"Would it make any difference if I did?" he asked, grinning. "I remember how you could eat as a kid."

"Not those ice-cream bars again?"

"Nope. The fried chicken at the Labor Day barbecue. I didn't know a forty-five-pound kid could eat that much."

"Your mother made the best fried chicken in the world," Cate remembered. "Best potato salad, too. Brad always loved it." Her smile faded, and she pushed her plate away.

"He loved just about everything," Jesse said. His voice wasn't sad, but warm with the memory. "That was the first thing you noticed about him—his enthusiasm. He was one of those rare people who see and appreciate the beauty in everything around them, wasn't he?"

"Yes," Cate said reflectively. "He was. That was one of the things that made him so easy to love."

They fell silent while the waiter returned to clear their plates. A murmured word from Jesse and he brought coffee, then disappeared again. Jesse added cream to his cup, stirred and sipped.

"Do you miss him?" he asked quietly.

"Not the way I did at first. I thought the pain would go on and on forever, but time eventually does heal all wounds."

"But the scars remain."

"They have to. I don't believe a thinking person would want to forget entirely. We are what our past has made us. We learn from the pain as well as the joy."

In the pause that followed Cate could hear the soft rattle of dishes and cutlery and the low murmur of conversation as the room began to fill with people.

"You're right, of course," Jesse said softly. "It's just hard to see that when you're hurting."

"Was it hard for you to understand that things would get better?"

Cate half turned on the velveteen seat to watch his face. In spite of herself she looked at his eye patch. Jesse saw, but took no offense. He nodded, half smiling.

"I knew from the beginning that this eye was lost, but for a while no one knew if the other one could be saved. I spent one of the worst months of my life in a VA hospital in Long Beach, wondering if I'd ever see again."

"Oh, Jesse," Cate whispered, reaching to cover his hand with hers. "I never knew that."

"There would have been no way for you to learn of it. My parents had already moved to Orlando, and they were the only ones who were told. I didn't want them to know, but the marines sent the notification before I could stop it." He turned his hand over and clasped hers.

"You were still trying to spare them from the truth?"

"I'd rather they never knew. I think a lot of guys felt that way. The situation over there was completely outside any experience we knew. We felt like the people we'd left at home could never understand anyway. It seemed easier to let them believe what they wanted."

"So you wrote cheerful letters that had nothing to do with the truth?"

"Yes. Maybe it helped us, too. Maybe we felt we could alter our reality, make it into what we wanted it to be."

"How bad was it, Jesse?" she asked after a moment of silence.

"How bad?" He glanced at her and shrugged. "That's hard to say. How bad is bad? It was something boys from comfortable towns in Ohio couldn't even imagine. It was the unspeakable made real."

"How did you handle it? How did anyone handle it?"

"Some guys didn't." He looked into her eyes, his gaze shadowed by memories of the past. "Most did, though, by getting through it one day at a time and putting it behind them when they came home."

"The way you did?"

He nodded. "As you say, time is the great healer. The pain eases, the scars fade." He paused. "What was your nightmare about, Cate?"

His perception surprised her. "Brad," she said, "and the Memorial. He was on the other side of that wall, calling to me, but I couldn't reach him. I tried to, but the wall was between us, keeping him in, keeping me out." Jesse caressed her hand gently. "He was so real; I could see him so clearly. And do you know what struck me?"

"What's that?"

"He was so young. I'd forgotten how young he really was."

"How young we all were. That may have been a blessing. The young are more resilient; they bounce back. I see that in the kids I treat."

"Mmm-hmm." Cate shook her head, throwing off the memories. "Speaking of those kids, I'd like to watch you work."

"I doubt if that'd be much of a thrill. What would you want to see?"

"Anything. Everything."

"Everything?" Jesse asked her quizzically, and she laughed.

"I have an idea. I want to talk to you about it, if you don't mind."

"Of course I don't mind. Why don't you tell me about it on the walk home?" He glanced at their waiter, hovering near at hand with their check. "I think it's time for us to pay up and move along."

They walked out into a beautiful autumn evening. The western sky was fading from pink and rose to purple, and the lights of the city were coming on. The air was cool and crisp. Cate zipped her jacket up to her chin and stuffed her hands in her pockets. Jesse pulled one hand out again so he could take the heavy camera bag from her and sling it over his own shoulder.

"Now," he said, "tell me about your idea. What is it you want to do?"

"I don't know how you'll feel about it," she cautioned. "You might not like it."

"Why don't you try me and see? I'm pretty broad-minded." He grinned, and Cate began to hope.

She took a deep breath. "I want to do a magazine article about you."

Chapter Five

*W*hat?''

Jesse stopped short. Cate took three more steps before she realized he was no longer beside her. She turned and walked back to him. His face was rigid with horrified amazement. Clearly she had been premature in hoping he would like her idea.

"What did you say?" he demanded.

"I want to do an article on you."

"No! Absolutely not!"

Cate stared at him. Surely he would let her explain. "At least let me tell you the kind of article I had in mind."

"I'm not going to—"

"Jesse! Listen to what I have in mind. Please!"

He hesitated, then let his breath out in a noisy sigh. "All right, but I'm telling you up front that I don't want any part of it."

"You don't know that yet. Will you just listen to me?" She waited until he nodded. "Okay. I told you about the pictures I've sold to *Washington Month*. They like my work, and they want to see more. They've asked me to work up ideas for photo-essays on anything in the D.C. area that interests me. Being at the hospital today gave me an idea, the first one I've had that I like enough to work on. I think I can make an article out of it."

"An article on me," he said grimly.

"An article on the pediatrics unit, if you're going to have a fit about it," she retorted tartly. "I think a photo-essay on one of the doctors and his patients would be terrific, but it can be about the pediatrics unit as a whole, if it has to be."

"It has to be," he said shortly.

"Whatever. Don't you agree that an inside look at the hospital would be interesting?"

"Not really, no. I can't imagine why anyone would want an inside look, except voyeurs."

"Stop it, Jesse!" Cate snapped. "The rest of the world is frightened of hospitals, intimidated by them. They need to see the truth, with the mystery stripped away. It's not voyeuristic; it's tremendously valuable."

He shrugged. "I guess so," he said grudgingly. "As long as it's not one of those sappy articles about the valiant young doctors performing miracles every day."

"Who said anything about *young* doctors?" Cate shot back, bringing him up short.

He shook his head. "All right, I deserved that. I know you aren't the sappy-article type."

"I certainly am not! I want to show people the reality and help them understand it. I have no intention of sugarcoating or sensationalizing anything. Do you think the hospital brass would allow me to do something like that?"

"I couldn't say." He paused. "Do you really want to do this?"

"I really do."

"I can't talk you out of it?"

"You can't. And if you won't help me, I'll ask around until I find someone who will. I'm going to pursue this, with or without your help, Jesse."

"All right, then, I know who you can ask. Do you want me to set up an interview for you or something?"

"No, thanks. This is business. I'll arrange my own interview, but I'd appreciate it if you'd come and give your opinion."

"You *want* me to tell them my opinion? You know what I think about it."

"Mmm-hmm. I don't want you to lie about it, either. I want all the pros and cons understood and the limits clearly set before I start work. That way no one can change the rules on me in the middle of the game."

"I see. And once you start, nobody can stop you." He nodded slowly, grudging approval in his eyes. "Very crafty, Cate. You're sure you want me to tell them how I feel?"

"I do," she said firmly as they turned the corner and stopped at her gate. She handed Jesse the key and let him usher her through. "I'd rather you didn't scream and yell and throw things, but I'd like the administrator, whoever that is—"

"Mitchell Carlson."

"Mr. Carlson, to know your opinion and the opinions of the other pediatrics staff." At the top of the steps she waited for Jesse to unlock her door. "Would you...?" She paused, suddenly shy. "Would you like some coffee...or anything?"

"No, thanks."

Jesse set the camera bag inside the door and turned back to her. In the evening dimness of her landing he seemed very big and very close. She couldn't see his face clearly, but she could feel the warmth of his body, smell the faint tang of this morning's after-shave, mixed with hospital antiseptic and the dark scent of man. It was a heady combination, already familiar to her, calling to mind darkness and closeness and strong arms around her. Cate felt herself sway involuntarily toward him.

"I don't have time for coffee tonight, Cate," he was saying.

She pulled herself together with an effort and tried to listen to his words.

"I still have evening rounds to do. Here's Mitch Carlson's office number." He scribbled on the back of an envelope he dug out of his jacket pocket. "Don't call before nine; he's in at eight, but he doesn't take calls for the first hour."

"Okay," she said slowly. "Is there anything else I should know? Does he bite?"

"He seems kind of formal, but he's fair. You'll do fine. Call me when you have it set up, okay?"

"Okay." She nodded.

He bent and kissed her quickly on the lips. "See you tomorrow, Cate." He turned and loped down the stairs, and was stepping onto the sidewalk before she recovered enough to reply.

"Bye, Jesse," she said to the disinterested night, but he was gone. She turned and went inside.

* * *

"Well? Do I look professional enough for Mr. Carlson?"

Jesse, dressed in his customary costume of flannel slacks, shirt, tie and lab coat, gave her tailored gray suit an admiring inspection. "Cate, that's formal enough for Merrill Lynch!" He tapped her calfskin briefcase with his fingertip. "What kind of evidence did you bring?"

"Pictures, mostly. I brought a lot of prints—the ones I'm the most pleased with and the ones that are similar to what I'd like to do here—as well as a résumé and a credit sheet. I was up until two this morning making prints and some slides I want him to see."

"Wouldn't you have been better off getting a good night's sleep?"

Cate shook her head. "An occasional short night won't hurt me, but presenting something less than my best work might." She looked at her watch. "Shouldn't we be going?" The appointment was for three-thirty, and it was already three-fifteen.

"In a few minutes. Maggy Oswald's coming with us. She's very interested in your idea."

"She is? Good." Cate smiled.

"Don't get too excited yet. She has some reservations about it, just like I do." He frowned. "I feel funny going with you when I'm still opposed to this. I know you won't sensationalize things, but I still don't want to do this."

"I know you don't, Jesse. You don't have to remind me. If Dr. Oswald is more open-minded I'll welcome her input."

"I'm flattered to hear that," Maggy Oswald said from the doorway. She smiled at Cate. "I have to warn you, Miss Drummond, that I'm not wholeheartedly in favor of this idea."

Cate rose to shake her hand. "Frankly, I wouldn't expect to you to be—not until you've heard some details of what I want to do. Thank you for coming today, Dr. Oswald."

"Call me Maggy, please. And may I call you Cate?"

"Of course," Cate said, smiling.

"What about me?" Jesse asked plaintively. "What can I call you?" He stepped past Cate to kiss Maggy Oswald on the cheek.

"*You* can call me ma'am," she informed him loftily, and he was laughing as he straightened from kissing her.

Cate forced a smile, but it covered a stab of jealousy so sudden and intense that it astonished her. She bent over her briefcase to hide her face until she had herself under control. This woman was his colleague and his friend, she told herself; he could kiss her if he wanted to. Pasting on a smile, she zipped the case closed and straightened again, tucking it under her arm.

"Are we ready to go?" she asked brightly.

An intense and pressured ninety minutes later she and Jesse left Mr. Carlson's office. Cate walked quietly at his side until they had turned the corner and traveled fifty feet along the corridor. Then she stopped short.

"Cate?" Jesse stopped a pace farther on. "What's wrong?"

"Why wouldn't he give me an answer? Why do I have to wait?"

"For all the reasons he gave you. The hospital board, the legal people, everyone he has to consult. It'll only take a week or so to get your answer."

"Only?" she protested. "I have to wait a week, and you call it *only*? I'll go nuts in a week!"

"If you do, then you'll probably be the only nut taking pictures around here."

"Do you mean that?" Cate demanded. "Do you really think I'll get permission?"

"I think you probably will." Jesse's tone was glum.

"Even though you don't want me to?" she asked coolly. He'd made his opinion all too clear during the meeting, and Cate had been grateful for Maggy Oswald's more positive input.

"You wanted me to be honest," he reminded her, and she scowled at the floor as they walked on.

"I know, I know." She sighed. "I'm not mad at you for being honest, Jesse, but I wish you could be a little more open-minded about it. Don't you trust me not to do a schlocky piece on noble young doctors and sexy nurses in high heels?"

This time it was Jesse who sighed. "I know you aren't going to do anything like that. I just don't want to be exposed that way in a magazine."

"Exposed? Come on, Jesse, this isn't *Playgirl*! I promise not to take any nude shots of you!"

"Not even if I want you to?" Jesse asked with a wicked grin. "Even if I beg and plead?"

The idea struck like a blow. The thought of Jesse...nude. She already knew what she'd seen and touched of his body as if she'd photographed and studied him, memorized each plane and angle and curve. She'd had a brief taste of him, not enough to satisfy, but enough to make her crave more. She wasn't going to photograph him nude, though. She wouldn't be able to hold the camera, let alone operate it. She sucked in a deep, steadying breath and grinned at him.

"Serve you right if I did, Mr. Big Time. You'd drop dead of embarrassment, and you know it!"

They walked several steps. "Yeah," Jesse said at last. "You're probably right."

Cate glanced at his face, then looked down the hall ahead of them, hiding a smile. "No 'probably' about it," she said, saccharine-sweet, and dodged the swat he aimed at her.

"Five days! It's been five whole days, and nothing. Not one word!"

"He said a week. Five days is not a week."

"Oh, don't split hairs!" Hands outflung in exasperation, Cate whirled away from the line of prints she was hanging to dry. Her studio with its west-facing window was bright with the afternoon sun, but her face was thunderous. "Five days is a work week! I'm going crazy waiting, Jesse. I want this article, and the more I wait, the more I want it!"

"Just relax, Cate. After all, the worst they can say is no."

"And you'd be glad to hear that, wouldn't you?" she flung at him; then her arms dropped and her shoulders slumped. "I'm sorry, Jesse. That was uncalled for. It's just—"

"It's just that you want this so badly." Jesse moved toward her and she met him halfway, dropping her head onto his shoulder when he put his arm around her and pulled her close. "Why do you want this particular article so badly, Cate?"

"Just because." His shoulder was warm and firm beneath her cheek. She rubbed it absently to and fro on the crisp cotton.

"That's enlightening." Jesse's voice was gently amused.

"Because I know I can do a good article, an article that will move people, teach them something about hospitals, the people who work there, the kids who are patients, and maybe about themselves, too." She put one hand on Jesse's chest and pushed herself back to look up at him. "Because I think it's important," she said quietly. "Because it *is* important."

"Hey." He shook her gently. "It's important, but it's not the end of the world. We're not talking brain surgery here."

She gave a little spurt of laughter and relaxed. "We could be. It's a hospital story, after all."

"I think your answer will be yes," Jesse told her. "You just have to hang on for another couple of days."

"Aaack!" She mock-strangled herself. "I'll never make it!"

"Yes you will, and you aren't even going to brood about it anymore. I know just the therapy for you. Come on!" He turned and strode for the door, dragging her after him.

"Wait a minute!" She hung back. "What do you have in mind?"

"Therapy. An afternoon playing tourist. Have you been to the Washington Monument yet, or taken the White House tour?"

"Well, no, but—"

"Great." He pushed her toward the shelf of cameras. "Pick out a camera. You'll want to take pictures." Cate hesitated for a second, and he gave a quick mutter of exasperation. "How about this one?" He picked a camera from the shelf, but she shook her head.

"That's for portraits." She took it from his hand and set it back, then selected a Nikon and a medium zoom lens. "This one will be more useful."

Jesse watched her change lenses. "Can you use it indoors, too?"

"Yeah." She packed the camera in a small bag.

"Don't you need a flash or something?"

"Uh-uh. Fast film." She dropped several rolls of film into the bag and zipped it closed. She looked up. "I'm ready."

"Great!" He grabbed her hand and pulled her through the house and out the door. He didn't slow down for several blocks.

"Where are we going, anyway?" Cate asked as they hustled along the sidewalk. She was breathless.

Jesse slowed his pace slightly. "Why don't you relax and take some pictures and let me worry about the agenda? You just look for things to photograph." They walked out of the afternoon shadow of a George Washington University classroom building and into the sunshine again.

"Stop." Cate halted him with a tug at his sleeve.

"Why?"

"Because I see something I want to take a picture of." She pulled the lens cap off and dropped it in her pocket. "Look over there, at those squirrels on the telephone wire. They use those wires just like expressways, don't they?"

Jesse turned to look, and she snapped his profile, ignoring the squirrels. A river bird called raucously above them. Jesse swung around, following it, and caught Cate pointing the camera at him. She focused on his face and snapped the shutter again.

"What did you do that for?" he demanded.

"You told me to find things I wanted to take pictures of." She grinned, unrepentant. "So I did."

"Well, once is all right, but don't do it again, okay?"

Cate promised nothing, and as they walked through the governmental section of the city she turned her camera on Jesse between shots of the people and buildings around them. He protested, but there was little he could do to prevent her from taking pictures of him as well as the gargoyles and statues. They walked and talked and laughed together until the sun slid behind the tall buildings, leaving purple shadows in its place.

Cate took a picture of the Capitol dome, gilded by the last glow of the setting sun, then lowered the camera, pushing the film-advance lever. It moved heavily, and she turned the camera over to press the film-release button.

"What's the matter?" Jesse was watching her hands.

"I'm out of film. This was the last roll." The wind freshened, sliding around the corner of a building to tug at her hair as she began to rewind the film. She shivered and shook the auburn strands out of her eyes.

"You're cold, too." Jesse wrapped his arm around her shoulders and pulled her against the shelter of his body. "We'll get a cab home."

He stuck out his hand and, like magic, a cruising cab pulled over to the curb. Cate sank gratefully back into the cigar-scented warmth. The cab swung into traffic with a tooth-rattling jerk, and she braced herself against the seat.

"Jesse?"

"Hmm?"

"Are you as hungry as I am?"

He swayed with the movement of the cab and looked down at her. "I don't know. How hungry are you?"

Another jerk of the cab tumbled Cate across the seat and against his chest. He put his arm around her shoulders and braced them both against the movement. Cate stiffened for a second, but Jesse was warm and strong and held her securely as the cab lurched and swayed. After only a token argument with herself she gave in to temptation and relaxed. He turned her slightly so that she was tucked beneath his arm, leaning comfortably against his chest. Cate could feel the rhythm of his breathing.

"I'm starving," she replied to his questiion.

"I know just the thing." He leaned forward to rap on the plastic divider and direct the driver to a pizza parlor. "Pizza is all right, isn't it?"

"Sure." Cate wasn't hard to please. "I haven't changed that much since I was twelve."

"So you still like . . ." He searched his memory. "Pepperoni and green peppers?"

Cate dropped her head back to stare up at him. "That's right! How on earth do you remember something like that?"

"Memory like an elephant." He tapped his temple. "I never forget anything."

"Well, I still like pepperoni and green peppers, but when I was fifteen I learned to like mushrooms, too. How about you?"

"Everything but anchovies."

"Okay. Except no pineapple. Pineapple belongs on upside-down cakes, not pizza."

"No argument from me." As Jesse spoke, the cab pulled to a stop. He opened the door and slid out, pulling Cate into the curve of his arm again when she stood. He passed a bill through the window to the driver, startling him into a fervent "Hey, man! Thanks!"

Jesse just smiled and led Cate into the pizza parlor. It was dimly lit and cheerfully noisy, patrons cheering as they watched basketball on the television above the bar. Jesse led her to a high-backed booth at the rear of the long, narrow room and slid onto the bench beside her, rather than sitting down across the table.

Cate hadn't expected that, but she liked it. She liked having Jesse beside her, his shoulder touching hers, his leg brushing hers. Their wine came in a thick glass carafe, deep red, sweet and potent.

Cate sipped, and the sweetness clung to her lips. Without thinking she licked it off, then looked up to see Jesse watching her mouth. His gaze was dark with a message that disturbed her. She dropped her head to stare at her wineglass, toying with the stem.

"Cate." She felt Jesse's fingers under her chin, lifting her face with a gossamer touch, turning her to look at him. He gazed into her eyes for a long moment, then bent closer and kissed her mouth. He lifted his head an inch or two. "You taste of wine, warm and sweet."

Cate's heart began to thud against her ribs. She couldn't look away from Jesse's magnetic gaze. The eye patch slashing across his face did nothing to detract from his looks; in fact it added a hint of danger and mystery, of seductive secrets and conquering will. His gaze lingered on her lips for a moment; then he looked into her eyes again.

"You could drive a man over the edge," he murmured, and kissed her again. Lingering and sweet, his lips moved gently on hers, inviting her response, tentative and shy. When he sat back her breath was quick and shallow, and her heartbeat raced. He smiled, and the danger and mystery evaporated.

"After you eat this pizza, though, I'll probably be safe," he teased. "You'll taste of pepperoni and green peppers."

Cate plopped down to earth again with a sense more of relief than disappointment. Jesse could make her quiver with his seductive words, but he was going too fast for her, and she was afraid. She leaned into her corner of the booth, putting a little distance between them, finding it was easier to smile and laugh that way.

"It'll serve you right if that pizza is loaded with garlic! I warn you, though, even if it is I'm going to stuff my face. I'm about to starve."

Jesse looked up, over the high back of the booth. "Speaking of which..."

Their pizza, flanked by an antipasto and a basket of bread, was slid onto the table. True to his promise Jesse had ordered the pizza with everything but anchovies...and pineapple. Cate inhaled the fragrances with wholehearted approval, then filled her plate.

She ate hungrily, sampling everything but the hot peppers, and drinking two more glasses of wine. Jesse watched her with amusement and tenderness. She was flushed and laughing at something silly he'd said, and he thought he'd never seen anyone more beautiful.

A drop of sauce clung to her lip, and he took his napkin to dab it away.

"You weren't kidding about being hungry, were you?"

She swallowed hard and took a sip of wine. "Why should I lie? I couldn't fool you into thinking I had a dainty appetite anyway. You know better."

"No secrets from me, huh?"

She slid him a glance from beneath the silky fringe of her lashes. "Just a few secrets," she replied with a tiny smile, and attacked her pizza again.

Jesse felt his body tighten in response to that slyly flirtatious look. He felt pulled in two directions, the thirty-five-year-old Jesse MacLeod, M.D., slipping back in time to the eighteen-year-old Jesse who'd known little Cate since infancy.

He was never entirely certain if he was dealing with the woman or the child, or how much of the child lived on in the woman. Perhaps if he'd been around to watch her grow up he wouldn't keep having this problem. But then he would have had to watch her marry Brad at seventeen, a girl poised on the edge of womanhood, in a white lace dress, her hands full of roses.

She'd been a beautiful bride. While searching for her nightgowns the night she was ill he'd found a small framed wedding photograph tucked in a drawer of scarves and jewelry.

Brad had been a tall young man, with the bony lankiness of youth, but with a quiet maturity in his eyes. Cate had been simply radiant, her wiry energy transformed into a happiness that still glowed from that photograph after more than ten years. What had her thoughts been on that bright morning? What had she hoped for, planned for, prayed for?

And what had she spent the last ten years waiting for, cocooned in a too-safe existence that was only half a life? Jesse shook his head and bit viciously into his pizza. It tasted of nothing. It was the waste that infuriated him, the waste of lives, of dreams, of youth and hope.

When he allowed himself to think about it the old, well-remembered bitterness reached out to engulf him, taking the sunlight and warmth from the day, so he rarely allowed himself those thoughts. Deliberately Jesse tried to empty his mind of the darkness and the pain. He stared blindly at the tabletop, unconsciously rubbing his temple, the spot just beside the eye patch that always ached.

"Jesse?"

He jerked around to see Cate gazing at him, her face grave and concerned.

"Are you all right?"

He shook his head and blew his breath out in a sigh. "Yeah, I'm okay." He forced a smile. "I'm sorry, I just had something on my mind." He tried another smile, and it came easier this time. He indicated the remnants of the pizza. "Do you want that last piece?"

"Uh-uh." She sat back, shaking her head. "I couldn't eat another bite."

"It's nice to know you do get full sometimes." He signaled for the check, and Cate caught his arm.

"Can we get a doggie bag?"

"You want to take it home?"

"Sure." She grinned at his astonishment. "I'll have it for breakfast."

Jesse shuddered. "Tell me you don't eat it cold... please."

"Of course not!" she retorted huffily. "That's uncivilized! I heat it up in the toaster oven."

"That's a relief. Would you like the hot peppers from the antipasto, too?"

"I'll pass on those."

She maintained her dignity as they left the restaurant, despite the garishly decorated doggie bag she carried. Later she put it carefully away in the refrigerator, and Jesse had no doubt that she would indeed eat it for breakfast. His stomach rebelled at the idea. Rather than think about it, he concentrated on filling the coffee maker.

"Jesse?" Cate's voice brought him to the realization that he was standing there staring at dripping coffee. He turned to her. "What's wrong, Jesse? Please tell me."

Her eyes were soft and dark with worry, and when she walked up to him, Jesse closed his arms around her and clung tightly.

He buried his face in her hair, breathing deeply of her scent, warm and sweet with a hint of violets. He would remember that scent for the rest of his life. She was slim and soft and pliant in his arms, with the strength that women have, a strength that seems to come from deep inside them and is given freely to those they care for. He needed her strength. Standing in the middle of the brightly lit kitchen he took what she offered, then sought more.

He slid one hand up her spine, sensing the strength in her slender frame. He stroked the back of her neck, then tangled his fingers in her hair and lifted her face. She looked up at him with a hint of fear in her eyes, and more than a hint of desire. Her lips were slightly parted, and he watched them as he lowered his head. At the last moment he closed his eye. Lightly his lips brushed over her forehead, touched her cheekbone, the corner of her mouth, and then took her lips.

He didn't try to sway her or seduce her, but let himself sink into her, drown in her, in the sweetness and the vitality that he needed so much.

Cate could feel the need in him, though she didn't understand it. It was more complicated than simple passion. He wanted her, but more than that, he needed her. He needed something from her that she seemed to be giving him, though she didn't even know what it was.

And he was giving to her, as well. As the kiss deepened Cate answered him, her lips moving to seek and demand, her arms tightening to hold him close, her hands moving restlessly over his hair, his face, his shoulders.

She was melting and dissolving and drowning in the touch and the scent and the dark, sweet taste of him. There didn't seem to be any way to save herself, and she didn't want to try. She gave herself up to the wonder of it and let the dark waves close over her.

Chapter Six

"Cate. Oh, Cate."

Jesse groaned her name against the thin skin of her throat. The vibration of his voice sparked sympathetic vibrations all through her, little frissons of delight that ran along her nerve ends. This was craziness, and she knew it, but she couldn't bring herself to care. The delight was worth a little madness.

When Jesse suddenly released her, she nearly fell.

"No, Cate!" With an anguished mutter he spun away, half pushing her from him, and Cate clutched at the countertop to support herself. She was cold without his warmth, weak without his strength, alone and lost.

"Oh, God, I'm sorry, Cate." Jesse's voice was low and strained, his face dark with pain. "I'm sorry. I never meant for that to happen."

"Jesse?" She pushed herself away from the counter and took a step toward him, but he moved quickly away. She stopped. "Jesse, please tell me what's wrong."

He shook his down-bent head, the harsh light gleaming on his hair. He pressed his palm to his brow, then wiped it over his face.

"I'm sorry, Cate," he muttered. "I never..." He gazed across the distance that separated them, his face grim. He lifted his hands in a helpless shrug, then dropped them. "I'll call you."

Grabbing his jacket from the back of a chair, he was out of the kitchen and striding for the door.

"Jesse!" Cate called after him. "Where are you going?"

Her only reply was the slam of the front door.

It could have been seconds or minutes later when she crossed the kitchen on shaking legs to switch the coffee maker to low and pour a cup. Her hand was unsteady, and coffee slopped over the side of the thick stoneware mug onto the countertop. Cate swiped at it with a sponge, then carried her cup to the table and sagged into a chair.

She didn't understand. She just didn't understand. She had no idea what she could have done or said to make Jesse leave so suddenly, or to put that anguish in his gaze. She sipped her coffee, burning her tongue, but she ignored the pain. Staring hard at the scarred walnut surface of her grandmother's table, she tried to figure out what had happened. She forced herself to think, to concentrate, going over the things they'd said and done that afternoon from the time they'd left her apartment.

There had been nothing wrong that afternoon, nothing wrong in the cab on the way to the pizza parlor. And then she had it. She didn't know why it had happened, but she knew when.

Jesse had been fine until they were almost finished with dinner. Something had happened then, but she didn't know what it was. He had become quiet, too quiet, brooding over thoughts he hadn't shared with her. And it was those thoughts that had darkened his mood and caused him such pain.

She closed her eyes and tried to remember what they'd been talking about. Nothing of any import that she could remember. Jesse had been teasing, and then he'd become quiet, scowling at his pizza and rubbing his temple, where a small scar showed beside the eye patch.

Her eyes snapped open. He had revealed too much by rubbing that little scar. As a photographer she was an astute student of body language, and that little gesture had spoken volumes. That scar was from the war.

He'd been thinking of the war. Something had brought it to his mind, darkening his mood, plunging him into an angry depression. She hoped that when he'd sought her arms as solace she'd been of some help. His need had been clear, but whether she'd been able to assuage his pain she had no idea.

"Thank you, Mr. Carlson," Cate said calmly. Her fingers were relaxed on the telephone receiver. "Yes, that would be fine. All right. I'll see you at three."

She hung up and sat absolutely still for a moment, then erupted from her chair.

"I got it!" she shouted to the empty apartment. "I got the article!"

Hugging herself, she did a little victory dance around the kitchen, then subsided against the refrigerator, grinning widely. She wanted to celebrate, to share her terrific news with someone else, but there was no one to tell. With a sigh she dropped her arms, her shoulder slumping dejectedly. Damn it, she'd just gotten the best news she'd had in weeks, and she had no one to share it with.

There was one person. She snatched up the phone again and dialed quickly. The line buzzed, clicked, then the call went through.

"Renato's Restaurant and Deli," a pleasant male voice announced. "How may I help you?"

Cate took the phone from her ear to stare at it in amazement, then put it back. She *must* be rattled if she couldn't even dial the phone!

"I'm sorry. I'm afraid I dialed the wrong number."

"No problem, miss. Just remember us if you need a good meal or catering. Serving Georgetown for thirty-one years," he added cheerfully, and hung up.

Cate pressed the button to break the connection, then dialed again, slowly and carefully. This time she reached Jesse's office, but the receptionist informed her that he wasn't there.

"You can try the hospital, but the staff meeting is on Friday. He won't be available until after that."

"What time does it end?"

"Usually between three and three-thirty, but it might go later than that."

"Oh." Cate heard the disappointment in her voice and made an effort to pull herself together. "I'm meeting with Mr. Carlson at three. When you hear from Jesse, could you tell him that, and I'd like to talk to him as soon as possible?"

After assuring her that the message would be delivered the receptionist hung up, and Cate sighed again. She'd be able to give Jesse the good news soon, she told herself.

But maybe not soon enough.

At three forty-five Cate was sitting in Mr. Carlson's elegant office, nodding and smiling and taking occasional notes as she listened to him outline the direction he wanted her article to take. This was not news reporting, and since he was granting her permission to do a story on his facility, his input was important.

Mr. Carlson had readily agreed to the requirements Cate had outlined. She was free to express whatever opinions she felt, so long as she concentrated on one particular topic.

That topic would have to be discussed with Jesse, though, and Cate had a sinking feeling he should have been at this meeting. She was certain of one thing: he was not going to be pleased when he learned what had transpired. In fact, he was going to be livid.

"That's all, Miss Drummond. Do you have anything you'd like to ask?"

"Not right now, thank you." She smiled. "But I'm sure I'll have plenty of questions for the staff when I begin working."

Mr. Carlson returned her smile, his frosty manner softening into a courtly sort of charm. "I'm sure they will be happy to cooperate with you in every way. The public-relations office can help you with any historical background you might need." He rose, still smiling, but concluding the meeting. "I studied the samples of your work, Miss Drummond, and I found them very powerful. I'm not sure what makes a photograph communicate, but if that sort of message can reach the public about the work we're doing here, you will have done us a valuable service."

Cate let him usher her toward the door, then stopped. "I'm glad you feel that way, Mr. Carlson. Don't you think Dr. MacLeod should be consulted about his part in this, though?"

"No need for that." He was blandly unconcerned. "The renovation project was his idea in the first place. I'm sure he'll be delighted to help make it into a reality. I'm glad we're going to be working with you, Miss Drummond. Good day."

He smiled gravely and shook her hand, and then Cate was very politely ushered out the door.

She walked down the corridor, her head reeling. She had carte blanche to do the kind of article she most wanted to do. Mr. Carlson simply wanted her to focus her article on one topic, the proposed renovation of the pediatrics pavilion.

The hospital was raising funds for the work now, and publicity would attract attention to the project, which was much needed and long overdue. The logical assumption was that attracting attention would also attract funds. Mr. Carlson was entirely in favor of her article, as enthusiastic as Cate supposed he ever got about anything.

His only stipulation: that she focus her story on the creator of the plan for a radically renovated unit.

Her problem: the creator of the plan was Jesse MacLeod.

She found him in the pediatrics staff lounge, a small, cheerless room with a battered table and chairs and a sagging sofa, Naugahyde upholstered in a peculiarly repulsive shade of green. She was lucky; he was alone. The only sound in the room came from an ancient coffee urn, complaining noisily as it brewed. The urn did have one redeeming feature: it produced excellent coffee.

Jesse already had a cup, steaming gently on the table beside the journal he was reading. Cate walked in and pulled the door closed behind her.

"Hello there!" Jesse looked around and smiled. In the few days since he'd hurtled out of her apartment she'd seen him briefly several times. Neither of them had mentioned the incident. "What are you doing over here?"

Buying time, Cate walked over to the coffee urn and drew a cup for herself. "I got a phone call this morning." Her back to him, she concentrated on adding powdered creamer to her coffee.

"And?" Jesse prompted impatiently. He rose and followed her to the machine. "Is it good news or bad news?"

"I hope you'll think it's good news." Cate turned to him, smiling in spite of her trepidation. "I get to do the piece!"

"Congratulations!" Smiling proudly, he took the cup of coffee from her hand and set it safely aside, then caught her in his arms and pulled her close. He kissed first one cheek and then the other. "I'm really glad for you. When do you start?"

Cate pushed at his chest, levering herself back until she could look into his face. "Today, tomorrow, whenever I want. But Jesse, there's something you need to—"

"I knew you'd sell him with your work. It was a very impressive presentation." Jesse smiled proudly on her behalf.

"Thank you, Jesse, but—"

"There's a lot of power in your work. I know you'll—"

"Jesse, *listen* to me! Please, will you listen for a minute?"

"All right." He loosened his hold on her, and she stepped away from him. "What is it?"

"There's a stipulation to my doing the article, Jesse."

"A condition, you mean?" He frowned. "What is it?"

"I have to center the article around one person." She hesitated, loath to tell him the rest.

Jesse studied her face. Cate had the uncomfortable feeling that he saw more than she wanted him to. "Who is it, Cate?" he asked carefully.

She swallowed with difficulty. "You."

There was a long moment of silence. Jesse's gaze stayed level and unblinking on her face. He finally said, "You're kidding. This is a practical joke, and in a minute you're going to start laughing."

She shook her head. "It's you. I can do the article—if I center it around you, your life and your work here."

Jesse shook his head slowly from side to side, anger dawning in his face. "Me, my life and my work? How could you agree to something like that?"

"How could I refuse?" She threw out her hands. "I want to do this article. I have free rein as far as the opinions I express, the pictures I use. All I have to do is make you the central figure."

"Well, I'm sorry about the article, but I won't do it," he said flatly. He turned on his heel and stalked to the window to stare out at the uninspiring view of a parking garage across the street. "I refuse to cooperate with something like that."

Cate was torn by conflicting feelings. On the one hand she hated to do something Jesse resented so much, but on other she agreed with Mr. Carlson. Jesse would be the best choice. She wanted to do the article about him; she'd wanted that from the start.

"Jesse."

"What?" he demanded of the window.

"You don't have a choice about this," she said softly. He jerked around to face her again. "What do you mean?"

"The renovation of the pavilion. It's your plan, your idea."

"What's that got to do with anything?" he demanded angrily.

"Mr. Carlson feels that any publicity for the renovation project will aid fund raising."

"So I'm supposed to shill for the fund raisers?" He slammed his fist on the table. "Hell, no!"

"You don't have to shill!" Cate shouted back at him. "I don't do that any more than you do. It's explaining the need for the renovation, the same way your proposal explained it. Showing how the kids will have a better environment, a place to go to school, a bigger, better playroom. It's your idea, Jesse, your concept. You're the one who can—who *should*—explain the need for it. You're the one who can tell people what it will accomplish and how the kids will benefit."

She took two slow steps closer to him. "And if you can do that," she asked quietly, "don't you think you ought to? Especially if it will make it possible to get the money and do the work that much sooner?"

"In other words, I'd be a shill."

Cate sighed in exasperation. "Why don't you quit feeling sorry for yourself and start thinking about the sick kids who will benefit from this, huh, Jesse?"

"That's hitting below the belt."

"Maybe so, but it's true." She laid her hand on his arm, trying to reach past his hostility. The muscles beneath her fingers were steel-hard with tension. "Look, Jesse, I know how you feel about this. It wasn't my idea, but I agree with Mr. Carlson. You are the one who should present this to the magazine's readers. And I think—" she stepped squarely in front of him, forcing him to look at her "—that you should try to trust me enough to know that I won't put together an article that will embarrass you."

Jesse scowled at her for a long moment, then sighed heavily. "I know you won't write anything exploitive or cheap, Cate."

"Then why can't you accept that you're going to play a central role in the article and quit fighting something that's going to happen anyway?"

"It is, isn't it?" He wiped his hand tiredly over his face. "It's going to be done, regardless of how I feel about it."

"That's Mr. Carlson's stipulation. He seems to feel that you'll be more than happy to cooperate, since it will help to make your project a reality that much sooner."

"I don't *want* publicity!"

"I know you don't for yourself, but you have to think of it as publicity for the project, for the kids. When people think of Washington they don't think of seriously ill children, Jesse. They think of big buildings and statues and congressmen. You can open their eyes, give them something else to think about."

He stared at the floor for a moment, then sighed heavily. "Damn! I don't want to do this!" he warned, and Cate began to smile.

"But you will?"

He glanced at her, then scowled out the window again. "I warn you, though, that I won't let you get in the way or interfere with treatment."

"That's not a problem. Just tell me if I'm somewhere I shouldn't be."

"I will, you can believe it."

"But you'll cooperate on the article?"

"Yeah." The word came grudgingly. "Not that I have a choice."

She moved nearer, her smile widening. "You do have one choice, you know."

"Oh, sure," he grumbled. "What choice is that?"

"Well, we can do this the easy way, or..."

"Or the hard way. I should have seen that coming." Jesse took her elbows and pulled her close. He shook his head, an unwilling smile tugging at his lips. "You drive a hard bargain, lady. I want to be mad at you. I should be mad at you, you know, but I can't quite manage it."

"It's because you know I'm right."

"Don't press your luck." He shook her gently. "You may have won this round, but I think you owe me a little something in return."

Cate tipped her head to the side and flirted up at him through her lashes. She might be playing with fire but, flush with success, she was willing to take the risk. "What do you suppose I owe you?" she asked with a provocative pout. Her gaze flicked to his mouth and was caught there. She stared helplessly, longingly, at his lips. The payment he had in mind was no penalty at all.

He made her wait, until she swayed toward him, unable to help herself. And then he enfolded her in his arms and captured her mouth in a hard, hungry kiss.

"Morning, Dr. MacLeod."

The sky outside the windows was pitch-dark, the hallway empty save for the elderly janitor with his rolling bucket, mopping his way along.

"Morning, Ernie." Jesse returned the man's greeting with a smile and a wave, then stopped at his office door, fumbling in his pocket for his keys.

"Don't need to bother with your keys, Doc," Ernie said from behind him.

"I don't?" Jesse looked from Ernie to the door and back.

"The young lady got here about half an hour ago. I let her in so she could wait for you." Ernie leaned on his mop and frowned. "I hope that's okay, Doc. It's the young lady you was with yesterday."

"That's fine, Ernie. Her name's Miss Drummond, by the way."

"Cate. I know." Ernie smiled and turned back to his bucket. "A real nice young lady," he commented as he mopped. "Pretty, too."

Jesse looked around in surprise. "I didn't think you were on the lookout for pretty girls, Ernie."

"I may be old," came the dry reply, "but I ain't dead!"

Chuckling, Jesse pushed open his office door and peered in. Cate sat in his chair, fiddling with a camera she had set in the one small empty space amid his stacks of books and journals and papers.

His smile faded to a grim scowl as he watched her. Damn, but he didn't want to do this! He didn't want his life and work recorded for posterity, but Cate was so eager to get started. Jesse would have liked to share her enthusiasm, but all he felt was dread.

"Cate?" She looked up and smiled. "What are you doing here? It's not even..." He checked his watch. "It's not even six yet."

She shrugged and bent over her camera again. She was beautiful, even at this ungodly hour of the morning, her face fresh, her hair shining beneath the cold fluorescent light. Her expression was intent as she worked on the camera, doing something technical and confusing, her long, elegant hands dealing capably with the delicate mechanisms.

"You said you start work at six in the morning," she told him. "I figured I'd better be here early."

"All this so you can follow me around?" Jesse closed the door and hung his coat beside hers.

"You bet. If I hadn't gotten here before you, I wouldn't put it past you you to sneak off without me. You'll be pleased to know, though, that I'm only going to trail you for part of the day." She finished whatever it was that she was doing and snapped a lens cap on the camera. "Then I'm going to go see some of the kids and the other pediatrics staff. I don't think the public has any idea how many people it takes to run just one unit in a hospital."

"So you're going to show them?"

"If I can."

"Make *them* the stars of the article, why don't you? Better them than me!"

She grinned in reproof. "Not a chance, Jesse. I'm ready to get started whenever you are."

"I can tell. You're just dying to do this, aren't you?"

"Jesse, quit complaining. You won't even know I'm there."

"I'll know," he insisted gloomily. He riffled through his desk drawers, taking out a stethoscope, a pencil flashlight, an otoscope and the rest of his daily pocket luggage. He pulled on a starchy white lab coat and divided the impedimenta among the pockets. Cate was watching him when he looked up. "Well," he asked her, "do I look the part?" He felt like a fool.

"Oh, absolutely." Cate grinned, then lifted one of her cameras and snapped his picture. In spite of himself he flinched and turned away. When he looked at her again she took another picture.

"Damn it, Cate!" He stalked around the desk. "Are you going to be doing that all day?"

"You'll get used to it," she told him.

Jesse laughed shortly at that. He looked her up and down, the slim hips and long graceful legs in flannel slacks, the tiny waist wrapped with a snakeskin belt, the slender shoulders and arms...the small, high breasts beneath the soft silk blouse. She was smiling, and when she smiled her face lit up. It sounded trite, but it was true; she seemed to glow, her cheeks, her eyes.

He loved that glow. He wanted to give her enjoyment just to see that smile. Hiding a smile of his own, Jesse took another lab coat off its hook. He was going to hate having his picture taken, but he didn't hate having Cate around. He glanced along the length of her body once more.

"I'll know you're there," he said with complete conviction. "Here." He tossed the lab coat at her, and she caught it neatly. "Wear this. You'll look official, and it'll help keep your own clothes clean. It's got lots of pockets for film and stuff, too."

"Thanks." She pulled the coat on and buttoned it. It fit well. "You picked out the right size."

"Actually, I had Maggy Oswald pick it out for me." He walked to the door, but Cate caught his arm before he opened it.

"Jesse, wait a minute."

"Hmm?" He looked down at her.

"I know how you feel about this, and I'll try to be as unobtrusive as possible. I don't want to drive you crazy; I just want to do a good job."

He nodded silently and walked out the door.

Cate followed two steps behind, content just to watch him walk. The shapeless lab coat did something remarkable for his shoulders, and his sober gray slacks emphasized the length and muscular shape of his legs, one of the sexiest garments she'd ever seen. Or perhaps, she admitted to herself, it was the man and not the clothes.

If only he weren't so strongly opposed to the idea of being in this article. She was going to photograph him and write about him, because that was what Mr. Carlson insisted on. The article would be done regardless of Jesse's wishes, but she would be happier about it if he were a willing participant. Right now he felt he was being dragooned into participating in something he detested. It was up to her to persuade him otherwise.

She took three quick steps to catch up to him. "Where are we going first?" she asked.

"To make rounds. Up on the units."

Cate hung back as Jesse worked. She'd had only a vague idea of what "rounds" actually were, but she understood what he was doing as he went from one small patient to another, checking their charts to see how they'd fared overnight, examining each child and giving orders for further treatment.

She had snapped several pictures in the first two rooms, using her zoom lens so she could remain in the background, well out of his way. Each time she shot, though, the click of the shutter and the whirr of the autowinder as it advanced the film brought Jesse's gaze sharply around to her. She was surprised that he even heard her camera in the confusion of voices and movement, but he did, every time.

He walked toward the third child's room, talking quietly to a nurse who carried an armful of charts. He paused at the doorway and glanced over at Cate. He stared at her for a moment, frowning, then turned on his heel and walked into the room. A nurse and a couple of interns followed, along with Cate, who stopped just inside the door.

A girl of six sat propped up against a stack of pillows in the high bed. Thin to the point of almost frightening fragility, she had long brown hair and a hauntingly delicate face, with near-transparent skin stretched over fine bones. The over-bed table had been rolled in front of her, and she was working diligently in a fat coloring book, her tongue stuck out the corner of her mouth as she concentrated.

She looked up and smiled when she saw Jesse and the others.

"Hi, Dr. Jesse. I'm coloring a picture for you."

"Well, that's awfully nice of you. Can I see it?"

She shook her head quickly and covered the picture with her small hands. "Not till it's finished!" she commanded.

"You're a tough cookie, Melissa!" He grinned and waited for her to close the coloring book. Cate lifted her camera and focused.

"I'm a peanut butter cookie!" Melissa retorted, sending herself into fits of giggles at her own wit. "And you're a coconut pie!"

Cate snapped the shutter, capturing Melissa's laughter.

Jesse glanced over his shoulder, his mouth tight. Cate shrugged apologetically. There was only so much she could do to quiet the sound of the camera.

She waited until he turned back to Melissa, then focused again, zooming in to frame her picture more effectively. Jesse bent over the little girl, murmuring something that made her smile, his profile and her face filling the frame. When he smiled Cate pressed the button.

Jesse whirled around on her, his face dark with fury. "Blast it, Cate!" he snarled. "Will you stop snapping that bloody thing all the time? It's driving me crazy!"

Cate lowered the camera and took a step toward him, her eyes appealing for his patience. The room was deathly quiet.

"Jesse, there's only so much I can—"

"I don't care!" he spat at her. "I've had it with that thing. Just get out of here and let me work, will you?" Cate stared at him, stunned and shocked. "Go on!" he snapped. "Get out of here!"

Without a word she turned and walked from the room. The last thing she saw was Melissa's face, wide-eyed, shocked and scared at the anger in Jesse's voice.

Chapter Seven

Cate waited for him in his office. She knew he would come.

Less than ten minutes after Jesse had ordered her from Melissa's room she heard his footsteps pause in the hallway outside the door. Keeping a tight rein on her anger, she sat very straight and still on the uncomfortable side chair.

"Cate?" He spoke as he opened the door, but didn't see her until he stepped into the office. He closed the door carefully behind him. "Cate, you have to come back to the unit."

"Do I?" Her tone was icy, her face cool and set.

"Yes." Jesse sighed heavily. "I don't want to get into all of it right now, Cate, but you have to come back to Melissa's room and talk to her."

"She's a beautiful child, and in other circumstances I'd love to talk to her, but after being tossed out of her room

I fail to see why I should go back there." Cate didn't do anything so obvious as shout at him, but her clipped words had a definite bite to them. "And I think we certainly should 'get into all of it,'" she added tightly. "Right here. Right now."

"I know you're angry," he began in placating tones, and Cate's unnatural coolness burst into furious flame.

"You're right. I *am* angry!" She pushed herself out of the chair and faced him, fists clenched at her sides. "I can't remember when I've been this angry about anything! You were going to cooperate with me, Jesse, not order me out of the room! For heaven's sake, what were you trying to prove back there?"

"That I could make an ass of myself?"

Primed for battle as she was, it took a second for her brain to process his words. The angry breath went out of her in a little hiss, taking the fighting tension with it. Her shoulders relaxed.

"That must be the reason," she agreed with a touch of malice. He winced. "Damn it, Jesse, why did you do that?" She shook her head, unable to understand. "I wasn't in your way. I was staying in the background and using a zoom, and I wasn't asking questions or anything. What on earth did I do to deserve being thrown out?"

"Nothing. That's the trouble. You weren't doing anything wrong." He wiped his hand over his face. "I was on edge just waiting for you to take the next shot, but you weren't doing anything wrong. I've said how I feel about this thing, but I guess I feel more strongly about it than I realized."

Cate stared at him, trying to understand. "Jesse, I can't figure this out." She spread her hands. "You know what I'm going to do, you know that you're going to be a part of it, and yet you toss me out of the room. I don't get it."

"I—I guess I just felt invaded, exposed. Maybe I'll get used to it."

"It's going to be tough on both of us if you don't," Cate pointed out. "I'm not asking you to like this, Jesse, but you're going to have to accustom yourself to having me working around you. Do you think that's possible?"

"It'll have to be," he replied with a grim smile. "Otherwise you'll end up bashing me over the head with one of your cameras, won't you?"

"The idea has a certain appeal." Her smile matched his for grimness. "I have a job to do, Jesse. Please understand that."

"I'll keep it in mind." He stepped toward her, reaching for her hands. "Now will you come back with me, please? I'm in big trouble if you don't."

"In trouble with who? Or with whom?" Cate let him keep her hands in his and draw her gently closer.

"With Melissa. She's not going to relax until you come back up to her room with me and tell her you're all right."

"Tell her I'm all right? What does she think happened to me?"

"I yelled at you, and she's afraid I've hurt your feelings."

"Well, you did," Cate told him frankly. "But mostly you made me mad. I don't want Melissa to be upset, though, so let's go and reassure her."

Melissa was waiting for them, sitting up in bed staring at the door. Her cheeks were tear streaked, and the tip of her nose was red from cying. She glared at Jesse when he walked into the room, then smiled broadly at Cate. For the first time Cate noticed the crutches and prosthetic leg propped in the corner. With an effort she kept her face under control.

"What's your name?" the little girl asked Cate.

"It's Cate." She smiled, walking to the bedside. "What's yours?"

"Melissa." The little girl gazed up at her with wide, worried eyes. "Why did Dr. Jesse yell at you?"

Cate slid a quick glance at Jesse. "I think you'll have to ask him that, honey."

Melissa turned her clear, serious gaze on Jesse. Cate could see the back of his neck redden. "Why did you yell at Cate?" Melissa asked him gravely.

"I was wrong to do that," he said after a moment. "I was nervous and upset, and I took that out on Cate. I shouldn't have done it."

"Are you gonna tell her you're sorry?"

Jesse flicked a glance at Cate, and she had to bite her lip against laughter at the expression on his face.

"I'm sorry, Cate," he said quietly, and beneath the compliance with Melissa's request there was an undertone of sincerity. "I was wrong to yell at you that way."

"Thank you, Jesse." Cate turned back to Melissa. "I know he didn't mean to yell at me and upset you, Melissa. I'm not upset with him anymore."

Mellisa studied her face for a moment, then nodded gravely. "Okay. When Dr. Jesse gets done with his rounds will you come back and talk to me?"

"Sure I will. I'll show you how my camera works, too."

"Will you really?"

"Yes, she really will," Jesse interrupted. "But right now, we have to go and finish the rounds, all right, Melissa?"

"Aww! You always have to go finish rounds!"

"Yes, I always do," Jesse said, teasing the pout from her face. "And I always come back, don't I"

Melissa brightened. "Yeah, you do. I'll finish your picture for you, okay, Dr. Jesse?"

They took their leave in a flurry of goodbyes and promises to return. Out in the hall Jesse took Cate's arm and pulled her to a stop.

She looked up inquiringly and he smiled. "Thank you."

"For what?"

"For getting me off Melissa's hit list. I don't know if she would ever have forgiven me."

"Oh, come on." Cate tucked her arm through his and they walked on. "She's a little girl who idolizes you. She'd have forgotten all about it."

Jesse shook his head. "She's a little girl who can carry a grudge, and she was awfully mad at me. I'm glad you came to my rescue."

Cate shrugged. "If it means that much to you, I'm glad I did, too," she said, smiling. "Can we get on with these rounds now?"

"Your wish is my command." He hesitated, gazing at her face.

"What are you looking at?" Cate asked after a moment.

"At you," he replied softly. "Just at you. You're very beautiful." He kissed her on the lips, quick and hard, then caught her hand and led her toward the next patient's room.

Her lips still tingling from the kiss, Cate followed and watched, shooting pictures of anything that caught her eye. Jesse did his best to ignore her, and after a while she could tell that the snap of the shutter no longer broke his concentration.

Sometimes she photographed Jesse, sometimes one of his small patients or a nurse, or the strapping, breathtakingly handsome respiratory therapist who crawled on the floor and made elephant noises to persuade a reluctant two-year-old that he would enjoy his treatment.

Rounds took two hours, and with the pressure of Jesse's hostility off her, Cate found it fascinating to watch him work. The rakish, sexy, even dangerous pirate in the eye patch was a different man with his small patients. He made them laugh with funny faces and nonsense rhymes, explained as best he could the things he had to do to them, and enlisted their cooperation whenever possible. And when they cried he held and comforted them with tenderness and understanding.

She hovered in the doorway as he rocked a wailing three-year-old who'd just had a blood sample taken from her fingertip. Cate had watched his face. The finger prick had hurt him more than it had the baby. He'd spent nearly ten minutes rocking her, murmuring wordless comfort as she wept out her fright and confusion along with the hurt.

Her sobs slowed to sniffles and shaky hiccups. A huge tear clung to her lashes, then dropped to her cheek. It slid slowly over the plump curve, and Jesse bent his head to murmur something into her riot of golden-blond curls as he wiped the tear away. Holding her breath, Cate snapped the shutter, then waited, camera poised. Her instincts were right, for the little girl looked up at Jesse, answered his murmur and broke into a broad, wet-eyed grin. Cate didn't need to see the proofs to know she had two exceptional pictures.

"What have you been taking pictures of all morning?" Jesse threw the question over his shoulder as Cate followed him out of the little girl's room.

"Anything and everything. You, the other people, the kids. I took some pictures of the building, too, like that big window at the end of the hall."

Jesse turned around to look at the window in question. "Why would you want to take a picture of that?"

"That window says as much about the age of the building as five pages of text." Cate studied it. "I don't know if I'll use it, but I've got the shot just in case."

Jesse gave the window a last glance and shrugged. He didn't see anything special about it, but if she did, who was he to argue? He pushed open a door. "Come on in here. I'll get the charts."

"In here" was a dingy, windowless cubicle off the nurses' station. It was about the size of the average broom closet, lit by a glaring fluorescent fixture and furnished with an ancient dull-gray desk, three metal chairs and a telephone. When Jesse rejoined her, he had his arms full of charts. His tall, muscular frame seemed to fill the tiny room, making it seem even more claustrophobic.

"There!" He dropped the charts onto the desk with a clatter. "This'll be boring, but it won't take long."

Cate sat down on the chair in the corner. It wobbled unnervingly, and she switched to another chair. "Don't worry about me, Jesse. I'm not here to be entertained. Just do what you do every day, and I'll hang around and watch."

"You're the boss." He shrugged and bent over the charts.

Watching Jesse, Cate screwed a filter onto her lens to compensate for the color distortion of the fluorescent light. She was reluctant to admit, even to herself, how much pleasure she took in the sight of him. She was going to capture that, as much for herself as for her article. She raised the camera, focused and shot.

"Huh?"

Jesse's head jerked up at the sound of the shutter. Cate smiled and lowered the camera to her lap.

"It's just me, doing my job."

"Yeah." He glanced from her face to the camera and back again. "I've been trying to ignore it."

"It'll get easier."

"I hope so." With a last hostile glance at the camera, he went back to his charting.

Cate leaned back in her creaking chair and watched him writing rapid notes and flipping the multicolored pages of the charts. He had strong hands with elegantly long fingers, quick and deft as he changed a child's dressing, moving with neat economy as he wrote... working magic when he touched her skin.

Cate jerked her head, physically pulling her gaze away. She stared out the door at the activity in the nurses' station. Quick heat burned in her cheeks, and she glanced warily at Jesse. He was scribbling rapidly, unaware of her discomfort.

He frowned slightly, concentrating, his lips firm, his chin set. His jaw was square, smooth from his morning shave, the tanned skin taut over the bones, with a faint satiny sheen to it. It was warm and smooth, and she wanted to touch it, to stroke his face, kiss him. She caught her breath and shifted uneasily in her chair.

"What are you writing?" she blurted.

"Charts." He didn't look up.

"I know, but what things do you write on them?"

"A daily record of the patients' condition and treatment. What I observed when I saw them this morning, any treatment that I performed and whatever treatment I ordered."

Cate craned her neck to look sideways at the neat columns of handwriting. "What about their emotional condition, the way the kids feel? Do you write that down, too?"

"Oh, yes." He shut the chart he was working on with a snap and half turned in his chair to face her. "That's important for any patient, but especially for kids. We try to keep their lives as nearly normal as we can. That's why the renovation project is so important."

"I thought it was because the building's so old."

"That's part of it. This building's functional, but it's too much like a hospital. The kids, especially the ones who are here for a long time, need normalcy."

"Their parents stay here with them, don't they?"

"For most of them at least one parent can stay. They have to sleep in armchairs, though, and make do with the public rest room out by the elevators. There are no facilities here for them to shower or change clothes, and some of them stay for weeks while their children are undergoing treatment."

He leaned back in his chair, crossing his ankle over his knee and folding his arms. Cate watched the heavy cotton of his lab coat strain across his shoulders and over his biceps. She jerked her gaze back to his face.

"What about the other facilities you want to add? Why are they needed?"

"For normalcy. That's basically all it is. These kids have been removed from their normal environment and placed in one that is profoundly abnormal. They're sick, they're in pain and away from home, and they're in a place with little dull-colored rooms, with only a few toys and books and games, with no place to go to school."

"They need a real playroom, that's obvious. And I can see why kids ought to continue school, but do they really want to?"

"More than you would guess. In spite of all the complaining kids do about school and homework and teachers, school is one of the most powerful links they have with their normal lives. When you're sick you can't go to school. Continuing to go to school reminds them that normal life is going on and that they're working to return to that. That's crucial, even if the child isn't going to return to normality."

The words fell from Jesse's lips like stones, leaving a reverberating silence in the room. Cate had avoided thinking about that all day, but the ever-present specter could not be ignored.

"They're still kids," Jesse said quietly. "Even when they're dying, even when they know they're dying, they're still kids. They still need kid things, like toys and school and silly jokes." He began to smile again. "I couldn't count the knock-knock jokes I've been straight man for."

Cate managed to return his grin. "So I can look forward to lots of knock-knock jokes?"

"And a healthy dose of nine-year-old humor. Brace yourself, and try to remember what amused you when you were nine."

"Oh, gosh!" Her face fell at the thought. "Rubber spiders and squirt guns?"

"At the very least." He shuffled the charts into a pile and stood. "Are you ready to go?"

"Sure!" She hopped up. "What's next on the agenda?"

"Medical staff meeting. You may not have been bored by this, but the meeting will put you to sleep."

Contrary to Jesse's gloomy predictions Cate found the meeting fascinating. She didn't understand most of what they discussed, but she understood the group dynamics. The meeting was noisy, somewhere between an animated discussion and a small riot. There was icy sarcasm and table thumping, to say nothing of the shouting and name-calling. It reminded her of hostilities at the UN.

Perched on a chair in a corner of the room, Cate watched the faces, letting the emotions flow around her. Nobody noticed when she snapped the shutter. She stayed for over an hour, but when the meeting settled down to a relatively sedate discussion of charting procedures she slipped out the door.

She wanted some time on her own to write up her impressions and ideas, and she wanted to spend some time with the kids.

That was where Jesse found her, late in the afternoon. He stopped just outside the door of the solarium-playroom. Cate didn't notice him.

She was sitting on the floor in a pool of sunlight, surrounded by toys, with Melissa close beside her and Chad Martin, another of Jesse's patients, sitting on her lap. Chad frowned in concentration as she showed him how to focus her Nikon. Jesse wondered how many other photographers would entrust a thousand-dollar camera to the hands of a seven-year-old.

"Just turn the bumpy ring—like this—until you can see clearly, all right?"

"Okay." Chad nodded his understanding.

His small brown face was very serious as he stood, clutching the camera carefully in his hands. He walked a few steps away from Cate and Melissa, then turned back to them, the afternoon sunlight gleaming on his bald head, and aimed the lens at Cate and Melissa.

"Say 'cheese,'" he commanded.

They obliged him with broad smiles, and Melissa began to giggle. He focused carefully and snapped the shutter. Melissa applauded, and Cate came to her knees as he ran back to her, his face split by a wide, proud grin. She enfolded him in a fierce hug.

Melissa sat clapping and laughing, her crutches beside her, her prosthetic leg extended stiffly in front of her. Cate's cheek rested where the boy's hair should have been, and Jesse saw in her face the angry grief, the will to protect, the raw hurt. He understood those feelings all too well.

He hoped she was ready to deal with them. This was only her first day, and already she felt the fury and the frustration. Jesse wondered how she would handle these kids, if her involvement would deepen until it hurt both them and herself. He ignored the fact that he had never been able to distance himself from his patients. When he moved into the room she looked up.

"Hi, Jesse." She smiled, then sniffed hard before she continued. "We've been taking pictures of the playroom."

"And Chad's been taking pictures of you, I see."

"Yeah!" Chad piped excitedly. "And Melissa taked one, too!"

"You did?" Jesse looked at her with smiling wonder.

"Yeah!" Melissa struggled to rise to her feet, frowning with the effort of manipulating crutches and the prosthesis that replaced the leg she'd lost to bone cancer. "I took a picture of Cate and Chad. And when Cate gets it out of the camera she's gonna bring it for me!" Erect at last, she clumped over to Jesse. He swung her into his arms.

"I'm glad you two had a good time, but it's getting late. I just saw the dinner cart outside, and you know what you're having tonight?"

"What?" Chad and Melissa demanded in unison.

"Guess." Jesse grinned at them. "It's your favorite."

"Macaroni and cheese?" Chad asked, and Jesse nodded. "Yippee!" he yelled, and thundered out of the room, tossing goodbyes over his shoulder at them as he ran.

"Bye, Dr. Jesse." Melissa kissed his cheek and he set her carefully on the floor, steadying her until she was balanced. "Bye, Cate! I'll see you tomorrow!" She hurried in Chad's wake.

Smiling, Cate watched her go, then sank onto one of the child-size chairs, her knees under her chin. "They love their macaroni and cheese, don't they?"

"It's one of their favorites. Dietary makes a special recipe for the kids on chemo, lots of calories, lots of protein, to keep their strength up."

Cate's smile faded. Not just simple macaroni and cheese, but lots of calories and protein for the kids on chemotherapy. Nothing was as simple as it seemed.

Jesse nudged the red-and-white spotted rocking horse with his toe, setting it gently rocking. "The first thing Melissa wanted to do was ride this guy, wasn't it?"

Cate nodded. "She loved it."

"She loves anything to do with horses," Jesse said, grinning. "Her parents have a little farm in West Virginia, and she pesters them no end to get a horse. They have a mule, but he's a poor second to the horse she has in mind."

"Is the mule named Elmer?" Cate asked him.

"Yeah."

"She told me about him. Apparently she spends a lot of time in the barn talking to him."

"She probably needs someone to talk to," Jesse said, gazing past her at the curving wall of long, many-paned windows.

The solarium would have looked perfect furnished 1930s-style, with painted wicker furniture and Boston ferns. That was about when it had been built. It was dingy, almost dreary, in spite of the sunshine streaming through the windows and the toys scattered around. He half closed his eyes, and he could see the room he wanted, cheerful and colorful, with games and toys to challenge young minds and provide some simple fun.

He gazed out the window. "I have a warning for you, Cate."

"A warning? About what?"

"About you and the kids. I know how you feel about them. It shows in your face, and believe me, I can understand it. It's natural to want to protect them, to make everything all right, but you can't protect them from what's happening and you can't make everything right again."

"Your point, Jesse?" she asked coolly.

"My point is that you can't allow yourself to get too involved with them, even though you want to. Keep a little distance."

Cate stared at him. He sounded so cold, so clinical, so unlike the Jesse she thought she knew. "Keep my distance," she repeated with distaste. "Just watch them and take their pictures and ignore what's going on inside them?" She looked away. "Sure, Jesse. No problem."

The silence was broken only by the soft ticking of an old schoolroom clock over the door.

Jesse looked at Cate, her arms wrapped around her legs, chin resting on her knees. Her scowl had faded, and she was gazing at the red-and-white rocking horse.

"Penny for them," he said softly. She glanced at him, then at the horse.

"I can't keep my distance, Jesse," she said softly. "I know that's well-meant advice, but I can't do it. I can still see Melissa on that horse. She calls him Thunder. When she was rocking him, I could see that in her mind she was riding a real horse. And not just any old horse." Cate paused. "Not an ordinary horse, but a fiery steed with flashing eyes and prancing hooves. She rocked fast, so she could feel the wind in her hair, and she was powerful and free. When she was riding that horse in her mind, no crutches or prosthesis could hold her back." Cate turned to look into Jesse's face. "That's why she wants a horse of her own so badly, you know. It would return to her some of what she lost when she lost her leg."

"You're probably right. She's been powerless to stop the things that have happened to her. It's only natural that she'd seek some way to have a measure of control over her life again."

Cate was silent for a moment. "Do you ever wonder," she asked softly, "why such terrible things happen to children? Do you ever wonder if there is any justice?"

"No" was Jesse's unhesitating reply. "I don't wonder because there is no justice in disease or accident. Tragic events happen. Tragic events can't be explained or justified or even understood. That's a fact of life."

Cate looked up at him, her eyes clouded with doubt. "That's true, unfortunately, but do you accept it? Is that why you can tell me to keep my distance? Have you gotten so used to it that you accept the tragedy and the unfairness?"

He turned his head to look at her, and Cate involuntarily recoiled from the dark anger in his gaze.

"No, I don't accept it." His voice was quiet and deep, vibrating with emotion. "I fight like hell against it every day. And if the day ever comes that I feel myself starting to accept it, that's the day I'll quit medicine."

Chapter Eight

Look at this one." Cate lifted a dripping print carefully from the rinsing pan and held it up for Jesse. "I like it."

The late-afternoon sunlight slanting into her studio was closed out of the tiny half bath she had converted into a darkroom.

Jesse leaned over her shoulder and studied the picture in the red glow of the safety light. Melissa grinned back at them, her flyaway brown hair escaping from its braids as she rocked the red-and-white horse. Though the image was static, the impression of movement was strong. The horse was rocking hard, Melissa's braids swinging with the motion, her face flushed and shining with triumph.

"That's..." Jesse searched for the word he wanted. "That's really good, Cate...more than good. You can *feel* the speed and how she loves it."

Cate nodded with satisfaction and clipped the print to the line to dry. "That's what I was trying to catch."

She had spent two full days photographing at the hospital. Some of the pictures captured exactly what she'd been seeking, but many, indeed most of them, fell short of her standards. Like all photographers, she knew she might easily shoot an entire roll of film to get the one picture that communicated the message she wanted. The wastebasket in the corner was already half-filled with her rejects, pictures that weren't composed or framed or exposed exactly right.

Hanging proudly on the line, though, carefully developed and printed, were two fuzzy photographs of her, smiling broadly, sitting in the playroom, first with Chad, then Melissa. Those pictures would be matted and presented to the kids.

Cate studied the others with a highly critical eye, while Jesse seemed to approve of everything except pictures of himself.

"I don't like this one." He touched the edge of a wet print.

Cate looked at it. She had taken it while Jesse was examining an infant. He was peering into the baby's eyes with his ophthalmoscope, one hand cradling the baby's head. He had been making funny noises, and the baby was gazing raptly up at him, eyes wide and fascinated. Cate thought it was a particularly good picture, telling a great deal about the way Jesse worked with children.

"I like it," she disagreed with him. "It might or might not be one I'll use in the article, but I'm certainly going to keep it."

She covered the pans of chemicals, and opened the dark room. Sunshine spilled in, and she switched off the safety light as she led Jesse out into the studio.

"I don't know why," he muttered. "This one, then." He pointed out a shot of the staff meeting. He was arguing his case for the establishment of a schoolroom in the Peds wing, his passion and conviction clear. "I don't know what's the matter with it. It's better than the others but I still just don't like it."

"I know what's the matter with it." Cate glanced at the picture. It was composed well, perfectly framed, and made a clear emotional statement. It could hardly be improved.

"Well?" Jesse demanded. "What's the matter with it?"

She turned to him, smiling patiently. "You're in it. That's all that's wrong with it."

"No, no, there's something else." Jesse bent to study the print more closely, but Cate took his arm and pulled him away.

"There's nothing else. You like the pictures of the kids and the hospital and the other staff members, even if they're badly composed or exposed wrong. The only ones you don't like are the ones that you're in. Face it, Jesse, you're going to be the centerpiece of this story, so you're going to be in at least half the pictures."

He scowled, his lips tightening to a severe line. "I hate that, too. I really hate it!" he said heatedly. "This thing should be about the hospital or the kids, something other than me!"

"You're wrong." Cate's voice was quietly certain. "I know you don't believe me, but what will sell the article and the idea to the readers is you."

"I don't think so," he grumbled. "And I hate all those pictures of me!"

"You know what it is?" Cate pinned up the last print and turned to grin at him. "You're shy."

"I'm what?" His expression was outraged, but Cate knew her remark had struck home.

"You're shy. I don't know why I didn't think of it before, but it really embarrasses you to see yourself in pictures, doesn't it?"

He grimaced. "I just don't like looking at myself much."

"So how do you manage to shave in the morning?" she teased.

"I don't look at anything but what I'm shaving. There's not much to look at, anyway."

He reached up and touched the strap of his eye patch, adjusting it a fraction. Cate was sure he hadn't done it deliberately, but the small, unconscious gesture said far too much. She knew that memories of the war returned to haunt him at times, and she felt a stab of guilt.

"Jesse?" she asked carefully. "Does it bother you to see pictures of yourself wearing an eye patch?"

"It doesn't exactly make my day to see myself in pictures, regardless, but it's not the patch that bothers me. I just don't want the publicity."

"But your eye... Could you have gotten a glass eye or something? Something that might have looked more natural?"

"Not without plastic surgery. The ophthalmologist explained it all to me in the hospital. It would have taken a couple of reconstructive operations, and it would never have matched the other side of my fact exactly. At the time, it just didn't seem to be worth all the trouble."

"I see." She looked down at the floor for a moment, struck by a powerful wave of guilt. "I never thought that you might be uncomfortable about the patch," she said unhappily. "It should have occurred to me, but it didn't, because you seem so much at ease wearing it." She moved over to him, resting her hands on his forearms and looking up into his face. "I'm sorry, Jesse. That was insensitive of me."

"It's not the patch, Cate. Don't think that. I just don't like publicity." He shrugged and cupped her elbows in his hands. His grin was lopsided and wry. "It's nothing that you did. I'd be uncomfortable with it even if I didn't have a face that scared little children."

"Jesse, please! Don't say that."

Cate ached for him. He'd never been a vain man, but it couldn't have been easy to adjust to disfigurement as well as the loss of an eye. She reached up to stroke his cheek, letting her fingertips trail over the narrow leather band. His skin was warm, the slight rasp of his afternoon beard contrasting with the cool, smooth leather.

"There's nothing wrong with your face, Jesse. Nothing at all." She leaned close, resting her hands on his shoulders, and rose on tiptoe to kiss his lips.

For an instant Jesse was utterly still; then his lips moved against hers. His arms slid around her waist, and he pulled her against his body as he took over the kiss. Cate couldn't imagine Jesse needing reassurance of his attractiveness, but he kissed her with a kind of questioning need. His arms tightened around her waist until her body was pressed to his from neck to knees, and she wrapped her arms around his neck, holding him close.

His body was big and hard and solid, solid as a rock she could cling to in a storm. And cling she did, while his mouth teased and tasted, sought and found. The rush of wanting caught her by surprise, leaving her without defenses against the melting she felt inside, the weakening and softening that made her mold herself pliantly into Jesse's embrace. His lips asked a question and hers answered, parting and allowing him to deepen the kiss. She tried to tell him with her lips and her hands that there was nothing his injury could do to make him less attractive.

She was shaking when at last he broke the kiss, shaking and weak-kneed, her heartbeat thundering in her ears so that she could barely hear the ragged note in Jesse's breathing. He pressed her face into his shoulder and rested his cheek on her hair. She felt his chest lift and then relax in a deep sigh.

"You're sweet, Cate," he murmured into her hair. "Sweet to worry about me. But you don't need to. I've long since dealt with what happened to me."

She didn't believe that for a minute. She knew the demons still haunted him. "Have you?" she asked against his chest, hoping he might open up to her. "I don't know that you've dealt with the past any more than I have." A pause. "And I'm beginning to realize that there's a lot that I haven't dealt with yet."

Jesse moved his cheek gently against her hair. "I don't know, Cate. I think I've dealt with it all. Maybe I haven't." His arms tightened around her in a hug before he let her go. "It's nice of you to worry about me, even though I don't need it." He glanced at the prints once more. "I just can't get enthused about being the object of all this publicity, that's all."

"Keep reminding yourself that it's all for a good cause and it won't bother you so much."

"You think not?"

She nodded.

"If they want to put my face on a magazine cover, though," he threatened, "all bets are off!" He dropped an arm around her shoulders and led her toward the door. "Now, let's forget about the article and the publicity and the fund-raising and taking pictures of anybody—especially me! What would you like for dinner?"

Cate considered, then grinned. "Anything at all ... as long as I don't have to cook it!"

"Okay. How about coming to dinner at my hide-away?"

"Your apartment?" She'd been to his apartment, in a high-rise building near the Watergate, several times. It was modern, convenient, efficient, and not at all homey, more like an expensive hotel room than a home, in spite of the few pieces of art and the books and journals that showed Jesse lived there. She'd never heard him refer to it as a hideaway.

"Nope. My hideaway. It's about an hour outside Arlington. We can get some stuff on the way and fix dinner there."

"You have a hideaway an hour from Arlington?" This was the first Cate had heard about it. "How often do you go there?"

"I usually go on the weekends I'm not on call and sometimes a night or two during the week."

"Have you been there since we met? It's been nearly three weeks."

"No, I've stayed in Washington. That's another reason for me to go. I need to check on the place."

"I can understand that, but, Jesse, why have you stayed away from it for almost a month?"

He smiled down at her, and the message in his gaze made her cheeks warm and her heartbeat quicken.

"Because I've had a reason to stay in the city," he said softly. His gaze locked with hers, holding her immobile as he bent to gently kiss her lips.

"*Now* will you tell me where you're taking me?" Cate looked out at the thick woods streaming past the windows of Jesse's four-wheel-drive station wagon and braced herself for the next stretch of road. It was black-top, as narrow and winding and liberally dotted with potholes as the last stretch. This road, such as it was, was lifting them into the first foothills of the Blue Ridge, and Cate had been hopelessly lost since they left the express-way half an hour before.

"You'll see when we get there." Jesse's reply was the same unsatisfactory one he'd been giving her since their departure.

"*If* we get there."

Unconvinced, Cate turned to look out the window. Through a gap in the trees she could see a picturebook valley falling away from the road, gilded by the last rays of the sun. Its patchwork fields were November-bare, and its red barn, which looked exactly the way a red barn ought to look, caught the sun on the southwest side. The valley disappeared, replaced by the endless trees, and she turned to Jesse again.

"Is there a road to this place of yours, or do we leave the car and backpack the rest of the way in?" Her question wasn't entirely facetious.

"There's a road." He slowed for a curve, then swung onto another blacktop road leading off to the left.

"Dirt, gravel, or paved?"

"Paved road, gravel driveway."

"How long's the driveway?"

"Half a mile."

"Flat?" she asked, without much optimism.

"Hilly. It goes up pretty steeply."

Cate was silent for several moments. "Jesse, is this place of yours civilized? I mean, do you have plumbing, and electricity and stuff?"

Jesse laughed aloud at that, and after a moment Cate chuckled, too. She knew she sounded silly, but she was feeling kind of timid. She'd never traveled this far into the Virginia countryside, and she was unprepared for its remoteness and wildness. All she'd seen for what seemed like miles and miles were trees, trees and more trees. The tiny villages scattered along the road were mere hamlets, places that time seemed to have forgotten. The last one was called Old Tavern. Once past it, they'd driven through virtually unbroken forest.

"Yes, it has plumbing," Jesse replied patiently to her question. "And bottled gas for the stove and water heater, and a generator for electricity. I don't know if there's enough fuel to run it tonight, though."

"Do you use candles?"

"Oil lamps. It's surprising how much light they give."

"I suppose it is." Her voice was less than enthusiastic. She'd always been a city girl, accustomed to her urban comforts. She didn't particularly enjoy discovering this cravenly unadventurous streak in herself, but their trek into the country was bringing out the coward in her.

Make that a trek into the wilderness, she thought, watching the forest grow darker and thicker as day became evening. "Jesse?" Her voice was embarrassingly thin.

"Hmm?"

"Are we almost there?"

"We're thirty yards from the drive." He began to brake, slowing the wagon to make a right turn onto a narrow, well-maintained gravel drive. The drive led into a Stygian tunnel beneath overhanging trees.

Cate was glad they'd arrived...at least, she thought she was glad. She didn't realize she was clutching the door handle tightly as Jesse downshifted and the wagon growled its way up the steep drive in low gear.

It was every inch of the half mile he'd estimated, all of it seemingly straight up, and Cate was frankly afraid of what she'd find at the end of it. A tiny hovel with monstrous trees looming over it, no doubt. A decrepit log cabin, surrounded by underbrush, ideal for trolls and gnomes....

Or a positively beautiful two-story stone house, sitting in a large, grassy clearing atop a knoll that commanded a view of the hills for miles around it. Jesse braked to a stop in front of the wide veranda that wrapped around the house, and for several long seconds Cate could only stare, captivated by the beauty of it all.

The rising moon gilded the slate roof, glinted off the east-facing windows and made the clearing, dotted with pines and shrubs that would flower in the spring, a place of magic. Cate wasn't even aware of opening her door and climbing down from the wagon, but when Jesse joined her, she caught his arm and held it tightly, still gazing in wonder at the house.

"Cate?"

"Yes?" For the first time she pulled her eyes away from the house.

"Will you come into my home?"

He inclined his head in grave invitation. It was an invitation into much more than his house; it was an invitation into his sanctuary, into a part of his life that he guarded jealously. Cate understood all that, and she went willingly.

"Oh, yes!" she breathed, and let Jesse take her arm to lead her to the door.

He ushered her across the yard and up five steps to the broad, board-floored porch. The front door was a wide slab of dark oak, inset with two small panels of beveled glass. Jesse unlocked it and swung it wide.

"Welcome to my home, Cate," he said gravely.

She glanced at his face, then stepped into the house, and into enchantment. A brass oil lamp waited for them on a marble-topped table in the hall. Jesse turned up the wick and lit it, and by its soft glow he showed her the living and dining rooms, furnished with an intriguing assortment of antiques. She would have liked to linger and explore, but Jesse kept her moving with the air of a man who's saving the best for last.

"There are four bedrooms and a bath upstairs," he told her, urging her past the graceful dining table, topped with a pair of beautiful pewter candlesticks. "The kitchen is back here."

With a last, longing glance at the dining room she followed him through the swinging door, then stopped short.

The kitchen was a huge room, running all the way across the rear of the house. The living room and dining room were beautiful, but the kitchen was captivating, a room she might enter and never wish to leave.

As the golden lamplight pushed back the darkness she could see the details. The room was floored with flagstone, much scrubbed and worn with age. A vast fireplace, built of the same blue-gray stone, dominated the far end of the room, ten feet wide and high enough for a man to walk into and stand upright. The fire grate had been replaced by an ornate cast-iron stove that stood inside the fireplace, with cut wood filling a basket beside it. Several copper utensils hung from a blackened iron rack above the stove, and the thick wood beam that formed the mantelpiece was lined with pottery jugs and bowls.

The stove was comparatively modern, only forty years old or so, white enamel with five burners and an oven that had to be lit with a match. There were no cabinets and countertops as such, but a tall Hoosier cupboard and an enormous Victorian sideboard stood ready to store dishes and foodstuffs. A work surface and eating area was provided by a massive oak table, its top a single thick slab. The many windows were curtained with gingham, and a chintz settee beside the iron stove provided a spot to sit and rest.

The kitchen could not have been improved upon. It was perfect. Cate surveyed it in silence, then looked up at Jesse, who stood close beside her. He was smiling at her in the lamplight.

"This is beautiful, Jesse. The word is inadequate, but it's absolutely and utterly perfect! Do you use the pot-bellied stove for heat?"

"Yeah, especially when the gas runs out, but sometimes I just want the feel of it. That's why the settee's there. I can sit there and read, or just think."

"I'd like to sit there and just think," Cate said, gazing at the stove. "Could you light it now?" she asked, her expression eager.

"Sure. It takes about fifteen minutes for it to warm the room. By that time we'll be ready to eat."

"I'm ready to eat right now!" Cate shrugged out of her leather jacket and draped it over one of the ladder-back chairs standing around the table. "I didn't realize it before, but I'm starved!"

"Let me get the stove going; then I'll cook the hamburgers while you make the salad, okay?"

"You're the boss." Cate gave him a snappy salute, then had to dodge a swipe at her bottom. She trotted out of the kitchen to retrieve the bag of groceries Jesse had left in the hall. When she carried it back Jesse was crouched beside the big gas stove, fiddling with something on the back of it. "What are you doing?" She set the bag on the table.

"Turning on the gas." He waved her over. "Come here and I'll show you how." Cate stood behind him and craned forward to look over his shoulder. She leaned too far and lost her balance, catching herself with a hand on his back.

"I'm sorry," she said breathlessly.

He shrugged, and she felt the muscles shift beneath her palm. She left her hand where it was.

"Don't worry about it. See this handle? You turn it until it's pointing toward the wall." He demonstrated. "That lets gas into the line. Then, when you're ready to cook, you turn the burner on and light it with a match." He turned and rose, placing his hands at Cate's waist to move her back out of the way. He took a wooden kitchen match from a cup on the shelf above the stove. "You light it just like this." He demonstrated, and a burner flared to life. "Now, where's that hamburger?"

"Here." Cate fished the package of ground beef out and handed it to him. "Where do you keep your knives?"

"Over there," he said, pointing to a drawer. "You can wash the salad stuff in the sink. The water won't be hot yet—I just turned the heater on—but the cold will run."

With a nod Cate crossed to the sink to begin work. The meal was quickly prepared, and neither of them said much until they had eaten hungrily for several minutes.

"Well—" Jesse set the last piece of his hamburger on his plate and leaned back "—that makes a difference."

"Oh?" Cate looked up, her mouth full. She swallowed hard. "What difference does it make?"

"I think I'll live now. I was in danger of starving to death."

"Well, don't blame me for that. You're the one who suggested driving halfway to Georgia to have dinner." She popped the last of her hamburger into her mouth.

"Do you think it was worth it?"

"Oh, yes! This is wonderful. It's a big surprise, too."

"A surprise?" He looked puzzled. "How's that?"

Cate hesitated. She didn't want to offend him with the blunt truth. "After seeing your apartment," she said carefully, "I wasn't sure what your country house would be like. Frankly, I didn't expect anything like this."

Jesse's lips twitched for a moment; then he let the laughter out. "You don't need to sugarcoat the truth, Cate. I know what that apartment's like, but I can put up with it for the sake of convenience. I guess I've been putting all my energies into this place.

"You've expended them well. At the risk of repeating myself I'll say it again: I love it."

"I *know* I'm repeating myself, but I'll say it again: I'm glad you do." He glanced at her empty plate. "If you're finished, we can have our coffee and dessert over by the wood stove."

"Can we toast our toes by the fire?"

"Whatever you want."

Jesse was as good as his word. They installed themselves on the small settee with coffee and the box of pastries they had bought in Washington. Cate slipped her shoes off, tucked her legs up under her and let Jesse pull her into the curve of his arm. Nestled close against him, she gazed into the fire and nibbled a rich cookie filled with apricots and almonds. She turned and lay back across Jesse's lap so she could look up into his face.

He was a man out of a dream, gilded by firelight, his features thrown into strong relief. For just an instant she wished for her camera. If she could capture him this way...

Several buttons of his shirt had fallen open as he cooked, and the firelight gleamed on the strong muscles of his chest. She could see him as a pirate, dressed in breeches and boots and a loose shirt with billowing sleeves. He would wear a cutlass at his belt and a gold ring in his ear.

"Taste this," she said, her voice a breathless whisper. She lifted the cookie to his lips. "It's delicious."

He took a bite, his lips brushing lightly over her fingertips. Cate shivered, and he brushed his hand over her arm and shoulder. "Are you cold?"

"Oh, no," she murmured. "Not cold at all."

Jesse's lips touched her hair. "You like it here?"

She turned her cheek against his chest, sensing the strength beneath the cotton shirt. She shifted gently, nestling more closely against him. His arm was behind her head, and she could feel the slow, steady beat of his heart beneath her cheek.

She liked the feel of him, the sense of being safe and secure and protected in his arms. She thought she could stay this way forever. A log broke and fell into the fire in a shower of sparks.

"I could stay here forever," she finally replied to his question.

"I'm glad you like the house," Jesse said after a moment. "Because you're going to have to stay here tonight."

Chapter Nine

It took a few seconds for the meaning of his quiet words to sink in. Then Cate jerked upright, twisting around to stare at Jesse.

"What do you mean, stay here?"

He gestured at the windows. "Look out there."

Cate looked. The curtains were open, and beyond the small panes of glass she could see only a milky grayness. "What is that?"

"It's fog. I should have called for the weather forecast before we drove out here, but it's been so clear that I didn't think we'd have any trouble."

"We can't drive back in the fog?" Cate asked, already knowing the answer.

"Umm-umm." He pulled her gently back into his arms, and she could feel the small movement behind her as he shook his head.

She looked at the window. The fog swirled and shifted eerily against the glass. Cate shuddered and turned her gaze back to the golden flames dancing behind the stove's slatted iron door. The fire was warm and cheerful in contrast to the blankly forbidding grayness outside.

She didn't have to be told twice that they couldn't drive through that fog on a narrow, winding, precipitous road. The road had been nerve-racking in the clear afternoon light; it would be frightening in darkness, and impossible in fog.

So they would stay here until the fog lifted. That wouldn't happen before dawn, perhaps not before noon. They would spend the night together... again.

"It won't be too bad," Jesse was assuring her. "It's very civilized here, as you said before. There are four bedrooms for you to choose from, and the bathroom has real, live hot water."

"I'm not worried." She turned her head to smile up at him. "One thing I can be sure of is that you'll take care of me. After all, you took good care of me when I was sick." She remembered something that had bothered her about that time. "Jesse?"

"Yeah?"

"After I was sick... you left that morning and said you'd see me."

"Yes, I did." He waited patiently for her to make her point.

"But you didn't call. You didn't come by or anything. I didn't even see you again until I went to the hospital with your gloves."

"Mmm-hmm."

"Jesse," she asked, "why didn't you call me?"

"I was waiting."

"For what?" Cate demanded sharply, propping herself on her elbow. She was leaning on Jesse's stomach, and he moved her elbow. "What were you waiting for?"

"I was waiting for you to be ready. I would have called you in another couple of days, but I was waiting for you to get over your embarrassment. You felt so bad that morning and seemed so uncomfortable with me around, that I didn't want to come back too soon. I didn't want— I don't want you ever to be nervous of me, or uncomfortable with me. I wanted to give you some time."

Cate held his gaze as long as she could, then bent her head to look down at her hands. "Oh," she said very softly.

Jesse moved, settling her comfortably against him. He folded his arms around her, holding her securely. "You thought I was giving you a not-too-subtle brush-off, didn't you?"

Wordless, Cate nodded.

"I'm sorry about that, Cate. I meant to make things easier for you. I didn't know I'd made them worse."

"I should have known you wouldn't just leave me hanging. I guess I wasn't thinking very clearly."

"You had an excuse."

"For acting like an idiot? Oh, right."

"You'd been pretty sick. You were overemotional because of that."

"It's nice of you to say that, but I was still acting like an idiot."

"Stop it!" Jesse shook her. "You weren't acting like an idiot then, but you are now."

"Oh." Cate dropped her head, her hair falling forward to hide her face.

"You're nervous again, aren't you?" Jesse whispered just above her ear.

Cate shrugged.

"I'm sorry we're stuck here tonight, Cate, but it won't be too uncomfortable, I promise."

"I know it won't. You probably even have spare combs and toothbrushes, don't you?"

"Yes, I do. My mother raised me to be a good host." She could hear the smile in his voice. "But it's not the toothbrush that you're nervous about, is it?"

She shook her head in silence.

"Oh, Cate." Jesse turned her in his arms and pulled her cheek against his chest, holding her securely. "Please don't be afraid to be alone with me. You know I wouldn't hurt you for anything."

She rubbed her cheek against his sweater. "Maybe it isn't you I'm afraid of."

"Mmm?" The deep rumble of his voice came from beneath her ear.

"Maybe..." Her voice was barely a whisper. "Maybe I'm more afraid of myself."

Jesse went very still for a moment. Then his cheek came down to rest softly on her hair. Neither of them spoke as the flames leaped and danced behind the iron-barred door.

Over an hour later Cate watched as Jesse piled ashes over the last embers in the stove. "Will they go out before morning?" Cate asked.

"Nope. In the morning I'll just have to stir up the coals and add some more wood." He straightened. "I'll show you the bedrooms, and you can pick the one you like."

"This sounds like a luxury hotel—my choice of bedrooms!"

She laughed and followed as he led the way upstairs. They had sat together without speaking as the fire burned down, lost in their thoughts, their closeness, in the hypnotic flickering of the flames. Jesse hadn't broken the silence until the last log burned through and fell into the grate.

It was late and time to sleep, he'd suggested calmly. Cate tried to match his relaxed manner as he took her on a tour of the upstairs rooms, but she doubted that she fooled him. When he showed her into the last bedroom, though, she knew it was the one she wanted.

It was the smallest of the four, tucked under the eaves at the rear of the house. It had a sloping ceiling and two dormer windows, and a beautiful acorn-finial bed covered with a handmade quilt. The walls were papered in soft shades of rose, echoed in the cushions on a small rocker in one corner. The curtains were unbleached muslin with a deep ruffle. Jesse lit a small lamp on the chest of drawers and the room was filled with its warm glow.

"This one," Cate said, turning to smile over her shoulder at him. "This is the room I want."

"Are you sure you wouldn't like the one across the hall?" Jesse looked around uncertainly. "It's a lot bigger than this one."

"This one's perfect." She looked at it again smiling happily. "This is…it's the room I wanted as a child." She spun around, gazing at him uncertainly in the flickering light. "It's okay, isn't it? Or would you rather I took one of the others?"

"No, not at all. You take the one you want."

Cate grinned sheepishly. "I sound like a little kid, don't I?"

"There's nothing wrong with that. Sometimes I think the child in us is the best part of us." He lifted the larger lamp and stepped back. "I'll put some stuff in the bathroom for you. You'll have it first, whenever you're ready."

"Okay," Cate replied, as calmly as she could

She was trying her best not to be nervous and childish and silly, but it was an uphill battle. She listened until Jesse's footsteps went back downstairs, then bolted to the bathroom. He had left a lamp lit for her and set out towels, comb and brush, and the much discussed toothbrush. He'd also left her a pair of his pajamas and a robe. The pajamas were pale blue cotton, still crisp and creased, obviously never worn. The robe was soft white terry, frequently worn but freshly washed, carrying the faint scents of bleach and fresh air.

She hurried through her bath, hand-washed her underthings and hung them on the rod to dry, then buttoned on the pajama jacket. She turned up the sleeves until her hands showed, then tried on the pants, but they were a lost cause, far too big for her slender hips. After several futile attempts to make them stay up she folded them neatly and left them on the small chest beneath the bathroom window. The jacket reached halfway down her thighs, adequate to protect her modesty. She pulled the robe on over the jacket, wrapped the thick terry cloth around her and tied the belt securely.

A glance in the mirror did nothing for her ego. Her face was scrubbed clean, her hair brushed, and she looked about thirteen years old, swathed in the overlarge robe. That wasn't entirely a bad thing, she realized. This was a dangerous situation, and maybe a little insurance wasn't such a bad idea. The robe covered her bare legs and swaddled her body in shapeless folds, removing any vestige of seductiveness. She gave herself a last disgruntled glance, then shrugged and carried her lamp from the bathroom.

She stopped short in the doorway of "her" room. Jesse was bending over the bed, turning it down and sliding a hot water bottle down to the bottom of it. He straightened and smiled as he saw her.

"There you are. Are you warm enough?"

"Yes. Yes, I'm fine." She plucked at her terry-cloth lapel. "This is nice and warm."

"Not much of a fit, though." He looked her up and down and shook his head. "So much for your glamorous image, Cate."

"What glamorous image?" she asked, grinning. "And believe me, if you think this robe is a bad fit, it's only because you haven't seen the pajamas!"

"So—" Jesse folded his arms and waited, his lips twitching with laughter "—show me how they fit."

"I can't," she giggled, pulling the robe closer around her. "The shirt is huge, but the pants are enormous. They're so big I couldn't make them stay up. I left them in the bathroom." Jesse's face went still, the laughter dying form it, and Cate found herself babbling nervously on. "The shirt will be plenty warm enough, Jesse. It's as long as a nightgown. I'll be warm...." Her voice trailed away.

Jesse cleared his throat. "That's good." His voice was rough. "If the hot water bottle cools off just take it out and put it on the table." He brushed past Cate, then stopped in the doorway, half a pace from her. "Good night, Cate. Sleep well."

"Thank you. It's—"

Jesse reached out to touch her cheek, and the banal words died in her throat. His fingertips feathered over her skin, across her cheekbone and under her hair to cradle the nape of her neck. With the lightest of pressures he drew her toward him.

Boneless, her body swayed into his. She couldn't suppress a little gasp as they met, melting together. Her head tipped back, her lips parting expectantly. Slowly, very slowly, Jesse bent to kiss her, brushing his lips lightly across hers until Cate could wait no longer. She reached up to grasp his face and pull him down to her.

As if her movement had released whatever controls he'd put on himself, Jesse abandoned all pretense of restraint. His arms closed around her, crushing her against him.

She went to him willingly, eager for his touch, his kiss, hungry from the days of waiting and wanting, and trying to ignore that wanting. He filled her senses with his scent, his touch, the rasp of his beard against her face, her neck. Cate wound her arms around his neck and kissed him with all the passion she'd pushed out of her life for so many years. She might never have felt passion in her life—certainly she'd never felt *this* kind of passion for any man.

She was weak at the knees. Her breasts ached, heavy and swollen, echoing the ache low in her belly. She was trembling, burning with the heat that was pulsing through her veins. She wanted Jesse so badly that she couldn't think, could only feel.

She was pure sensation beneath his mouth, every nerve vividly aware of Jesse, of his hard, muscular strength, big and warm and vitally male, of the way her slimmer, softer body molded to his. They fit together like two pieces of a puzzle, the curves and hollows of their bodies meshing perfectly as he drank his fill of her mouth.

Cate rose on her toes to come even closer, sliding her hands restlessly over his shoulders, around the back of his neck, through his hair, echoing the movements of Jesse's hands. His passion was evident, but he kept it tightly reined. He caressed her back, her shoulders, her throat, through the terry cloth of the robe. He never pushed the thick fabric away from her body, never touched her skin.

"Oh, Cate." He breathed her name, a groan against her throat, and his arms tightened around her until he was almost hurting her. Cate didn't mind the hurt; it was the closeness she wanted.

And then he pushed her away. He let her go so suddenly that she staggered backwards, falling against the tall pine chest and catching herself awkwardly by grabbing at its top. Against the lamplight from the hallway she could see only a tall, broad-shouldered silhouette.

"Cate, I—" His voice was low and harsh. His hand lifted, reaching toward her, then fell back to his side. "Good night, Cate." He turned on his heel and was gone.

Cate slumped against the chest, staring uncomprehendingly at the doorway. The lamplight receded toward Jesse's room, at the other end of the hallway. A door opened, then closed, cutting off the light.

Why had he gone?

Cate pushed herself away from the chest and walked on shaking legs to the wide bed where she would sleep...alone.

Why had he gone? That was a stupid question. She knew perfectly well why he'd gone, and why he'd gone at that moment. If he hadn't left her then, he wouldn't have left her at all.

She untied the belt and slid Jesse's robe off her arms, trying to ignore the picture her shameless mind created of that robe swathing Jesse's nude body as he stepped from a shower, warm and damp and fresh. She dropped it across the foot of the bed and crawled beneath the bedclothes. The sheets were comfortably warm from the hot water bottle, but the chill within Cate couldn't be banished so easily.

She was glad he'd had the strength to leave her. There was a powerful attraction between them, but they were far from ready to act on it. They might never be ready.

She was glad he'd had the strength to push her away, since she certainly had neither the strength nor the will. She was glad he'd left her before things got out of hand.

Things were out of hand before you ever came to this house, her mind pointed out. She ignored it, rolling onto her side to curl into a small ball, her arms wrapped around her knees.

She was glad he'd left her.

She was glad.

She *was*.

It took an eternity of tossing and turning and pillow punching for her to fall asleep. When she awoke it was pitch-dark and freezing. She curled herself into a tight ball and massaged her icy toes fruitlessly. She was cold, the bed was freezing, and the room was frigid. She had no idea what time it was, since her watch was downstairs in her purse, but an interminable several minutes of trying to get warm were unsuccessful.

There was no help for it. She had to have another blanket, or she'd freeze to death before she got back to sleep. Quietly Cate slid out of bed, flinching as her feet met the icy boards. She pulled Jesse's robe around her and padded out into the hall, seeking another blanket.

The darkness was not quite absolute. She could dimly make out the deeper patches of murk that marked the doorways of the other rooms and the lighter patches that were the windows at either end of the hall. She felt her way along the wall, trying to remember where she'd seen a big, pine blanket chest. The chest was her best bet to find more covers, but she couldn't remember where it stood. Somewhere in the hall, against the wall between two of the doors.

How hard could it be to find a large pine chest? The blob of darkness in front of her might even be it. She reached out and bumped a small piecrust table, upsetting the vase that stood on it.

Biting back a gasp, she grabbed for the vase and caught it just before it toppled to the floor. Very carefully she set it back in place. Shaking from the close call, Cate leaned against the wall and waited for her heartbeat to slow.

Think, she ordered herself. Think about it. The chest she'd seen was much bigger than this little table, so she had to look for big blobs in the dark. The darkest part of the hall was in the center, farthest from the two windows. She found the chest there by the simple expedient of stubbing her toe on the corner of it with excruciating force.

"Ow!" She fell onto the chest and managed to crack her shin on the edge before lurching against the wall with a thump. "Eee!" she breathed, clutching her wounded toe as hot lances of pain stabbed through her foot.

It's only a toe, she told herself. It's only a toe, and it'll feel better in a minute, and oh, how can it hurt this much!

"What the hell?"

The demand came from just behind her. Startled, Cate whirled around, pivoting on her uninjured foot, lost her balance and fell to the floor, landing heavily on her derriere.

"Cate?" Jesse asked incredulously. "Are you out here?"

"Yes." Her voice emerged as a squeak.

"What on earth are you doing?" Surefooted as a cat in the darkness, he stepped neatly around the chest and crouched to pull her into his arms. "Did you get hurt? Are you all right?" He ran his fingers lightly over her limbs, searching for evidence of injury.

"I'm okay." Her voice was a little stronger now, and exasperated. "Or I will be when my toe and my shin and my backside quit hurting!"

"Your toe and your shin and your—" He broke off. "What happened? And why are you out here, anyway?"

"I came out to look for another blanket. I didn't want to wake you up."

"Then you shouldn't have fallen over every piece of furniture in the hall!" There was laughter in Jesse's voice. Cate didn't know whether she wanted to laugh with him or smack him. "You came for a blanket. Were you cold?" He felt for her hand and closed it in his. "Good Lord, Cate, you're freezing!"

"No fooling. I practically rolled myself into a ball trying to get warm in bed, but it didn't work. I figured another blanket would do it."

"You need more than a blanket to warm you up," Jesse said grimly. He ran his hand down her leg to her icy foot and ankle. "Put your arms around my neck." He slid his arm behind her shoulders.

"What?"

"Put your arms around my neck," he repeated impatiently. "Unless you want me to drop you and complete the damage." He slid his other arm beneath her knees and began to lift her. Cate hastily clasped her arms around his neck and hung on.

"Jesse!" She tried to make her voice imperious, but she was starting to shiver again, and it came out thin and quavery. "What are you doing with me?"

"I'm going to get you warm."

"But my room's the other way."

"I know. I'm taking you to bed with me."

Astonishment held Cate silent and frozen long enough for Jesse to carry her into his room and deposit her on his wide pine bed. The sheets were smooth muslin and still held the warmth of his body.

"No, Jesse! I can't sleep in your bed." She pushed herself up, but Jesse caught her before she could scramble to the floor.

"Of course you can. I slept in your bed," he reminded her. He slid in beside her and flipped the bedclothes up over them both. "Lie down."

He wrapped a strong arm around her shoulders and pulled her down beside him. He nestled her close against his naked chest, his body curving around hers. He began to relax, then raised his upper body again and propped himself on one elbow.

"You've got to get this thing off before you freeze to death inside it."

He pulled the robe open, dragging it off her arms and pulling it from beneath the covers. He tossed it away and lay down again, wrapping her in his arms and draping his leg over Cate's, warming her with his own heat.

Cate held herself rigidly still for several minutes, but as the warmth of his body began to seep into hers, she started to relax. And as she relaxed, as her muscles warmed and loosened, a new sort of tension began to grow inside her. Jesse's arms were closed around her, one supporting her head, the other draped over her ribs, just below her breasts. His hand, warm and relaxed, was a hair's breadth from the undercurve of her breast. His leg lay over hers, heavy and warm, the coarse hair rasping softly, excitingly against her smoother skin.

She shifted slightly, her back moving against Jesse's chest, her derriere against his belly, and he tensed behind her. She could feel his breathing, not as slow and regular as it had been before. Cate lay very still, fighting to steady her breathing, her heartbeat, fighting the clamor within herself.

Slowly, very slowly, Jesse moved, turning her in his embrace until she faced him. She couldn't have resisted even if she'd wanted to. The arm beneath her shoulder held her close as he touched her face, stroking his fingertips over her cheekbone and then across her mouth, feather light. Cate caught her breath sharply as his fingertip pressed at her lower lip. A kind of madness was growing in her, a wildness she'd never acknowledged.

Half shy, half temptress, she parted her lips to brush his fingertip with her tongue, then caught it in her teeth. She heard the catch in his breathing, saw his teeth gleam in the darkness above her as he pressed her onto her back, his body covering hers. His thumb followed his fingertip across her lips and then was replaced by his mouth. The kiss was slow, lazy, hot with a heat that began to beat through Cate's veins.

This time she wouldn't pull away. There was strength in her, but no strength to deny what she wanted so badly. Her strength was all in her wanting now, the power of all that she had suppressed and fought against released at last.

Jesse kissed her again and again, slow and gentle, then deep and demanding, and her body began to clamor with demands of its own. She twisted beneath him, inviting more, demanding more, her movements instinctive, enflaming.

She could hear ragged breathing, hasty, whispered words, but didn't know if the breathing and the words were his—or hers. He pulled impatiently at the pajama top that swaddled her. A button popped, and the fabric was dragged away, freeing her body.

Cate wound her arms around his neck, and the soft mat of hair on his chest brushed over her nipples, sending a thrill of sensation through her to coil in a heavy knot low in her belly. Jesse cupped his hands on her shoulders, enjoying her silky skin. He stroked down the graceful line of her back, past her waist, and gasped against her neck when he found no panties, but only satin skin. Then his hands moved again, and Cate began to tremble.

She twined herself around him and gave herself up to him. He searched her body with his mouth and hands, seeking and finding points of delight she'd never suspected. He found her breasts, the nipples taut and aching with desire for him, her slender waist, the soft curves of her hip and thigh, and the throbbing center of her. The heat flamed and burned as he touched and kissed and nipped and caressed. Her breasts were swollen and sensitive under his touch, her limbs lax as the waves of arousal swept over her, pulling her deeper and deeper.

She knew no more shyness; there was no place for shyness where he took her, but only want and desire and this man whom she needed more than she needed air to breathe. She took him with her, her hands working the same magic for him, reveling in her power to excite as she reveled in the strength and the beauty of him.

They were so different, hard and soft, strong and yielding, yet they fit perfectly, his larger body moving with her smaller one in the oldest dance of all. And then his mouth captured hers again as he took her, and together they slid over the edge and into a whirling, spinning eternity.

Neither knew when the last quakes and tremors eased, for as their bodies cooled, sated but still entwined, they slid into sleep together.

Chapter Ten

"Melissa!" Cate cried in mock outrage. "Don't you dare take a picture of me with my hair looking like this!"

"I'm going to! I'm going to take your picture!" Melissa crowed gleefully from her perch on the play table.

Her prosthetic leg lay discarded on the floor, and her crutches were propped against the table beside her. She held one of Cate's "old" cameras, a semiautomatic thirty-five millimeter fitted with a basic fifty-millimeter lens. With that camera and that lens, even Melissa could take reasonable pictures, and with all the practice she was getting, she was turning into a fairly proficient little photographer.

"Tell you what," Cate said, lifting her Nikon with its heavy zoom lens and autowinder, "I'll take a picture of you, and you take a picture of me. If we do it at the same time we'll get pictures of each other taking pictures."

Melissa puzzled that out for a moment, then nodded. "Okay. I'll count three. One..." She lifted the camera and waited for Cate to do likewise. "Two..."

Cate focused, then zoomed in until Melissa filled the frame. Her fine, mouse-brown hair was escaping from its braids, the sun turning it into an aureole around her head.

"Three!" Melissa cried. She snapped the shutter on her camera, and Cate held her shutter button down, firing several frames of film and catching Melissa's triumphant grin as she lowered her camera.

"Very good!" Cate applauded. "I think you can be a photographer if you want to when you grow up, Melissa."

"No, I can't," the little girl stated with the absolute conviction of her six years.

"You can't, huh? How come?"

"'Cause I'm gonna be a ballerina." Melissa seemed to see no incongruity in a child with only one leg having such an ambition. "Or a fireman. My brother Timmy says I can't be a fireman because I'm a girl, but I saw a girl fireman on TV the other night. Girls can be firemans, can't they, Cate?"

"Sure they can, honey." Cate tried very hard to keep the quaver out of her voice. She almost succeeded.

Melissa slanted her a secretive glance. "You know what else I'm gonna do?"

"What's that?" Cate smiled

"I'm gonna get married," Melissa whispered.

"You are?" Cate gaped appreciatively. "Who are you going to marry?"

"I don't know yet." Melissa shrugged that problem off. "Are you gonna marry Dr. Jesse?" She looked up, limpidly curious.

"I don't know," Cate replied after a startled moment. "Why would you think that?"

"Because you're so pretty, and Dr. Jesse likes you."

Reason enough to get married, Cate thought, and hid her smile. "I like him, too."

"Good!" Melissa smiled excitedly. "Do you want me to ask him to marry you?"

"No, no, please don't do that, honey!"

"Why not?" Melissa asked, crestfallen.

Cate bent close to whisper. "Because men like to ask first. It makes them feel better."

"It does?" Melissa didn't think that mattered, but when Cate nodded, she sat back thoughtfully. "I guess I won't ask him, then."

"It's better if you don't, sweetie."

"There you are, Melissa!" said a cheerful voice from the doorway. "It's time for your checkup, little girl."

Dr. Maggy Oswald stood there, smiling at Melissa. She nodded pleasantly at Cate. "Hello, Miss Drummond," she said. "Has Melissa been posing for you?"

"Actually, she's been taking pictures of me."

"Have you really?" One of Dr. Oswald's carefully groomed eyebrows lifted, and she smiled at Melissa.

She was always immaculate, even when she was dressed in the baggy hospital greens, always polite, always correct. Cate could have disliked her heartily if there hadn't been a genuinely warm and caring woman behind all that correctness.

"When they're developed, can I have one, Melissa?" She turned to Cate. "I have several of Melissa's drawings, but I don't have any photographs by her."

"Will you hang it on your wall?" Melissa asked.

"Of course. I'll hang it in my office along with your drawings"

Melissa was carefully easing herself off the table as they talked, struggling to balance with one crutch. Dr. Oswald made no move to help, though she watched the girl intently. Cate fought her own urge to jump to Melissa's aid. She wouldn't be doing Melissa a favor by lifting her down. She had to learn to do things for herself, even if the process was frustrating and difficult.

Melissa hung from the edge of the table for a moment, then wriggled an inch farther. Her toe touched the floor before she dropped the rest of the way and turned to grasp her other crutch and grin at them in triumph.

"Dr. Jesse!" she cried, looking past the women. Cate's head jerked up.

Her heart lurched, then began to pound slowly and heavily inside her ribs. He stood behind Maggy Oswald in the doorway, grinning at Melissa, who made her way over to him.

Cate couldn't keep from staring at him. She knew she had never seen a man so beautiful, yet she dreaded coming face-to-face with him. She'd been avoiding him all day, ever since he'd dropped her at her apartment to change clothes.

They'd left the Virginia hills before seven in a clear dawn that held only traces of the night's thick fog. Cate's mind was fogged, though, clouded and confused with guilt and dismay.

They'd had no time to talk things out that morning. Jesse had already shaved and dressed when he woke her at six. They'd eaten a hasty breakfast and hurriedly packed up their few belongings. Cate had been stiff and embarrassed, disinclined to talk; she dreaded discussing what had passed between them last night. She had feigned tiredness, curling into her seat and closing her eyes as they began the drive to Washington. Pretense became reality after a few minutes, and to her surprise she slept all the way home.

Jesse shook her awake as he drove through Georgetown, and when he stopped the car at her apartment she scrambled out with a quick goodbye. She knew he intended to kiss her, and she didn't think she could bear it.

"Cate!" he called before she could close the car door.

"Yes?" She bent and peered into the car, but she couldn't bring herself to meet his gaze.

"What's the mat—" The radio disc jockey brightly announced that the time was 8:10 a.m. "Damn!" He struck the steering wheel with his fist. "There's no time now! Look, Cate, we need to talk." She stared silently at the gearshift knob. "I'll see you at the hospital," he told her. "You will be there later, won't you?"

"Yes." She nodded at the gearshift. "I'll be there."

"I'll see you." It sounded more like a threat than a promise. He shifted into first. Cate backed up, and as she swung the door shut, she heard him repeat his words. "I'll see you."

Cate almost hadn't gone to the hospital. She would have stayed home if she hadn't promised to see Melissa.

Now Melissa reached Jesse at the playroom door, and he lifted her to give her a hug, then shook an admonitory finger under her snub nose.

"You be a good girl for Dr. Maggy and let her look in your ears and eyes, okay?"

"Okay." Melissa gazed up at him adoringly. "And I'll stick out my tongue real far, too."

"That's the way. See you later, Melissa." He squeezed Maggy's hand briefly. "I'll talk to you later on, Maggy."

"I'll call your office." With a smile and a little salute for Cate, Dr. Oswald shepherded Melissa down the hall.

They were alone. Cate bent her head over her camera and fiddled with the lens until Jesse's hand closed over hers, stilling the nervous movements.

Cate stared at their hands, his larger, more tanned, stronger than hers. She wouldn't look up; she couldn't.

"You've been avoiding me." It wasn't a question, so she made no reply. He took the camera from her hands and set it on the table beside them. He placed it there very carefully, a little afraid, she knew, of damaging her expensive equipment.

He owned a camera, but it wasn't the same. He'd shown her a few pictures he'd taken, and she'd managed not to laugh.

When he was satisfied that the camera was in no danger of falling he stood before her and tipped her face up with his fingertips.

"Why?" he asked.

"Why what?" She wouldn't give an inch.

"Why have you been avoiding me?"

Cate pulled her chin free of his hand and looked down. "Why do you think?" she muttered sullenly. She'd hoped he wouldn't realize she had been dodging around corners all day, trying to stay out of his path. She'd known it couldn't last, though. She had hoped to have her thoughts sorted out by the time she saw him again, but that hadn't happened, either.

"Because we made love?" he asked softly. "Is that any reason to avoid me?"

"Jesse!" Her face flaming, she glanced at the open door. "Anyone could hear us in here!"

"Then we'll go to my office." He picked up the camera Melissa had used and headed for the door. "Come on."

With all the enthusiasm of a child on her way to the principal's office, Cate gathered up her equipment and followed. Inside his cubbyhole of an office Cate set her camera bag down and perched on the lumpy chair while he closed and locked the door.

"Now, why," he repeated, very gently, "have you been avoiding me all day?"

"I—" Cate shrugged. "I wanted some time. To think."

"Time to think." Jesse walked around the desk and seated himself. The chair creaked in protest as he leaned back. "And did you? Think, that is?"

Cate kept her head down. "I tried to."

"Reach any conclusions?"

She shrugged.

"Avoiding me isn't going to help. We need to talk."

Talk about what? Cate wondered desperately. Talk about how we made love? Talk about how we kissed and caressed and made sweet, sweet love? She could just see them having a nice, civilized conversation about *that* over tea and crumpets.

"I don't know what good talking is going to do," she muttered mutinously, staring at the linoleum beneath her feet. It was a thoroughly obnoxious shade of gray-green. "Thinking certainly hasn't gotten me anywhere."

"It's gotten you feeling unhappy and guilty, for no good reason."

Cate's head snapped up at that. She glanced quickly at Jesse, then stared down at the floor again. He saw too much, saw things she wanted to keep hidden.

"We made love, Cate," he said quietly. "There's nothing terrible in that. We're adults, we're unattached...we care a great deal about each other. You have no reason to feel guilty."

Slowly she dragged her gaze up to his face. Her eyes were dark with unhappiness. "Then why do I feel guilty, Jesse? Can you answer me that? If it's all so great, why do I feel so bad?"

"I don't know why," he said slowly. "I could make a guess, but I won't. This is something you'll have to settle for yourself." He dropped his stethoscope and the other pieces of his pocket luggage into the desk drawer and shoved it closed, then stood. "Let's go get some supper."

Alarms and warning sirens went off in Cate's head. It was supper, after all, that had started all this. She was shaking her head as he walked around the desk.

"No. No, thank you, Jesse. I don't—"

"Scared?" Softly spoken, the word was a challenge, a dare. There was still enough of Cate the girl in her to make it impossible to resist. Her chin came up and her eyes flashed.

"Not at all," she said firmly. "What did you have in mind?"

"Deli and a little conversation." He approved of the quick flare of anger in her eyes.

Cate studied his face for a moment, then nodded. "All right."

He parked the car a block from her home, and they walked the rest of the way, stopping to buy bread from a German bakery, cold cuts from a deli, and dessert from a newly opened, trendy French *pâtisserie*. He unpacked their purchases and began assembling sandwiches while Cate set out plates and cutlery and poured iced tea.

"I remember a time," he said, watching her take a too-big bite of her pastrami, onions and mozzarella on a kaiser roll, "when you wouldn't touch pastrami. You said it was poisonous."

"I was convinced at the time that it was. If you'll remember, I used to hate yogurt, too."

"You mean you actually eat that stuff?" His face was a study in horrified distaste.

Cate laughed. "I've changed from the kid you remembered, Jesse. I've changed a lot, but sometimes I get the feeling that when you look at me, you still see a twelve-year-old."

"I didn't mean for that to show." She just smiled, and he shrugged. "I hate to admit it, but sometimes I do have trouble separating the adult Cate from the child."

"I can tell," she commented dryly.

Jesse tried to scowl at her, but couldn't quite manage it. "That's a part of it," he said after a moment. "It's a part of what makes the closeness between us so easy, and so unnerving. We share a history. We can laugh at silly things, at private jokes, the way people who've been married for a long time do."

The remark caught Cate off guard. It was a little bit frightening. Before she had a chance to digest the idea, Jesse went on.

"It's that shared past that's made all this such a surprise, I think." He half turned in his chair and gazed at the far wall. "If we had met as strangers and been attracted to each other this way, I don't think we'd have been so astonished. That kind of instant chemistry isn't common, but it's not unheard of. What's kept us both uneasy is the old business of thinking of each other like brother and sister." He swung the chair around and pinned her with a level gaze. "We're not brother and sister, Cate."

"I know," she whispered, and looked away. "I know."

Jesse held her eyes, his gaze dark, dangerous. "We're lovers, Cate."

Cate's breath caught in her throat. For a moment her heart, her breathing, everything seemed to stop as she remembered what it felt like to love him, to be loved by him.

She shoved herself roughly to her feet and took two agitated steps away from the table. Her back to him, she clutched the edge of the countertop, her fingers whitening from the pressure. "You said you weren't going to talk about that anymore." She turned to face him challengingly.

"I know what I said, but maybe I was wrong. Ignoring it isn't going to make it go away." He rose, and as he walked toward her, Cate found to her mortification that she was shrinking back against the cabinet. His face twisted. "Don't be afraid, please, Cate. Don't ever be afraid of me."

"I'm—I'm not," she protested unconvincingly.

He reached out to take her shoulders and ease her toward him. "Don't be afraid," he repeated. "Not of me, or of your feelings." He touched her cheek, and the gentle pressure of his fingers seemed to light a flame that shot through her veins to ignite the warmth deep in her belly.

Cate looked up into his face, the face of a man she'd loved and trusted all her life. She still loved him, but she wanted him now, and it was the wanting that scared her. Her tension showed in her eyes, and Jesse took his hand away.

"Don't be afraid, Cate."

He dropped his hands and stepped back, and Cate moved quickly away. "That's easy for you to say." She spoke lightly.

"Not really, but that's all I ask. I know you're a little bit thrown by all this, but try to relax and stop worrying about it. Worrying never solved anything." He walked back to the table. "You know what solves your problems?"

"What's that?"

"Food. Come back and finish your sandwich."

"Food? Since when did food solve anything?" She scoffed, but she moved back to the table.

"Since I was in med school. I missed so many meals then that I learned any problem looks smaller on a full stomach."

"I wouldn't know about that, but I'd hate to let this pastrami go to waste." Cate grinned and took a big bite.

"How are you getting along with Melissa?" Jesse asked when they were finishing their coffee and pastries.

"I'm crazy about her. She's delightful, and so smart. I'm continually surprised at her observations of the world. Without ever being told she reaches a lot of pretty astute conclusions."

"I thought you'd get along. Especially after she got so mad at me for yelling at you. I think she sees herself as taking care of you."

Cate smiled. "My protector?"

"In a way. She protected you from me, didn't she?"

"Very effectively, too. I only wish I could protect her."

Jesse nodded. "We all do. I think she's a pretty special kid myself. I'm glad you like her, but don't spend all your time with her. You'll get hurt, and you might hurt her, too."

Cate understood his point, but she didn't accept it. Frowning, she traced a random pattern on the tabletop. "I don't agree with you, Jesse. I don't see how caring can hurt. And if I spend a little extra time with Melissa, it's only because she doesn't have her mother staying at the hospital. She's just a little girl, and she gets so lonely between her mother's visits...." She looked at him uncertainly. "I'm not sure that I can explain this, Jesse."

"Try." He leaned his elbows on the table, watching her face.

"When I look at Melissa, I see a lot of myself. My mother lived with me, she was with me physically, but she wasn't really there, if that makes sense. She didn't have enough energy left after working all day to give me more than the minimum. I know that she loved me, but she never seemed to have the time or energy to listen to me." She shrugged. "That might be why I spent so much of my time tagging along after you and Brad and Mike. It's why I spend so much time with Melissa."

"Because you see yourself in her?"

"In a way, but mostly because I'd like to be to her what you were to me."

Jesse just stared at her for a moment, too touched to speak. He'd always liked Cate, even when he called her a pest and a nuisance, but he'd never realized how important he was to her. It was a humbling revelation.

He reached out to take her hand. "Cate, I never knew—"

He was interrupted by his beeper's piercing alarm. "Damn!" He pressed the button to silence the maddening sound. As he crossed the room to the phone he stroked her hair lightly. The silky softness of it lingered on his fingers as he dialed his answering service.

Cate watched him, not listening to his brief conversation. She could see the tension creep into his shoulders. She knew that he had to go.

"I have to go to the hospital." He hung up the phone and pulled his coat on.

"Is something wrong?"

"Yeah." He kissed her quickly on the lips. "I don't know how long this'll take. If it's not too late I'll come back when I get done." He was gone before she could reply.

The evening was suddenly endless and empty. Cate washed the dishes and wiped the counters and shook the tablecloth, and was halfway through cleaning the stove, which didn't need it, when she realized what she was doing. She tossed the sponge back into the sink with a soggy splat. She wasn't ready to go to bed, but cleaning an already clean kitchen just because Jesse wasn't there was silly.

She wondered what he was doing. She wondered if he was right to warn her about her feelings for Melissa. She wondered what he had been about to say to her when his beeper went off.

She took a cup of coffee into the living room, curled comfortably in the chintz wing chair and fell asleep, still wondering.

The doorbell woke her after midnight. She stumbled out of the chair, stiff and chilled, and hurried to open the door. Jesse stood outside, a cold rain blowing around him. A sudden gust spattered rain into the hallway, and Cate grabbed Jesse's soggy coat sleeve.

"Come inside! You're getting soaked out there."

He walked into the light, and Cate stared at him, shocked. His face was gray, lined with anguish and inexpressibly weary. He was cold and soaked with the rain, and she hastened to pull his wet coat off him and toss it on the coatrack.

"Jesse, are you all right?" That was stupid. He wasn't all right at all; he looked terrible. She turned back to him, resting her hands lightly on his forearms. "Jesse, how can I help?" she asked softly.

"Just . . . hold me," he muttered, and pulled her into his arms.

He held her in a desperate embrace, so tight that she thought her ribs would crack, but Cate wound her arms around his waist and held him with all her strength. She could feel him trembling, and when she pressed her cheek to his, it was damp. He buried his face in her hair and gradually his trembling eased, the rigid tension in his body beginning to relax.

"Jesse?" She stroked his cheek. "Can you tell me what happened tonight?"

He took a deep breath, his chest rising and falling within the circle of her arms. He hesitated so long that she reached up to touch his face.

"If you don't want to talk about it . . ."

"No. I'll tell you." He sighed heavily again. "Maybe it'll help." He bent his head and buried his face in the curve of her neck, and his hands slid up her back to cup her skull. "I was called to the hospital for Doug Paton."

"The little boy with liver cancer?" Cate held Jesse tightly; she could feel him beginning to tremble again. Her hands were spread across his back, and the muscles there were rigid with tension.

"He'd gone into a coma. That's why they called me. I knew when I went that there was no more I could do, but . . ."

"But you had to try," Cate finished softly.

"I tried," he agreed after a moment, "and I failed." His fingers closed on a lock of her hair, hurting her, but Cate never noticed. "Damn it, he died! With all we can do, we still can't do enough! He was only seven years old, Cate, only seven! And he died, and there was nothing we could do to stop it!" His voice broke on the last words, and he buried his face in her hair again.

It was a long time before he began to relax. Cate stood in his arms, held him, stroked his hair and wished fervently that she could do more to ease the pain that racked him. She massaged the back of his neck, kneading the taut muscles with her fingertips, then pressed her lips softly to his cheek. Blindly he turned, seeking her mouth, kissing her with a desperate intensity.

The kiss smoldered and flamed, and then his hands began to move over her body again with fevered need. Cate began to tremble as the need grew and bloomed in her, as well. She caught his face in her hands, kissing him with something near to his own desperation. The fever burned in them, and suddenly Jesse swung around to the hallway and pulled her along as he strode quickly to her bedroom.

He kicked the door closed, closing them in, closing the world out of the small charming room with the wide, high bed. They tumbled across the bed, pulling at each other's clothes, the need too great to be denied. Jesse had loved her slowly and gently, now he loved her fast, with urgency and a dark desperation, caressing and kissing and pushing her, pushing them both to the edge and then over.

Cate came slowly back to earth, cradling Jesse in her arms, her legs tangled with his, their bodies damp with a light sheen of perspiration. As the heat left her blood she shivered and reached down to pull the bedclothes up to cover them. Exhausted, Jesse was already falling asleep as she tucked the quilt warmly around him.

He muttered and turned on his side. Cate curled herself up behind him, one arm draped over his ribs to hold him close. She brushed her palm lightly over the soft hair on his chest and he stirred, mumbling something that might have been her name. Cate went very still until he'd relaxed again, then adjusted her position and let herself relax, as well. Her lips were against his hair, and she kissed him gently.

She was sleepy herself, but oddly thoughtful.

Now she understood Jesse's warnings against involvement with the kids. He wanted to spare her this kind of pain. It was already too late. Cate was too fond of Melissa.

She refused to worry about herself, though. She knew that pain was a part of living. You couldn't hide away from life; she knew, because that was what she'd tried to do in the years following Brad's death.

She'd been so utterly lost when he died, a teenage widow, unable to cope. When Brad's mother offered her a home she'd accepted gratefully, unable to face living alone in the tiny house she'd shared with Brad. Doris had helped Cate through her grief, and perhaps Cate had unwittingly helped Doris cope, too. At Doris's insistence Cate had gone to college, and when she'd earned her degree in photography they had opened a photo studio together.

Cate took the pictures while Doris ran the business, and together they were surprisingly successful. Cate had settled into a comfortable routine with Doris and never even thought of moving out to live on her own. When a man asked her out she turned him down, uninterested in dating, content to live in the comfortable shell she and Doris had built for themselves.

She'd never considered breaking out and had been absolutely flabbergasted when, after seventeen years as a widow, Doris announced that she was marrying a man she'd met through the business and moving with him to his home in Phoenix.

Cate had been even more astonished when Doris insisted they sell the business and the Columbus house. She had forced Cate to accept all the proceeds of the sales and had coaxed, cajoled and browbeaten her into moving away from Columbus. She needed to start living again, Doris had told her; she needed to get out of that too-safe, too-familiar environment. At the time Cate hadn't understood what she meant.

She understood now. Beneath her hand Jesse's chest lifted and fell in a steady rhythm. She curled close, warming his body with hers. She understood what Doris had meant, because now she was living again, and it was thrilling . . . and terrifying.

She didn't want to think about the pain she would feel if anything bad happened to Melissa. Her mind refused to even contemplate the pain she would feel if Jesse went out of her life.

And it could happen so quickly, so easily. Only a woman widowed young could know how quickly tragedy could strike. One day she'd been a teenage bride, certain that life would always be easy and good. Then a military car had pulled to a stop in front of her little house and she had learned just how fleeting happiness could be. She couldn't take love for granted anymore, and neither could she take it lightly.

She loved Jesse. In the warm darkness of her bedroom she could admit that, but not in the daylight, not out loud. Jesse had never said he loved her. He cared for her, she knew that, but she'd known he cared for her when she was six.

He wanted her, but men wanted women all the time. Wanting was easy; it was the loving that was hard.

Did Jesse love her?

She didn't know the answer to that. She only knew that he had needed her tonight, and she had been able to help him. For now that had to be enough.

Chapter Eleven

It looks good...as much as you have of it." The editor's voice was unenthusiastic, damning with faint praise.

"Well, thank you...I guess."

Cate propped the telephone receiver on her shoulder and wondered what problems John Dorset had found in her work this time. She'd sent her rough outline for the photo essay to the editor in chief of *Washington Month* a week ago. A tall, thin man of about forty, John had a perpetually dismayed manner. The exact opposite of the bluff and blustering editor of the Perry White tradition, he was a quiet, somber man.

She'd never known him to show either anger or enthusiasm, only this hangdog consternation about the material he received. She theorized that he didn't want to waste energy shouting at his writers, so he tried to "guilt" them into line. His method, though unorthodox, seemed to work, for he put a lively, intelligent, entertaining magazine on the newsstands each month.

He sighed deeply, and Cate smiled.

"What's the problem with the article, John?"

"It's the doctor. What's-his-name. MacLeod."

"Jesse? What about him?"

"You know the guy. He's a friend of yours, right?"

"Yes. He's a childhood friend. Why?"

"Because the article's supposed to center around him. All you have on him is work, work, work. That's all right, but we need to see something of the man, as well, something of his private life."

"I'm not doing a tabloid exposé, John."

He sighed again, unutterably patient. She could almost see his lugubrious face. "Did I say anything about exposés?" He waited for an answer. "Did I?"

"No, you didn't say anything about exposés." Cate matched his patient tone. She couldn't resist teasing him just a little. She'd always suspected that a sly sense of humor lurked beneath John's dour exterior. "What *do* you have in mind?"

"Nothing sleazy; just a little something personal, in addition to the job. Where does he live? What does he do to relax? Who's his girlfriend? That kind of thing."

"He isn't going to like it," Cate predicted with conviction. "I'm pretty sure he won't be willing to let us use anything on his social life. He has a weekend house in Virginia, though, out in the Blue Ridge. Do you think a couple of shots of him out there would be enough?"

"Is that all you can get from him?"

"I'll be lucky to have his cooperation for that much. I told you before: he's only doing this under duress from the hospital administrator. The article is supposed to be about the pediatrics units and the renovation plans. He doesn't want the personal publicity in the first place, and anything he sees as an invasion of his privacy is really going to turn him off."

"So don't invade his privacy," John said. "I have faith in your powers of persuasion. Just give me a little of the man behind the doctor, all right?"

"Yes, sir!" Cate replied snappily. "You're the boss."

"It's nice to know that somebody thinks so." John wasn't laughing, but she could hear the humor. "Get me the new version when you can, okay?"

"As soon as I can," she promised, and hung up wondering if the promise had been rash. Jesse wasn't going to like this development at all.

"I really hate this," he muttered angrily. "I feel like I'm being invaded. Like the whole city of Washington is going to be peeping through a window into my life." It was Friday afternoon, and they were on their way to spend a weekend at the house in Virginia, taking pictures.

"I've noticed." Cate had listened to a steady stream of complaints since the angry eruption that followed her announcement of her plans. Her patience was wearing thin. "You've managed to make your feelings excruciatingly clear. Jesse, I know you don't want to do this, but can't you at least be a better sport about it?"

"Why should I?"

Cate blew her breath out in an exasperated hiss. "Because if you cooperate with the photographer the whole process will be a lot easier on both of us."

Jesse glanced at her, scowling. "Cooperate?"

"Cooperate," she said severely. "For Pete's sake, Jesse, he wanted pictures of you with your girlfriend! You should at least be glad I talked him out of that."

"You had an ulterior motive," he shot back. "You didn't want your picture to end up in that magazine along with mine."

Cate let that one pass. "I've thought about how to minimize the invasion of your privacy, Jesse. I won't show the exterior of the house, and I won't give its location, either. No one will be able to identify it."

"You can do that?" He looked at her in surprise.

"Sure I can. I'll show a little of your life outside the hospital, but I don't have to give away private information. I don't even have to say what state it's in, for that matter, just that it's in the mountains. Those mountains could be in Maryland, for all anyone needs to know."

"Mmm-hmm." Jesse nodded. "I'd appreciate that."

"I'm glad. All you have to do in return for the favor is smile for the camera."

"Now that," Jesse said with exaggerated iciness, "is asking entirely too much!"

As Cate dissolved into giggles he turned into the drive.

Unloading their weekend bags was easy, but unloading Cate's equipment was a major project. To photograph inside she'd brought lights and stands, reflecting umbrellas and a tripod, in addition to her usual heavy bag of cameras and lenses.

"What is all this stuff?" Jesse demanded as he tried to maneuver an armload of equipment through the doorway.

"It's my studio stuff. Since we're going to be indoors, it'll be a big help."

"You've been taking pictures indoors at the hospital and haven't been using all this junk." With a clunk and a clank he pulled the stands into the entry hall and piled them noisily beside the stairs.

"I've been taking pictures of moving targets," Cate told him. "I can't run along after you and the kids with a bunch of lights, can I?"

"That would make you kind of conspicuous." He looked at the heap of equipment. "Is there anything else?"

"Nope. This is it."

"That's a relief!" He stepped carefully over the aluminum legs of her tripod, caught her hand and pulled her past the camera bag. "Do you have to start taking pictures right now?"

"Actually—" Cate went willingly into his arms, welcoming the security of his embrace, the excitement of his touch "—I wasn't going to take any pictures at all until tomorrow."

"Ahh." He considered that for a moment, and his arm tightened around her waist while his free hand stroked up and down her back. "Did you have any plans for this evening?"

"Mmm." Cate tipped her head back to flirt up at him through her lashes,. "No plans at all. How about you?"

"Well…" Jesse's lips curved into a small, secret smile. "I did have a plan…of sorts."

Cate watched the movement of his lips, remembering the touch and taste of him, the magic his mouth could make for her. She loved him so much it seemed to fill her to overflowing. She could no longer remember why she had felt uneasy, why she had avoided Jesse after they made love for the first time. This was so right; how could she ever have thought it was wrong? When she met his gaze again her cheeks were flushed and her breathing shallow.

"What…" Her voice was oddly breathless. "What did you have planned?"

"Well—" he brushed his lips across her ear, his breath sending warm thrills over her skin "—first of all . . ." He kissed her earlobe lightly and then the exquisitely sensitive spot just below it. Cate's eyes closed; her head fell back. "I think I'd like . . ." He nibbled at her neck. "Some dinner."

Jesse's lips were still moving against her throat, and it took several seconds for the meaning of his words to penetrate the haze in her brain. When it finally did she shoved him away with such force he nearly fell onto the heap of camera equipment.

"Hey!" he protested, all wounded innocence.

"You rat!" She was torn between fury and laughter. "Just for that *you* can fix dinner!"

"Will you come and watch me cook?" he asked plaintively.

"And have you rope me into helping out?" She shook her head. "Not a chance! I'm not even going to be in the same room. You can just go on into the kitchen and cook your little heart out. I'm going to take this stuff in the living room and get it sorted out for tomorrow."

"Aww, come on, Cate . . ." If she hadn't seen the sharp glint of mischief in his gaze she might have relented. He reached for her, but Cate put out a hand to ward him off.

"No deal, Jesse." He stepped back, trying not to smile. "You may call me when dinner's ready," she added haughtily, hoisted her camera bag and sashayed into the living room.

Jesse took her at her word, and she heard nothing more from him for thirty minutes.

"Come and get it!"

His bellow echoed through the house. Cate put down the lights she'd been arranging, dusted her hands on the seat of her jeans and strolled with great dignity into the kitchen. Jesse stood at the stove, a dish towel tucked in the waistband of his jeans, forking spaghetti into a serving bowl. The table was set, and a salad and a bowl of spaghetti sauce already rested in the center of it, flanking an arrangement of autumn mums and two of the oil lamps.

He had done all this for her. She stopped short just inside the door. "It's beautiful," she breathed.

"It ought to be," Jesse replied without turning around from the stove. "It's my mother's recipe, and you'd be hard put to find a more gorgeous spaghetti sauce on this earth." He turned, bowl in hands. "And if you want some before it gets cold you'd better hurry up and wash your hands."

"That's not what I meant and you know it, Jesse!" She hurried across to the sink to wash. The spicy aroma of the sauce was making her stomach grumble hungrily. When she took the chair Jesse held for her, she laid a large manila folder on the table.

"What's that?" Jesse tapped the folder as he walked around to his chair. He passed her the bowl of spaghetti.

"Thank you. These are the pictures for the article." She served herself a generous portion of pasta.

"You've picked them out already?" He took the bowl when she passed it to him and handed her the sauce in exchange.

"Not the final set. These are the possibilities, without all the duds I culled out." She ladled sauce over her pasta and sniffed the rising steam appreciatively. "This actually smells like it could be your mother's sauce."

"You doubted my word?" he protested. "It's hers, all right. I made her teach me how to make it. My dad had to eat spaghetti for four days before I got it right."

"I'll take your word for it. I just don't remember you being particularly interested in cooking."

"I wasn't, until I got out of the service. After years of marine cuisine I figured I'd better learn how to cook for myself before I was poisoned."

Cate sputtered with laughter. "So you got your mom to show you how?"

He nodded as Cate sampled her spaghetti. "I demanded that she teach me how to make all my favorite things."

"Mmm! This is wonderful! What else did you have her teach you?"

"Meat loaf, pot roast and Swedish meatballs."

"You didn't learn her apple pie?" Cate was dismayed. "That was always so-o-o good!"

"I tried the pie." He set down his fork and gazed across the lamp flame at her, shaking his head. "You know, I really did try, but there's something about piecrust that I could never get a handle on. Hers is always great; I think I'm doing exactly the same things, and mine comes out like cement."

"Maybe it's the touch. They say you need a light touch for pastry."

Jesse reached out to take her hand in his, and Cate's mouth went dry. "Don't I have a light touch?"

He turned her hand over and stroked the ball of his thumb across her inner wrist. Cate felt the warmth shoot from her arm to her center. She couldn't have spoken. He knew the answer anyway.

For an endless moment he held her gaze; then he lifted her hand to his lips and pressed a kiss into her palm. "Eat your dinner, Cate." He put her fork in her hand and closed her fingers around it. "Go on," he urged. "Eat."

Cate stared down at her plate. He knew exactly what he was doing to her, and he was enjoying it. Well, maybe she could give him a little of his own medicine. She looked up slowly, meeting Jesse's gaze across the lamp flame. She lifted her glass and sipped the dark, potent wine Jesse had poured for them, then, with a flick of her tongue, caught the drop that clung to her lips. Jesse watched her mouth, and she could see the quick flare of desire in his face. She hid her smile.

"Eat your spaghetti, Jesse. It's getting cold."

"I—" Jesse's voice was rough and husky. He looked sharply at Cate, then sat back, the tension leaving his body as laughter took its place. "Yeah, Cate, I'll eat."

"And then you can look through the pictures." She took a bite of salad and grinned at him. The glance he shot her before he bent to his plate again said he understood her very well, and he would let her get away with it . . . this time.

When they'd finished he stacked the dishes in the sink, but refused to do more. "I'm not taking time to wash them now." He shook his finger at her in warning. "And don't you try to sneak down here and do them in the morning, either. I'll wash them myself."

"There's no reason why I shouldn't help," Cate pointed out, but Jesse was adamant.

"You're the guest, and you aren't washing these." He dried his hands and took her shoulders to steer her back toward the table. "Now, show me these pictures."

Cate dumped the prints out on the table and shuffled through them. "I haven't put them in any kind of order, but I have a pretty good idea of the number of pictures I want to use on each topic. There will be some of you, the kids, the hospital and the other staff." She extracted a print from the pile and passed it to him. "I like this one."

Chad grinned at them from amid a tower of playroom blocks. His happy smile contrasted poignantly with his chemotherapy-bald head.

"Mmm-hmm." Jesse nodded agreement as he studied it. "This says a lot without words."

"It was great to see him go home." Cate smiled at the picture. "Do you think he'll be all right?"

"As far as I can tell at this time. His test results show he's in remission now. He'll be checked every couple of months, but it looks good."

"And his hair will grow back?"

"Now that he's off the chemo it'll grow back as good as new."

"I'm so glad."

"So's Chad. He's sick of wearing a baseball hat. Did you get to say goodbye to him?"

"Yeah. He took home those pictures I printed for him, too. I told his mother to watch for the article."

"He has the pictures of you? He'll probably stick them on his wall." Jesse passed the picture of Chad back to her. "Along with his Pete Rose poster."

"It's nice to know I rate the same wall as Pete Rose." Cate selected another print. "Here."

One by one they studied the pictures, making decisions to use some and to reject others. Cate could trust Jesse's opinions on pictures of anyone and anything except himself. Those pictures he uniformly disliked.

"I give up!" she finally exclaimed in disgust. "You hate every single picture with you in it! I'm not even going to ask you about any more of them. I'll just pick the ones I like and the heck with your opinion!"

"And the heck with me, too, huh?" Jesse took a picture from her fingers and slid it back into the envelope. He caught her hand and pulled her toward him.

"I don't know about that." Cate let herself be drawn out of her chair and onto Jesse's lap. She wound her arms around his neck. "You have your good points."

She brushed her lips across his cheek and heard his quickly indrawn breath. With a heady sense of her own power she rubbed her cheek against his, enjoying the rasp of his beard on her skin, breathing the heady scents of him: spicy cologne and spaghetti sauce and the warm aura of man. She touched her lips briefly to his jawline, the hard angle of his cheekbone, his temple. The heat of the stove had brought out the wave in his hair, and an unruly lock fell onto his forehead. Cate brushed it back, surprised, as always, to feel how soft it was.

She loved to touch him, to explore and discover the varied textures of him, strong muscle, soft hair, smooth shoulder, rough jaw. She didn't know if she was as fascinating to Jesse as he was to her.... She hoped she was. She wanted to be fascinating for him; she wanted to be beautiful for him.

"Mmm." Jesse's face was buried in her neck, his hands sliding over her back. "You have good points, too. Like right here—" he slid his palm over her shoulder "—and here." His hand traveled down the length of her spine, as he said, "And here." His hand stopped, and Cate caught her breath.

"Jesse," she whispered on a wave of need, and bent to seek his mouth with hers. He caught the kiss and returned it, deep and seeking, heating her blood, melting her bones. She barely noticed when he slid one arm beneath her knees, the other around her shoulders and lifted her to carry her out of the room.

He carried her up the stairs with strong, steady strides.

"Like *Gone with the Wind*," she murmured, and Jesse paused halfway along the upstairs hallway.

"What's that?" He kissed her brow, then her throat as her head fell back against his arm.

"Like *Gone with the Wind*," she murmured. "You carried me up the stairs just like Clark Gable."

He chuckled softly. "Clark Gable was better looking." He nudged open the door of his bedroom and carried her through.

"He had big ears." Cate nipped at his lobe. "I like yours better."

Jesse stopped at the bedside and let her feet slip to the floor. He closed his arms around her waist and held her, content for the moment just to kiss her. Cate needed his kisses, but the kisses only fed the need for more. She wanted more than kisses, she wanted all of him, and as the heat began to build she tugged at his clothes, pulling his shirt free of his jeans to slide her hands beneath and find his body.

His back was warm, the skin smooth beneath her hands as she explored the firm ridges of muscle, the line of his spine. Jesse turned with Cate still firmly in his arms and sank slowly to the bed, pulling her down with him. Cate went willingly into his embrace, twining her arms around him and clinging.

The heat grew, beating in their blood as laughter faded into need and passion. There was danger here, Cate thought as Jesse kissed the base of her throat, pushing the neck of her polo sweater aside.

There was a storm in the air, dark and dangerous and exciting. Jesse moved quickly, dragging the sweater over her head and tossing it aside. He caressed her shoulder, touched her breast, and she could feel the thunder in the distance.

"Do you know how I've thought of you?" he murmured against her skin. "Do you know how I've wanted to touch you like this?'' He brushed his thumb over her nipple, and Cate gasped, twisting helplessly beneath him. ''And this?'' he cupped her small breast in his hand and found the taut peak with his lips.

It was as if a river of fire was running through Cate, and in a burst of impatient need she began to pull at his shirt buttons. Her fingers were clumsy and slow, too slow. She needed him; she had to be next to him without the barriers of cloth. She fumbled with the buttons, drawing out the process and unintentionally driving Jesse closer to the edge.

His mouth left her breast to take her lips again in a kiss of hard, driven need. The same need was burning in Cate, and she answered him with a fierce demand of her own. The storm was growing, the thunder and lightning and wind pulling them into a whirling vortex.

Impatiently, desperately, they kissed and touched and caressed. Jesse felt her tremble beneath his hands, his lips. Wherever he touched her, her skin heated until she burned in his arms, all the fire and passion in her released for him alone. He fought for control, but she thwarted him with soft hands and sweet lips.

She pressed her mouth to his throat, his chest, nibbling and tasting and driving him, faster and faster, toward the edge. The last of their garments were thrown aside, and skin met skin, slid and clung and teased and tormented. With a low groan Jesse trapped her body beneath his, pressing her to the mattress and holding her there. His control forgotten, he took her in a burst of need, smothering her soft cry of triumph with his mouth.

The thunder and lightning crashed around them, and they were swept into the heart of the storm.

Jesse came slowly back to the dim, quiet room. The wick in the lamp had burned low, and the flame spluttered irritably inside the chimney, casting a weak, irregular glow. The quilts and blankets were pulled over them, enclosing them in a nest of warmth. He held Cate in his arms, securely nestled by his side, her body warm and sated.

He felt the same heaviness in himself, exhaustion and exhilaration together. He slid one hand down her side, savoring the silky skin, sensing the flesh and muscle beneath, the deceptively fragile body. There was a strength in her that didn't show on the surface, a different sort of strength from a man's. He stroked the narrow curve of her hip. So different, such a marvelous difference. She stirred beneath his hand, moving with the lazy contentment of a sleepy cat.

Cate felt Jesse's arms tighten around her as she moved, as if to keep her close. He had no reason to worry. She wasn't going anywhere. There was nowhere else she wanted to be, nowhere on earth. She reached up to stroke his cheek. Jesse. How long had she known him without knowing him at all? She lowered her head and tucked it beneath his chin, caressing his chest, absently brushing her fingertips through the soft mat of hair.

"Cate?" His voice was a deep rumble beneath her ear.

"Hmm?"

"You hungry?"

After a moment of startled silence she gave a little spurt of laughter. "After all that spaghetti?"

"Well, are you?"

She thought about it a moment. "Yeah. You know what I want?"

"What's that?"

"Chocolate chip cookies. Suddenly I have this really tremendous craving for chocolate chip cookies. Do you have any chips?"

"I might. Or a couple of chocolate bars we can chop up."

Cate propped herself on her elbow to smile down at him. "Did you have your mother teach you how to make chocolate chip cookies like hers?" she asked hopefully.

"Of course."

"And?"

"And what?" Jesse asked, puzzled.

"And did the lessons work? You said you still can't make apple pie. Can you make cookies?"

"I should make you wait and see...."

"Jesse!" She ran her palm down his chest. The ridged muscles of his stomach tightened beneath her hand. "I can make you talk...." Her fingers moved again.

"All right!" He caught her hand in his. "The lessons worked, okay?"

"Okay!" She sat up. "How long will it take to make 'em?"

"It hasn't been *that* long." Jesse looked up from dropping blobs of dough on a cookie sheet. He was barefoot, dressed in jeans and an unbuttoned shirt.

"You said fifteen minutes." Cate gathered the folds of her lavender peignoir around her and perched on a tall stool beside him. She dipped a fingertip into the bowl and scooped out a bite of dough. Jesse swatted at her with his wooden spoon, but she was too quick for him. "It's been twenty minutes already," she informed him haughtily.

"So we had to hunt for the chocolate chips. Aren't you glad we found them in the end?"

"I'm glad I decided to search all of the cupboards until they turned up."

"I just can't figure out why you put them away with the canned tomatoes. Seems like an odd combination." Quick and deft, she snitched another bite.

He filled the sheet and carried it across to the oven. "We all have different approaches to the logic of storage arrangements. It made perfect sense to me."

"Some logic. I'll bet you just stuffed them in the first space you found." Cate took advantage of his absence to take a huge bite of cookie dough.

Jesse turned from the oven and saw her. "Eat enough of that and you'll make yourself sick."

"An old wives' tale. One of the healthiest foods you can eat is cookie dough."

"Right up there with sugar sandwiches." He walked over to her stool and planted his hands on the tabletop on either side of her, trapping her there. He bent his head close to hers. "I'm a doctor; why don't you ask me what's healthy?"

"What's healthy?" Cate's heart began to thump against her ribs. She laid her hands lightly on Jesse's arms, feeling the coiled-steel tension there.

"Oh . . . this." He nuzzled her neck, then followed the low-scooped neckline of her gown with his lips. "I like this purple thing," he murmured. "Whatever it is."

"It's a peignoir, you peasant," Cate teased in a breathless whisper.

"I like it." His mouth moved over her skin, scorching hot. "It makes me feel very healthy." His arms closed around her, pulling her off the stool and into his embrace. Boneless, Cate's body molded to his.

"The cookies," she protested with the last of her strength. "They'll burn."

"I set the buzzer." Jesse slid the peignoir off her shoulder, pushing the ribbon strap of her gown after it

and following their path with his lips. "We have eight to
ten minutes to kiss . . . and . . ."

They made the most of those minutes.

Chapter Twelve

The scent of coffee, rich, warm and seductive, tugged her toward consciousness. Cate squirmed and shifted restlessly, reluctant to wake. She buried her face in the pillow, but she couldn't escape it, calling to her, pulling her out of sleep. With a sigh she admitted she was awake, stretched beneath the bedclothes and rolled over, squinting against the bright morning sun.

"About time you woke up, sleepyhead."

Jesse stood beside the bed, smiling gently down at her, a steaming mug of coffee in his hand. As Cate blinked sleepily at him, he sat on the edge of the bed. The mattress dipped beneath his weight, and Cate let herself roll toward him until her body rested against him.

She studied him with heavy-lidded eyes. Casually dressed in faded jeans and a flannel shirt, he was the most beautiful man she'd ever seen. His cheeks were freshly shaven, and his hair was still damp from his shower. She could smell the freshness on him, the clean scent of his skin, and wanted nothing more than to throw herself into his arms and bury her face in the open throat of his shirt. Blushing, she lowered her eyes to hide what might show in them.

"I was beginning to think you were going to sleep all day," Jesse said, and she smiled at him.

"How long have you been up?"

She started to push herself up against the pillows, then remembered with a jolt that she was naked beneath the bedclothes. She could feel the quick heat in her cheeks as she pulled the sheet to her throat and slid one arm out for the coffee. After what had passed between them last night it was silly to be shy, but she couldn't help it.

"Over an hour." His smile was smug as he handed her the coffee.

"I don't know why you need to be so self-righteous about waking up early. After all, some of us like our sleep." She sipped the coffee. "Mmm, this is delicious. What time is it, anyway?"

"A few minutes after eight."

"I don't need to apologize, then. Eight in the morning can hardly be called sleeping all day." She tipped her head to the side to study his face. "Why were you up so early, Jesse? Couldn't you sleep?"

Jesse's smile was warm with an intimate knowledge that brought the heat to her cheeks again. "I slept fine. I have some errands to run, though, and when I woke up I figured I might as well get up."

He reached out to trace a fingertip down her cheek and onto her throat. "You looked so cute sleeping, I didn't have the heart to wake you."

Cate struggled against the wave of desire his touch sent through her. "Well, I'm awake now," she said, her mouth dry. "What kind of errands do we have to do?"

"Not we, just me." He smiled, taking any sting out of the refusal. "I have to pick up some more bottled gas, and fuel oil for the generator. It'll take a couple of hours, so I'll get it over while you have your breakfast and lounge around here like a lady of leisure."

"Are you sure you don't want me to go along?"

"I'd love for you to go along, but you'd be bored to death. And if I get this done early you'll have the rest of the day to take pictures of me posing by the fireplace like the squire of the manor."

Cate giggled. "Serve you right if I did. I could make you wear a smoking jacket." She considered for a moment. "Do you know anyone who can lend you a dog, though? The squire of the manor has to have a faithful hound sitting at his feet."

"Would I have to smoke a pipe?" Jesse was trying hard not to smile. Cate could see his lips twitch.

"Of course. The picture wouldn't be complete without a pipe." She smiled sweetly at him and sipped her coffee.

Jesse sat back, folding his arms. "That's out, then. As a physician, I can't be photographed smoking. It's bad for your health."

"You should tell that to Dr. Gold," Cate retorted. "I never see him without a cigarette."

"I know. We're working on him, though. Either peer pressure or browbeating will work eventually."

"That sounds ominous. Are the rest of you going to tie him up and take away his cigarettes?"

"If all else fails. We'll probably just wear him down with snide remarks and dirty looks, though." He leaned closer and brushed the tumbled hair off her forehead. "Will you be all right here until I get back?"

Cate laughed. "I'll probably pine away to nothing if I'm left alone for two whole hours." She shook her head at him. "Don't worry about me. I'll be lazy and get up slowly, and I probably won't even be finished with breakfast by the time you get back with all your household fuels. Go on." She flapped her hand at him. "Get going. The sooner you go, the sooner you'll get back, right?"

"That's it." He smiled and bent over her, planting his hands on either side of her shoulders and pressing her back against the pillow. "You take things easy, and I'll be back before you know it, okay?"

"Okay." She was breathless. Her lips slightly parted, she waited for him.

Jesse bent still closer until his mouth was a fraction of an inch from hers, his breath warm and gentle on her skin. "Sweet," he whispered, and kissed her.

His lips were warm and mobile, teasing, tasting, fanning the embers of last night's fire. She rolled closer, curving her body around him as he sat. The sheet fell away from her back, and Jesse couldn't resist. He stroked his hand down the smooth line of her spine, and Cate shivered with the quick flare of desire.

Just when they would have burst into flame again he drew away, pulling the bedclothes up to cover her, his gaze lingering on her lips. His smile was rueful.

"I'll see you in a little bit, my Cate." He pushed himself off the bed and walked quickly to the door, where he paused. "That pink sweater you brought is really pretty, but it's cold today. If you want something warmer there are sweaters and things in the dresser."

A quick wave and he was gone. Cate sighed and relaxed against the pillows, smiling as she listened to his feet on the stairs. The front door closed with a bang, and a moment later she heard the engine spring to life and then the crunch of gravel as Jesse drove away. She sipped her cooling coffee, then tipped the mug up and drained it.

She set the empty mug on the nightstand and stretched luxuriously. This was the way to wake up, with coffee and a kiss in bed. She slid deeper into the bed, pulling the covers up to her chin and half closing her eyes. She was utterly and completely relaxed, her body warm and alive with Jesse's loving. She didn't know if she'd ever been so content.

Through the screen of her lashes she watched the morning sunlight flicker on the drapes. She really should get up; it was after eight in the morning. On the other hand, she was warm and drowsy, and it would be so easy just to close her eyes and drift back into sleep.

But if she didn't get up, and right now, she would still be asleep when Jesse got back, and then he would know just how lazy she was.

With that thought she shoved back the covers and sat up, shivering as the chill air struck her naked skin. Jesse had picked up her peignoir from wherever he had tossed it when he stripped it off her last night and laid it across the foot of the bed. She pulled it on, grateful for the garment and the thoughtful gesture.

Thoughtful. Not just tender and loving and impossibly sexy, but thoughtful. She'd never realized just how thoughtful Jesse was, though he'd been doing thoughtful things for her all her life. She'd taken them for granted as a child; it was only as an adult that she'd learned to appreciate this kind of caring. It was a rare gift, she knew, and should be savored and appreciated.

Well, she did appreciate it, just as she appreciated the fresh towels waiting for her in the bathroom and the bar of scented soap he must have purchased just for her. Bathed and dried, she returned to the bedroom to dress.

Her small bag sat on the luggage rack, and she smiled as she pulled out a pair of jeans. There had been no discussion last night of which room she would use. There hadn't been much discussion at all, though the cookie baking had been a success.

They'd been kissing when the oven timer went off and had jumped like burglars caught in the act. Though they'd eaten the warm cookies, washing them down with the obligatory cold milk, their thoughts hadn't been on dessert.

Teasing, flirting, Cate fed Jesse a bite of her cookie. He turned the tables on her, catching her hand to lick the melted chocolate from her fingertips. Even now, in the bright light of day, Cate could remember the heat shooting through her, the way she had weakened and melted at his touch. They teased and tormented each other, making a game of their wanting, until need overwhelmed playfulness and they could wait no longer. They'd left the cookies on the table.

For all she knew the cookies were still there, along with the spoons and the cookie sheets and the bowl with the dried-up traces of dough stuck in it. If she hurried she would have time to clean up the mess while Jesse was out running his errands. Cate zipped her jeans and looked through the few clothes she had brought with her. She had packed two blouses and the sweater Jesse had mentioned. She lifted the thin sweater out, frowning at it.

It might be a good idea to take Jesse up on his offer of something heavier. In spite of the sunshine it was cold outside, and a little extra warmth would be nice. At least she could see what Jesse had. She folded her own sweater back into her bag and went across to the tall dresser. She wasn't sure where to start looking, since the dresser had six drawers.

The bottom. If this was her dresser she would probably put sweaters in the lower drawers. She pulled the bottom one open, with difficulty, and found two blankets crammed into it. Shaking her head, she wrestled it closed again. The next drawer contained several pairs of shoes, the one above it, medical textbooks. Only a man, she thought with a smile, would put this kind of stuff in a dresser. He probably kept his T-shirts in a shoe box somewhere.

She opened the next drawer and found that he kept T-shirts in the dresser after all, hundreds of them, in all the colors of the rainbow, as well as white. She lifted a few to see if sweaters might lurk beneath, but the drawer was filled with nothing but T-shirts. She pushed it closed again. She struck pay dirt in the next drawer.

Inevitably, it seemed, he had chosen to put thick sweaters in a shallow drawer. They stuck behind the dresser front and rolled back as she opened the drawer. Something unseen fell clinking into the bottom.

"What does he have in here with his sweaters?" she asked the air around her. "It sounds like nuts and bolts."

Smiling indulgently, she pulled one of the sweaters free and pushed another out of the way. Something else small and metallic tinkled to the bottom of the drawer. Intrigued, she took two sweaters off the stack and shook them gently. Nothing. When she lifted the last one, though, a manila envelope slid from its folds. The size of half a sheet of paper, the envelope was worn and creased, and heavy for its size.

When Cate picked it up the contents slid out, clattering into the half-empty drawer. The noisy little objects weren't nuts and bolts, they were medals, military medals stored in the envelope along with some folded papers. Carefully Cate picked up one of the medals and turned it over in her fingers.

A Purple Heart. Jesse's Purple Heart from the war.

There were several other medals, as well as those little ribbon-covered bars that generals wear pinned on their uniforms. Cate had no idea what they all meant; the Purple Heart was the only one she recognized, but she knew their significance. Jesse had been highly honored for his service.

And he had hidden these symbols of honor away in a drawer. She sighed. He'd hidden them away, just as he tried to hide the memories away. Unfortunately, he didn't seem to realize that the only way to defuse the power of the memories was to face them, to deal with them by grieving, by acknowledging the truth, and then to let them go.

She looked at the envelope. It was from Mrs. Joanne MacLeod in Orlando, Florida. His mother had sent these to him. Cate prodded the sheaf of folded papers with her fingertip. They were faded clippings, several years old, from newspapers and magazines.

She carefully unfolded the first one. It was from the Columbus newspaper, with a large headline proclaiming Jesse a "Local marine sergeant hero." He had crawled through a firefight to drag three men to safety, losing an eye in the process.

And very nearly losing his life. With the papers and medals in her hands Cate sank cross-legged to the floor, staring at the article in horror. The newspaper account was frighteningly graphic about the danger he had faced and the severity of his injuries. The other clippings were similar. She read through them all, some from newspapers, some from magazines. The last piece of paper she unfolded astonished her; it was the cover of *Newsweek* with Jesse's face on it.

The picture was the one they had taken of him at boot camp, a yearbook type of photograph, with Jesse staring gravely and stiffly into the camera and wearing his dress uniform. He was very young.

The accompanying article was about the heroism of many of the soldiers and sailors and marines in Vietnam, but the story of Jesse's rescue was central. Of the men he rescued, two had survived, and they had been interviewed. The third man Jesse had dragged out of the line of fire had died of his injuries.

She spread the clippings and medals out on the rug and stared at them with tears in her eyes. Why hadn't she known any of this? The story of Jesse's heroism had been reported around the country, so why hadn't she known about it? She looked at the dates again, and this time she understood. These stories had been published the week after she learned of Brad's death. Jesse had been injured in the same spate of intense fighting that had killed Brad.

She had gone down into a deep, dark pit at that time, and it had been months before she finally began to emerge into the light again. She hadn't read magazines or newspapers during that time, hadn't watched the television news, had barely been aware that there was still a world around her. It was hardly surprising that she'd never known about this.

Had Jesse deliberately hidden these things away? Or had he simply forgotten where they were? The articles all praised his heroism, his courage, his sacrifice. He must be proud of the medals and the articles; he had to be proud of saving the lives of two men who would otherwise have died.

Of course, given the organization of his dresser, he might have simply felt the sweater drawer was a good place to keep these things. She gathered everything up again and slipped the medals and clippings back into their envelope, folding the top securely closed. Had Jesse deliberately hidden these things, she wondered again, or was this a simple matter of forgetfulness?

Cate weighed the envelope in her palm, wrestling with temptation. She studied the faded handwriting. Jesse's mother had sent him these clippings; she'd wanted him to have them. His mother had been proud of his bravery.

Well, Cate was proud of him, too. She wanted him to recognize what he'd accomplished, and she wanted to take the pain out of the memories that haunted him. She didn't know if he'd hidden these medals on purpose, but she did know that ignoring them, and ignoring the things they represented, wasn't healthy.

He deserved recognition for his past heroism as well as for his present work. He also needed to recognize what was happening within himself. He didn't want to face the memories and the pain, but he had to. He *had* to. She studied the envelope gravely for a minute longer, then nodded, her decision made.

Moving quickly, she went across to her overnight bag and slid the envelope inside, zipping it securely into an inner pocket. She returned to the dresser to choose a thick, cream-colored sweater, replaced the others, and closed the drawer again.

With the heavy sweater over her own plaid shirt she was cozily comfortable, if not the picture of chic. Jesse's sweater was marvelously warm, but the sleeves had a tendency to slide down over her hands, and the hem covered her bottom. Oh well, "oversize" was the latest fashion, wasn't it? She rolled and cuffed the sleeves, pushed them firmly up to her elbows and went to clean up the kitchen and get her breakfast.

Jesse must have known how her mind would work. The table had been cleared and the dishes stacked in the sink, with a large note taped above them.

"Do Not Touch These Dishes!" the note read. "I Will Know If You Cheat, And You Will Be Punished!!!" Cate laughed aloud and crossed to the stove to pour herself another cup of coffee. She would compromise with that awe-inspiring note. She would fix her breakfast, and if Jesse wasn't back by the time she'd finished eating, she would wash those dishes, note or no note.

When she heard him returning she was at work in the living room, setting up her reflectors and checking the room with the light meter. She stayed where she was as Jesse walked in the front door and strode down the hall to the kitchen. She heard the door swing open and waited for the explosion.

"Cate!" he bellowed. "What happened to these dishes? And where are you, anyway?"

"In the living room," she called.

He burst into the room, scowling thunderously. "What happened to those dishes?" he demanded again. "I left you a note—"

"And a charming note it was," Cate said, smiling sweetly. "Threatening me with grievous injury if I dared to wash the dishes. Very original, Jesse."

"So why did you wash them?"

"Did I say I did?" She gazed ingenuously across the room at him. "Maybe they washed themselves and then marched right back into the cupboard."

"Uh-huh." Jesse leaned against the door frame and folded his arms across his chest. He was still scowling, but Cate could see the smile lurking behind his frown. "And what were you doing while the dishes did their little samba around the kitchen?"

"I was watching, of course." Cate shrugged. "It was wonderful. When they were done I applauded."

Jesse's lips twitched. "You're certifiably nuts, you know that?"

"It's part of my charm." She smiled, and bent over her lights again. "Are you ready to be immortalized on film?"

"As ready as I'll ever be." He grimaced. "Couldn't you have talked that editor out of this?"

"'Fraid not. You don't talk John out of anything. All I want now are some good pictures that don't invade your privacy."

"What do you want me to wear?"

She glanced over her shoulder, surveying the jeans, plaid shirt and battered running shoes. "What you have on is fine. This is supposed to be you in the country, not dressed up."

"Okay." He shrugged. "You know what you're doing, I guess."

"I know exactly what I'm doing." She chose a camera from the bag and changed lenses. "Try to remember that."

"How could I forget?" he said, laughing. "You're a tough boss."

"Yeah," she replied absently, and straightened, camera in hand. "I want to do a few posed shots inside and then some candids outside. Go stand by the fireplace, okay?''

"Okay." He walked over to the fireplace and faced her stiffly. "Now what?"

"Lean your elbow on the mantel." She grinned over the camera, then looked through the viewfinder again. "Give me your best lord-of-the-manor look."

Jesse leaned against the corner of the mantel and looked quizzically at her. "I have no idea how to give you a lordly look."

"Sure you do," she urged. "Just look disdainful and supercilious, like you do when the residents do something dumb."

"Disdainful and supercilious?" He laughed, and she snapped the shutter, catching him with his head thrown back in full-throated enjoyment of her joke.

This was what she wanted, the essential man, the laughing man behind the intensely professional doctor, the tender man within the tough. She wanted to photograph the Jesse who collected antiques and laughed at dumb jokes and made chocolate chip cookies at midnight. And maybe she wanted the man who was her lover, as well, though those pictures would never be published. They would be for her eyes alone, for the times when Jesse was not with her.

And so she photographed him when he was posed, waiting for her to shoot, and when he didn't expect it, catching his many moods. She worked at it, pulling laughter from him with silly jokes and terrible puns, capturing a thoughtful expression when they talked about the hospital, a gentle smile at the mention of Melissa.

"I want to get her something," Cate said. They were walking toward the house after shooting in the fringe of the woods outside. "Some little souvenir from the Blue

Ridge. Will there be a store open in Old Tavern tomorrow?"

"Something will be open. Even though the tourist season is over, there's always traffic passing through there." Jesse looked down at Cate, who was walking beside him. "Do you think you ought to do that, though?"

"Take her a doll or a toy?" Cate shrugged and walked on, her hands in the pockets of her jeans, her camera swinging gently on its neck strap. "Why not?"

"You know why." Jesse caught her elbow and pulled her to an abrupt stop. The camera bounced heavily into her midsection. She steadied it automatically with her free hand as she looked up in surprise. "You're too close to that little girl already," he said harshly. "You're going to get hurt, and I don't want to see that!"

"Maybe not, but there isn't much you can do about it, Jesse." Cate felt her own anger growing. "I'm close to her, sure, and I'll probably get closer. She's so alone, only able to see her mother on weekends, if then. She needs someone around to care about her."

"She has a family, Cate, and she knows they care about her. Just because you've never seen them doesn't mean they don't exist."

"I know that! She's lonely, though, and I want to help."

"You want more than that." Jesse looked down into her face, his expression a mix of pity and exasperated anger. "You can't be her mother, Cate. She already has a mother."

Cate's mouth fell open. "Is that what you think I'm doing?" she asked, incredulous. "Trying to take her mother's place?"

Jesse was silent, his look reply enough.

Anger washed through Cate. "I am not trying to replace that child's mother, Jesse MacLeod. Whether you believe it or not!" She jerked her arm free of his grip and stalked toward the house, fighting back furious tears.

Cursing himself for being an insensitive idiot, Jesse strode after her. He wasn't convinced that Cate didn't see herself as a sort of substitute mother to Melissa. He knew that was a mistake, but if he was to persuade Cate to change her attitude, it was clear that he would have to be a great deal more tactful. And subtle, too. His broaching of the subject had been about as subtle as hitting Cate over the head with a baseball bat.

He'd seen the quick flash of hurt in her eyes, even before the anger. He cursed himself again. The last thing he wanted to do was hurt Cate; he wanted to protect her from hurt. Clearly he was going about it the wrong way.

"Cate." He caught her arm and pulled her to a stop a few steps from the back porch. "Cate, I didn't mean to be offensive."

"Oh?" She regarded him with chilly hostility. "What did you mean to be, then?"

"I don't want to see you get hurt, Cate. That's the only reason I said anything."

"I don't think I'm going to get hurt, Jesse." She stared defiantly up at him. "But, you know, if helping a little girl endure a frightening and lonely experience hurts me in the end, it will have been worth it. What are you expecting, anyway? Do you think I'll experience some kind of emotional collapse?"

"No, of course not. I know your strength."

"Then trust me to make my own decisions, will you? I don't want Melissa to become too dependent on me, but I won't abandon her when she has no one else. When her mother's visiting she doesn't need me, but when she does need me, I intend to be there for her." She narrowed her eyes on him. "You can't preach at me, anyway, Jesse. I know how you feel about those kids. You may hide it from everyone else, but you can't hide it from me."

Jesse sighed. "All right." He nodded and moved toward the house again. "You've got me there. I won't interfere anymore."

Cate followed him into the kitchen and set her camera on the table. "Jesse?"

"Hmm?" He turned from the sink, his face sober.

"I know you're just trying to help, but if you can deal with it, then I can, too."

"Yes." Jesse leaned back against the sink and folded his arms. "I guess you can." He was always a little surprised, a little intrigued, by her perceptive mind and her instinctive understanding. He smiled. "I keep underestimating you, don't I?"

"You always did." She smiled gently, her anger and hurt passing. "Even when I was a kid, following you around and making you crazy."

"You'd go to almost any length to pester me, wouldn't you?" He frowned ominously.

"It was worth it. It was so much fun to make you mad that I couldn't resist."

Jesse remembered something he'd long forgotten. He narrowed his gaze on her suspiciously. "Is that why you were always hiding in the bushes when I brought Mary Beth Lewis home from a date?"

"Mmm-hmm." She smiled, a sly, teasing smile that sent the familiar heat rushing through him. "I got quite an education that way."

"In between blowing raspberries and making yucky noises every time I kissed the poor girl? It's a wonder she didn't swear off boys altogether!"

"With a build like hers, the boys wouldn't have let her!" Cate retorted. "Of course, I was jealous of her," she added thoughtfully.

"What?" Jesse thought he'd misunderstood. He stood by the sink and watched as Cate placed three rolls of exposed film beside the camera and turned to face him. Her smile was ripe with meaning, those ravishing hazel eyes with the catlike slant heavy lidded and glowing green with promise. His heart began to thump heavily in his chest.

"I was jealous."

Cate sauntered across the flagstones toward him, her stride loose-limbed, with the gentle sway of hip and shoulder that made her such a pleasure to watch.

"I wasn't old enough to go out with you," she told him, "but I sure wasn't going to let you and Mary Beth neck on her front porch in peace."

She stopped in front of him and placed her palms on his chest. Her light touch seemed to burn through his heavy shirt. Jesse fought the sudden powerful urge to grab and ravish her. She slid her hands up, caressing his chest, then traced the line of his collar. Her fingertip brushed his throat provocatively, then his collarbone. Jesse fought to steady his breathing, wondering how much of this he could take. It was torture, and she knew it, sweet, sweet torture.

"I didn't want Mary Beth to kiss you that way," she murmured. "Because I wanted to be the one to do this...." She touched her lips to his jawline. "And this." She kissed his cheek, her breath a soft flutter on his skin. "And this." She kissed his mouth, and the tip of her tongue flicked out to brush across his lips. Jesse clutched the last shreds of his control.

She reached up, linking her arms around his neck, her slim, supple body molding to his, her breasts pressed against him, her belly, her thighs ...

And then his control snapped, just as she'd meant it to. With a low, feral growl Jesse wrapped his arms around her and let the flames take him.

Chapter Thirteen

Cate came awake to midnight darkness. She didn't know what had awakened her, but something had brought her up from the depths of sleep. She moved beneath the sheet, stretching, reaching, then stopped short. Sliding one hand over the sheet, she searched, but Jesse wasn't there. The bed still held his warmth, but he was gone.

She stifled the little taste of fear at the back of her throat. Where was he? She pushed the fear firmly away. How far could he have gone in the middle of the night, after all? Probably no farther than the bathroom for a drink of water. She rolled onto her side, peering around the room, dimly illuminated by the light of the late-rising moon.

He hadn't even left the room. He stood at the window, his back to her, starkly silhouetted by the moonlight. He didn't move as she watched, but stood motionless, his hands in the pockets of his terry-cloth robe, his head erect as he gazed out at the bare trees on the hillside. Cate lay watching him for several minutes, but he didn't move. There was something unsettling in his stillness.

He didn't appear to hear the rustle of covers as she slid out of bed and pulled on her robe. She padded across the cold boards to him.

"Jesse?" she whispered as she touched his shoulder. She didn't startle him, as she'd feared she might. Without turning he reached back to take her hand and pull her up beside him. "Is something wrong?" she asked quietly, her sense of unease growing.

"Only in my head," he replied after a moment's silence. "Only in my head."

Cate slipped her arm around his waist and leaned her head on his shoulder. He wasn't trembling. Instead he was too still. "You're thinking about the war." It wasn't a question. She already knew the answer.

"It comes back."

"And you have to think about it, even though you don't want to."

He nodded silently.

"You never talk about it, do you, Jesse? Not the reality you experienced. You may talk about politics and generalities, but not about the things you saw and heard and felt."

"You try to forget." His voice was so low she strained to hear his words. "You want to push it all away so that things can be normal again, but the memories sneak up on you when you least expect them."

He put his arms around her, pulling her into a hard, barely controlled embrace. Aching with love, hurting for him, she wished he would share the memories with her, lessen their power to hurt by bringing them out in the air.

He needed to do that. It would be painful, like lancing a boil, but she knew how much he needed to lance this particular boil and let the poison out. Cate glanced at her tote bag. She might have wondered earlier, but now she knew she was doing the right thing. Someone had to help Jesse face his past and come to terms with it. She had to.

She wrapped her arms around his waist and held him, her face pressed against his chest. She offered her closeness, her comfort, trying to ease his pain, even if he would not let her in to share it. Jesse didn't kiss her, but he held her tightly, one hand rubbing her back, the other stroking her hair, his muscles rigid with tension. The board floor struck cold on her feet, the air chilled her skin, but Cate never noticed. She held Jesse safe in her arms while he fought his private demons and the stars wheeled past in the sky.

"When will you develop the pictures?"

"Tonight or tomorrow. Do you want to look at them before I pick the ones I'll use?"

"No." Jesse grinned as he accelerated up the ramp onto the expressway. "It wouldn't accomplish anything. As you say, I don't like any pictures of me."

"I'm glad you've finally admitted that," Cate replied, grinning and sat back to watch the rain on the highway.

After beautifully clear weather on Friday and Saturday, Sunday had dawned hazy, and the haze had rapidly given way to low, sullen clouds and steady rain. The tires hummed on the wet pavement, and the wipers swished rhythmically across the windshield. The gray weather cut them off from the world outside the car, enclosing them in a warm, dry island of privacy. It was a nice feeling, Cate thought, this sense that they were the only two people in the world.

They might have been the only two in the world that morning, too. The gentle rain had cut them off from even the sight of the road below the house. Their conversation had been desultory, as if they had reached a level of closeness that didn't require words for communication.

She hadn't needed Jesse to tell her what he was feeling at midnight. She had seen the images of horror that haunted him, seem them in her mind's eye. As she held him in her arms she had watched those images gradually lose their power and fade, had felt the rigid tension drain from his body.

And when that tension had eased at last he had lifted her chin with his fingers and kissed her lips, and the healing magic had begun again. Cate didn't remember walking back to the wide bed; perhaps Jesse had carried her, or perhaps she had simply floated on air until she was lying in his arms again. They had made love wordlessly, effortlessly, each knowing intuitively what would pleasure the other most, when to hurry and when to wait, when to kiss and caress, when to be kissed and caressed.

The heat had flamed and grown, and in the end Cate had wrapped Jesse in her arms and legs and clung to him as the fire consumed them together. When she had awakened to a dim, gray dawn she had still been enclosed in his embrace, and the closeness of their minds had been unaltered.

He hadn't moved, but she'd known the moment he woke. She had rolled her head back on his arm and smiled at him with drowsy eyes.

"Good morning."

"Morning." His arm had tightened, lifting her lips for his kiss. She'd squirmed closer, and he'd slid one leg over hers, holding her a willing prisoner. "I won't ask if you slept well, since I know you didn't." He sighed, his chest lifting and falling beneath her cheek. "I'm sorry about that. I got up because I didn't want to wake you."

"Don't worry about that, Jesse, please. I slept like a log, and I feel wonderful. I'm glad I was able to help."

"Help?" he pulled her closer, pressing her face into his throat, and rested his chin on her hair. "I think you must be a witch, lady."

"A witch?" she protested against his skin. "I'm not sure I like the sound of that."

"A beautiful, mysterious, seductive woman who can work magic and cast spells? Why shouldn't you like the sound of it?"

"That's your idea of a witch, is it? No tall black hats and warts on the nose?"

"Nope. On the other hand, you'd look as sexy in a tall black hat as you do in everything else." Something warm and sweet bubbled up in Cate now as she remembered his words. When he said those things to her, she was sexy and beautiful—for him. And she had worked magic for him, as well, had helped him forget the pain and the bitter memories for a time.

"Penny for them." A penny dropped into her hand, which was lying open in her lap. Cate blinked and came back to the present, to the rain and the highway and the headlights of the other cars streaming past.

"A penny for what?" She turned the coin over in her fingers.

"Your thoughts. You were staring out the window and smiling at something."

"Oh." Cate slanted him a shy smile, then dropped her gaze to her lap again. "I was thinking about this morning," she said softly. Jesse's hand came across to cover hers, stilling her fidgeting.

"So was I." His voice was low and warm, with a smile in it.

Cate looked at him in the glow of the dash lights. She smiled, flirting. "I'm not really a witch, am I?"

"You're beautiful and magical and mysterious. Naturally you're a witch." He lifted her hand to his lips and kissed her palm. When he laid her hand in her lap again Cate closed her fingers over that kiss, holding it safe in her grasp. "I find witches enchanting," he said to the road ahead of them, then turned to look at Cate. "I find you enchanting."

"Oh, Jesse." She had to protest. "Don't say things like that. You'll embarrass me."

"You embarrass too easily."

"I don't think so," she retorted with a hint of tartness. "I just think you say too many embarrassing things."

"You'll learn," Jesse said with a little smile, and Cate sighed with amused exasperation. She glanced over her shoulder at the gift-wrapped package riding in the back seat.

"Do you think she'll like it?"

"The doll?" Jesse flashed Cate a quick grin. "She's going to love it. It's a great doll; she'd love it even if it wasn't a present from you."

"I hope you're right."

Cate had fallen in love with the brown-haired, gingham-skirted rag doll on sight. Handmade, the shop's proprietor had told her, by a woman who'd lived within two miles of the tiny hamlet of Old Tavern for all her ninety-one years. The doll wore a ruffled cap and a wide smile, embroidered in the same microscopic stitches as her bright blue eyes. She could have been modeled on Melissa, brown hair, blue eyes and all.

"I'm right. You'll see."

"Melissa?" Cate peered around the door frame.

Melissa sat propped against pillows in her bed, staring dispiritedly at the gray morning outside the window. She turned at the sound of Cate's voice and smiled wanly.

"Hi, Cate."

"How have you been this weekend?" Cate stepped into the room, holding her hands out of sight behind her back. "Did you have a good visit with your mother?"

Melissa's lip began to tremble. "Mama couldn't come," she muttered. "She called on the phone and said that Timmy's sick, so she had to stay home."

"That's too bad, sweetie. I know how much you miss her."

"Uh-huh." Melissa's woebegone expression said she was prepared to feel quite sorry for herself. Cate had other plans, though.

"I missed you this weekend," Cate said. Melissa's hangdog look lightened just a little.

"You did?"

"Mmm-hmm."

Melissa considered that for a moment, then shook her head. "No, you didn't."

"Well, why didn't I?" demanded Cate.

"You wouldn't miss me if you were with Dr. Jesse," she said with absolute conviction. "He's the handsomest man in the world." As if that said all there was to say. "Don't you think so?" Melissa demanded, staring up at her.

"He's very handsome," Cate agreed. She wouldn't have dared contradict her, even it if hadn't been the truth.

"Yes, he is. Are you going to marry him?"

"What?" Cate squeaked. She had thought that discussion was over with.

"Are you going to marry him?" Melissa repeated patiently. "I'd marry him, but I'm not old enough. I like you a lot, though, and I think you should marry him. I won't mind if you do."

"That's very generous of you, sweetheart, but don't you remember what I told you? I think I should wait until he asks me to marry him."

"What if he doesn't know he's supposed to ask you?"

"Then I guess we wouldn't get married."

Melissa scowled at the thought. "I think you ought to ask him." She looked at Cate's hands, which were still held behind her back. "What are you hiding, Cate?"

"A present!" Cate told her, and produced it with a flourish, grateful for the change of subject.

"A present?" Melissa breathed, wide-eyed. "For me?"

"Mmm-hmm." Cate placed the package in her hands. "Go on, Melissa. Open it."

Melissa pulled at the ribbon, hesitantly at first. She glanced at Cate, received a nod of encouragement and got into the spirit of it, tearing uninhibitedly at the paper. When the last of the paper was removed she slowed her movements again. Very carefully she lifted the lid and set it aside, then folded back the sheets of tissue and gasped.

"Is . . . ?" She glanced quickly up at Cate, then gazed raptly at the doll. "Is she for me?"

"Mmm-hmm. I picked her out especially for you."
Cate touched the doll's face lightly. "She had brown hair
and blue eyes just like you."

Melissa bent over the box. "She does," she said won-
deringly, and touched the doll's hair. She stroked her
small hand over the muslin cheek. "She's beautiful."

"Just like you are," Cate said.

Melissa didn't hear her. She was lifting the doll from
her box, patting her yarn hair, fluffing her ruffled skirt
and pinafore, studying her, entranced. She took the doll
into her arms and cradled her gently, then smiled up at
Cate.

"Does she have a name?"

"Not yet. She belongs to you. I think you should name
her."

"What should I name her?" Melissa asked. She turned
wide eyes on Cate and waited for an answer.

"I said *you* should name her!" Cate insisted, laughing. "Not me! What do you think would be a good name
for her? What kind of name would she like?"

"Gee..." Melissa studied the doll's face dubiously.
"How can I tell what she'd like?"

"Think about what kind of name you'd like if you
were her. Would you like Amanda? Or Suzanne?"

"Uh-uh." Melissa shook her head and frowned, her
lower lip jutting out in a pout of concentration.

"How about Melissa?" Cate suggested.

"Ewww, no! Melissa is a gross, yucky name!"

Typical. When she was a child Cate had thought Caitlin was the dumbest name in the world. At the time she'd
wished her name was Arabella. "What name do you like
instead of Melissa?" she asked.

Melissa looked up and smiled shyly. "You know what
name I like?"

"What's that?" Cate sat on the side of the bed, facing Melissa.

"Cate," Melissa announced. "I want to name her Cate, 'cause I love her and I love you."

"Oh, Melissa, thank you!"

Biting her lip against the tears that threatened, Cate hugged Melissa again, holding her close. She was so small, so fragile, she seemed nothing but skin and bones...and personality. There was so much life in her that it seemed impossible that she could be ill, that something so terrible, so frightening, could have struck her.

She pressed her cheek to Melissa's hair and swallowed the tears. "Would you like me to read you a story?" she asked. "Cate can listen to it, too."

"Okay. I'll pick one." Melissa rummaged through the stack of books on her nightstand and selected one. "Come sit here—" she patted the pillow "—beside me."

"I'll get as close as I can." Cate helped Melissa scoot over, carefully holding her IV line out of harm's way. "How about if Cate sits here, on your lap?" Together they seated the doll comfortably, settled Melissa in the curve of Cate's arm and she began to read.

"'And we had a good time at the beach,'" she read from the last page. "'Just Grandma and me.'"

Melissa sighed with satisfaction. "I like that story. My grandma doesn't take me to the beach, 'cause the beach is too far from our house, but she lets me help her make applesauce."

"She does, huh? How do you do that?"

"Well, first you take a whole bunch of apples..."

"Where do you get the apples?"

"From the orchard man. We go in Pop's truck to the orchard, and Grandma buys apples from the orchard man. He wears a yellow baseball hat, and he gives us the apples in big baskets."

"And you take them home and cook them?"

"Yeah, but we wash 'em first. In a tub by the pump. Grandma lets me pump the water. I can pump real good." She grinned proudly. "The apples float in the tub."

"The apples go swimming," Jesse said from the doorway. "And do you go swimming with them, Miss Melissa?"

"Noo!" she laughed. "You're silly, Dr. Jesse!"

"Yeah, but I'm cute."

Melissa giggled and shot Cate a glance heavy with meaning. He's cute, the glance said, and you oughta marry him. Cate raised a lofty eyebrow and looked down her nose at the girl with all the dignity she could muster, sending her into gales of laughter.

Jesse looked from one to the other. "What's going on here, anyway?" He smiled at Cate, but she could see the lines of strain around his mouth.

"Just a little girl-talk." Cate sent him a limpid-eyed look. "That's all."

"Yeah," Melissa giggled. "G-g-girl-talk." She clapped her hands over her mouth and laughed up at Jesse with her eyes.

"Do you like your doll?" he asked.

"Yeah." Her eyes were shining. "I named her Cate."

He glanced quickly at Cate, their eyes meeting in a message that was read and understood.

"That's a good name for her, Melissa. I think she looks like a Cate, don't you?"

"Yeah. I love her." She gave the muslin Cate a quick hug and kiss. "Are you gonna girl-talk with us, Dr. Jesse?"

"Boys can't girl-talk," he retorted. "That'd make it boy-talk, wouldn't it?" Melissa went off into fresh giggles. "Anyway, if you can take a break from the girl-talk, it's time for your lunch, and I need to take Cate with me for a while. Is that all right with you?"

"What's for lunch?"

"Ravioli and green beans and applesauce." Jesse waited for the verdict.

"Ravioli! Okay! I'll see you later, Cate."

Summarily dismissed in favor of pasta and applesauce, Cate said goodbye and followed Jesse to the nurses' station. He ushered her into the small room he used for consultations and closed the door behind them. When he turned to her, his face was grim.

"Jesse?" She stepped in front of him and laid her hands on his forearms. "What's the matter?"

"I just..." He sighed heavily and dropped his hands on her shoulders. He looked down at the floor between them for a moment, then raised his head. "I just got the Path report on the bone-marrow tap Melissa had Friday." Cate felt herself go cold. She was shaking her head slowly, denying his words as he spoke them. "It wasn't as good as we'd hoped, Cate. She's still got atypical cells in her marrow."

"What does that mean?" Cate asked through stiff lips. "What will happen now?"

"She'll have another course of chemo. It'll be a shorter one this time, but we have to treat her to eradicate all traces of tumor. I just hope to God this will do it, because she's not a good candidate for further surgery."

Cate began to shake. "What does that mean?" she demanded. "A short course of chemo... Not a good candidate... What does that mean, Jesse?" Her voice rose. "Does it mean she's going to die?"

"It means I don't know!" Jesse snapped back. He stopped, swore and pulled her against his chest, cradling her in his arms. "I don't know," he repeated quietly. "I wish to God I did, but I simply don't know."

Cate bit her lip hard, forcing back the tears. She took a deep, shuddering breath and stepped back, out of Jesse's arms. She was cold in spite of the warm room and her heavy clothes, freezing cold deep in her bones. She fumbled for a chair and dropped heavily into it.

Jesse watched and ached for her. Through his own pain and fury and frustration he could feel her agony as keenly as his own. He'd watched her reading to Melissa, cuddling her, giggling with her, all the while knowing the grim news he had to give her.

He understood what she felt, the shock and the anger, the helpless, impotent rage. He understood the need to find something—someone—to blame, some way to make sense of random tragedy. Everyone who loved a sick child felt that rage at some point.

When no culprit, no target for that fury, could be found, it was frequently turned on the doctor, who seemed to hold hope in his hands. When hope went unfulfilled the doctor was the one to take the blame.

Cate looked up, shaking her head. "Why do these things happen, Jesse? Why do they happen, and why to innocent kids?"

Jesse just shook his head. He didn't know the answer any more than she did. "You know," he said after a moment, "we're spoiled." He was aware that his remark seemed to be a non sequitur, but it wasn't.

"What?" she demanded angrily. "What are you talking about?"

"We're spoiled." He dropped into the room's other chair, which squeaked in protest beneath his weight. "We take too much for granted."

"Jesse, I don't have any idea what you're talking about."

"How many of the kids you went to school with died of diphtheria?" he demanded. "How many of them died from, or were brain-damaged or blinded by, measles? How many died of whooping cough, or summer diarrhea, or influenza?" His voice was harsh with intensity. "Hundreds, maybe thousands, of kids used to die of those things every year, Cate, and in other places in the world they're dying of those and other diseases right now. Gradually we've conquered them, and now we're trying to do the same with the more difficult diseases." He stared at her, willing her to understand. "Cancer never had a chance to kill kids when measles and the flu killed them first. I don't know why kids get diseases like this, Cate. I only know that kids have been dying cruelly and unfairly since the beginning of time."

She looked at him, her eyes dark with pain and confusion. "And what you're saying is that it never ends. That kids are going to go on dying."

"It looks that way."

"How do you deal with that knowledge? How do you face the fact that no matter what you do you're going to lose, at least some of the time?"

"I have to concentrate on the ones I win. Without treatment all the kids we see here would die. We save some of them. I want to think we can save them all, and until the worst happens I refuse to admit that we won't. Maybe it's naive or shortsighted, but I have to be optimistic."

"And you can still be optimistic in spite of the things that happen?"

Jesse shook his head. "I have no other choice. If I didn't believe I can make a difference, at least part of the time, I couldn't do this."

After a moment of thought Cate nodded. "But you do believe you make a difference?"

"I know I do. I know my success rate will never be one hundred percent, but I know that I have to keep trying."

"And do—" She took a deep breath. "And do you believe that Melissa will be one of the successes?"

Jesse ached to be able to give her a simple answer. "I could say yes, but that would be the easy way out. I think her chances are still better than fifty-fifty."

"What were her chances when she first came to the hospital?"

"With her disease? Her chance of surviving for five years was only twenty-five percent. The odds for her have improved considerably, but only if we treat the cancer as aggressively as we can." He watched the quick horror flick across her face at that grim statistic. "Don't scare yourself to death dwelling on it, Cate. Think of the positive. She's already ahead of the odds."

"Okay," she replied. "I'll concentrate on the positive. And say a prayer." She took a deep breath and stood. "You said something about lunch. I'm not really hungry, but I guess I ought to eat. You want to come?"

He did, and by the time they had gone through the cafeteria line and found seats in a far corner of the big room Cate was determinedly thinking positive. She was even feeling hungry again.

"How's the article coming?" Jesse sampled his cafeteria-special chili and nodded approvingly. "Is it almost finished?"

Cate pushed away thoughts of Melissa's disease. "Actually the first draft is done."

"It is? When did you get it finished?"

"Last night."

She didn't want to tell him how late last night. She'd worked nearly until dawn, photographing his medals and ribbons on a velvet cloth and weaving an account of his heroism into the text. "I left a draft and proofs of the pictures with Mr. Carlson's secretary this morning."

"Well, congratulations." Jesse extended his hand, and Cate gravely returned his handshake. "When do I get to see it?"

"Anytime you want." She smiled, thinking of her secret. She was glad he was showing interest in the article; it made quite a change from his initial reaction to the idea. She was eager for him to read it, eager to see if her words reached him. "You might even be able to get a copy from Mr. Carlson's secretary," she added with a smile. "I'm pretty pleased with the article, Jesse, and I think you'll like it."

Chapter Fourteen

Dressed in cream wool slacks and a fluffy pink sweater that Jesse liked, Cate was leaning over the big spaghetti pot when the doorbell pealed. Steam from the boiling water had her hair curling riotously around her face, flushed from heat and activity. She was fixing dinner for Jesse, in spite of his teasing doubts about her culinary ability.

He maintained that she was a much better photographer than she was a cook, and while that was undoubtedly true, she could fix a few things that wouldn't poison him. Spaghetti was simple enough to be safe, so she'd left the hospital at midafternoon to develop some film and fix dinner.

Jesse's last crack had been to hope that she didn't get her formulas mixed up and cook the spaghetti in developing solution.

The bell rang a second time, and she prodded the simmering spaghetti with a wooden fork. She nodded her satisfaction and hurried to greet Jesse, smiling in anticipation. The bolt stuck, and Cate had to fumble with it for a moment. It came free with a jerk, and she pulled the door open. It caught the edge of the hall rug, rolling it back, and she bent to free it.

"You must really be hungry," she said, laughing, as she bent over the rug. "You're about to ring the doorbell off the wall."

Jesse said nothing. When she straightened and looked at him, her laughter died away. He had obviously come straight from the hospital; he still wore his white lab coat beneath his raincoat, but it was his face that silenced Cate's happy banter.

Beneath hair ruffled by the wind or by his hand, his face was drawn and grim. Deep grooves scored his cheeks, and his lips were held in a hard line. Bewildered, Cate met his gaze and froze at the cold fury there. He didn't answer her teasing jest; instead he gave her an icy glance and pushed roughly past her. She hurried to follow him into the kitchen. He stood in the middle of the room, waiting for her.

She stopped in the doorway, several feet from where Jesse stood beside the table with his back to her. His head was bent, and he was studying something he held. At the sound of her approach he lifted his head and turned to look at her. His face was the face of a stranger.

Cate could feel the cold from where she stood, could feel the waves of anger beating at her. He was furious, with an icy, carefully controlled anger that frightened her more than heated shouting and storming would have.

"Jesse?" Her voice was high, thin. "Jesse, what's wrong?"

"What's wrong?" His voice was quiet, too quiet. He turned to face her fully and raised his hand, showing her the manila envelope he carried. He dangled it between two fingers like something soiled, then tossed it onto the table. It landed with a slap, loud in the too-silent room. Cate looked up at Jesse to find him watching her, stony-eyed.

"I took your suggestion," he told her in an ominously quiet voice, "and went to Mr. Carlson's office to see your article. They were happy to give me a copy." He smiled contemptuously. "They thought it was wonderful. They raved about it. Apparently you have a great deal of talent." His voice hardened. "Talents I never knew about."

Cate gripped the door frame with a white-knuckled hand. "You read the article?"

"Oh, yes, I read every deathless word." His sarcastic words hit and stung like small stones striking her. "With a recommendation like that, how could I do anything else?" He took a slow step toward her, then another. Cate found herself shrinking back against the door frame, away from the fury and the threat in his gaze. He was a pirate now, cold and cruel, the eye patch giving his face a frightening mystery. "Oh, it was fascinating reading, Cate. Your...exploration...went much deeper than I thought it would, revealed all sorts of interesting information...." His lips curved into a smile that wasn't a smile at all.

"Jesse I wrote the best article I know how—"

"It's good writing, all right. I just want to know why you did it," he interrupted harshly. He threw his arms wide. "What the *hell* did you think you were going to prove with that little stunt?"

"No..." She walked quickly into the kitchen, swallowing a sharp stab of pure panic. She'd wanted to reach

Jesse, but not this way. Fear left a brassy taste in her throat. She walked toward him, reaching out to touch his arm. "There was no stunt, nothing like—"

"Don't play stupid, Cate!" Jesse snapped, cutting short her protest. "And don't insult my intelligence." He shook her hand off his arm, then moved as quickly as a striking snake to catch her shoulders in a steely grip. "Where did you find that stuff, anyway?"

She didn't answer immediately, and he shook her. His fingers bit into her shoulders as she tipped her head back to look up at him.

"Come on, Cate," he urged with a contemptuously counterfeit camaraderie. "You can tell me. What'd you do, riffle the closets when I was gone?" He shook his head, disgusted. "You know, I don't even know where those things were. I'd forgotten about them...." His voice dropped. "Maybe I wanted to forget."

"They were in your dresser," she said quietly, wondering how to make him see her intent. "In the drawer with your sweaters."

"In the drawer? Good God, you really did it!" He shoved her away from him as if touching her soiled him. She staggered back and caught herself on the doorframe. "You actually searched the dresser?"

"No! That's not what happened! That wasn't it at all!" Cate shouted, desperate to make him listen, to make him understand. "You told me to get one of your sweaters to wear." She reached out to him, but he ignored her outstretched hands and the plea in her eyes. "Because it was cold. You told me to get a sweater," she continued more quietly, "so I did. The things were in that drawer, folded in with your sweaters. I found them when I took the sweater out."

"That's a convenient excuse, isn't it?" he sneered.

"I'm not making excuses! I don't need to. That's not an excuse; that's what happened!"

"No, it's not." Jesse shook his head sharply. He looked into her face, his gaze dark with anger and disgust. "It's only the beginning. You may have found those medals by accident, but it's no accident that they turned up in your article. Pictures of the medals, another version of all that war-hero drivel that was in the newspapers. Don't try to say that was an accident. For God's sake, Cate, you put all that nonsense in there without even mentioning it to me!"

He flicked the manila envelope with his fingertips, then looked at Cate the way he would look at an unpleasant lab specimen. "You didn't ask my permission. You didn't ask if I cared, if I wanted to have my past revealed." He slammed his fist on the tabletop, making Cate jump. "Damn it, you didn't ask if I wanted my privacy invaded that way!"

She watched him warily, shocked and afraid. She'd known Jesse would be surprised by her use of the medals and the story of his heroism in her article. She'd even thought he might argue with her about it, but she'd never expected this. He hadn't wanted to participate in the article at first, and he hadn't wanted her to photograph his house in the Blue Ridge, but he'd come around in the end. She'd assumed he would come around on this, as well. She'd hoped he would understand why she had mentioned his heroism.

And she had never imagined that Jesse, gentle, loving, passionate Jesse, could look at her with a cold disgust that seemed to penetrate her bones and freeze her heart. She might have been a stranger, a stranger he thoroughly despised.

"Jesse, I wasn't trying to expose you—"

"The hell you weren't!" he shouted, his anger bursting through his unnaturally tight control. "That was deliberate deception and manipulation. You used our relationship to do this article—"

"Oh, no! Initially I wanted to do the article because of you, yes, but my primary aim when I wrote it was to make people think about the hospital and the kids and get them to send money to help with the renovation."

"You used our relationship to do this article," he repeated implacably, "and you used our closeness to get information about me that I didn't want to reveal. You can't deny that, because it's true." His voice hardened. "I thought I knew you, Cate, I really did. I thought you cared about me."

"Jesse, I *do* care about you." Pleading, she reached out to him again and was ignored. "I love you! That's why I put in the stuff about your war record!"

"Love? You call that love? You don't know the meaning of the word. I don't know anything about you anymore. I thought I knew what you were like when you were a kid. I thought you were honest and forthright, and I didn't think you'd changed all that much since you grew up. It appears that I was wrong."

"I'm sorry it's upset you this way. I didn't want to hurt you; I just wanted to help—"

"Help?" he sneered. "Help with what? If you loved me like you say, you should have known better. My God." He shook his head and stared uncomprehendingly at her. "You didn't think about helping me, whatever that means; you didn't think about a damned thing except putting a little sensational spice in your article. Did you *read* those clippings? Did you read them all?"

Cate stood before him, palms out in an unspoken plea, begging for her life. "Of course I read them! I was shocked. I never knew you had dragged three men to safety. You're a hero.''

"You sound like those damned magazines with their tunnel vision!" he retorted. "Only one of them told the whole story. Do you remember reading that there were actually eleven men out there? Did you read that some of them were already dead, and that I couldn't get all the survivors out? Did it occur to you that I've been living with the guilt and the memories ever since? Did you read any of that?"

He took her shoulders again in a painful grasp, holding her captive, his face close to hers. Cate stared up at him, shaking and scared. "Yes, I read it. I was sorry you never shared it with me."

"It's not something I like to think about." His voice was low and shaking. "I had to play God, Cate! I had to choose which men would live and which would die! Did you ever think about how I might feel about having it all dredged up again?"

"Jesse, I know it's painful, but you need to think about it! You need to face it and deal with it!"

"Oh, do I, Dr. Freud? Tell me, where did you study psychiatry?" He flung her from him and spun away.

"I didn't have to study psychiatry to know that. I can see what—"

"You can see?" He cut across her words. "You can't see your hand in front of your face, Cate! Just do me the favor of keeping out of my life and out of my business, all right?"

Cate said nothing; there was nothing more to say. Numb, beyond further emotion, she walked across the room to open a drawer and take out the envelope of medals and clippings. She took them back to Jesse offered them to him.

"These belong to you," she whispered.

He took the wrinkled envelope and turned it over in his hands, studying it for a moment. With a contemptuous flick of the wrist he tossed it onto the table beside the other envelope. His Purple Heart fell out, tinkling onto the polished wood. "You found 'em," he said dismissively. "You keep 'em."

He turned his back on her and walked out.

Cate stood there long after he had gone. Alone in the middle of her kitchen, she stared at the two envelopes. She couldn't seem to move, couldn't think or even feel. Her arms dangled limply at her sides; her eyes burned. She loved Jesse. And she had turned what he felt for her into hate. She had overstepped her bounds and driven him out of her life.

A bubbling hiss and the smell of something burning finally broke through her stunned trance. She turned around to see through blurry eyes that the spaghetti was boiling over in a sticky, starchy flood onto the stovetop. She blinked, trying to focus on the mess, and the tears that filled her eyes spilled over onto her cheeks.

The afternoon was warm for November, the air heavy, the sky low and sullen, promising rain by the time commuters hurried home from work. Cate wandered along the Georgetown sidewalks, oblivious to the colorful shop windows and the equally colorful shoppers all around her. Lost in thought, she walked aimlessly, head down and hands jammed in her jacket pockets.

How could Jesse have misjudged her motives so completely? She kicked a pebble off the sidewalk. How could he have thought, after all they had been to each other, that she would use him in such a way? She hadn't manipulated or exploited him. At least, that had never been her intention. And it had never been her intention to expose him, either.

She'd only wanted to help him. She wouldn't have used the information about his heroism unless she'd thought it would help. She could see what the memories were doing to him, even after all these years, could see that he still had to work through the past. She had wanted to help him; that was all.

She had just wanted to help him work through it. She loved him. Weren't you supposed to help those you loved? She knew he needed to face this....

In the middle of the sidewalk Cate stopped short. The man walking just behind her crashed into her, shoving her into a lamppost.

"Watch what you're doing!" he snarled irritably.

"I'm sorry." Cate stepped out of the way and leaned against the post. With a sour look he detoured very pointedly around her.

Dazed, reeling from the truth that had just occurred to her, she made her way out of the flow of traffic. She had to think, and she couldn't do that in the middle of all these people. She walked on looking for someplace private. She found a tiny park between two buildings, a quiet patch of grass and shrubs surrounding a small marble fountain. She perched on the fountain's rim. She could be alone there. She could sit and think.

She had thought she knew what he needed, but how could she be so sure she was right? As Jesse had asked, where had she studied psychiatry? She had reached certain conclusions, but she didn't have a lock on any answers, did she?

And rather than simply bring the subject up and invite Jesse to share it with her, she had gone behind his back, using that information in her article, forcing the issue. Her approach wouldn't have helped him, she realized now. It would only have exposed feelings that were still raw and painful. She wouldn't have made the situation better; she would have made it worse.

Behind her, water tinkled musically into the marble basin. Lost in her thoughts, Cate barely heard it. She hadn't helped Jesse; all she'd done was remind him of a horrible experience he would rather forget.

In spite of what she knew about Jesse and the bitter memories that haunted him, she had blithely dragged out all the reminders of that bitterness and put them on display in her article. No wonder he was furious and disgusted with her! After all, what kind of woman would comfort a man when he was in pain, then publicly resurrect the reminders of that pain for the whole world to see?

What kind of callous, self-centered woman would do that? And what kind of woman would assume that kind of action would help the man she professed to love?

Cate began to shiver, but not from the cold. She had turned the article in. She had turned in the article that would bare Jesse's pain to all of Washington, and she had to stop it.

In a sudden, violent move she shoved herself up from the fountain's rim, frightening the pigeons, which had been lulled into complacency by her stillness. With a clatter of wings and outraged clucks they exploded into flight in front of her and wheeled overhead, chattering their disapproval as she hurried out of the park.

Cate reached the sidewalk, turned right and began to run.

The first drops of rain were spattering on the pavement when she dashed across the street and under the portico of the building that housed the offices of *Wash-*

ington Month. She shook the moisture off her hair and hurried inside, sprinting across the lobby to catch the elevator. Its doors were just sliding closed, but Cate managed to squeeze through at the last moment.

"You look like you've been running a marathon."

The elevator's other occupant, the young man who covered sports for the magazine, grinned at her.

She shook her head, fighting to catch her breath. "I just have to see John. Is he still here?"

"He was five minutes ago when I left to take some copy downstairs." Steve grinned, showing her his dimple. Women loved that dimple and the little-boy look it gave him. "When you're done talking to the big chief, how about having a drink with me? I know a great little bar over in—"

"No, thanks." Her abrupt refusal didn't even stem the flow.

"In Arlington. They have great Buffalo wings and fried zucchini. We can have a few laughs."

"Sorry, Steve." She shook her head firmly as the elevator slowed. "I'm not in the mood for laughs, and I have to go somewhere else as soon as I'm done here."

To her great relief John was still in his spacious office, reading a draft of the month's restaurant review.

"Come in!" he called in response to her knock. She pushed the door open, and he waved the pages at her in an uncharacteristic display on enthusiasm. "This review is okay, after all. A week after this hits the stands the whole city is going to be looking for Armenian food."

Cate wasn't sure if that was a good thing or not, but it wasn't what she needed to talk about. "That's great, John. I need to talk to you about my article."

"Oh, yeah, your article. I read it last night." His face settled back into its habitual sad-spaniel lines. He looked at her with weary dismay. "It's a very effective piece, Cate."

"I'm glad you think so." She sank onto a chair.

"You don't look glad."

Cate looked across the desk and met John's gaze. Beneath the spaniel's drooping eyebrows were a pair of very shrewd blue eyes. She shrugged. "I have to rewrite it."

"Why? I just told you it was fine."

"It isn't fine. I can't let the article be published as is, John. I have to make some changes in it."

"What changes?" He leaned forward tiredly, elbows on the desk, and watched her with steady, perceptive eyes.

"I have to remove all references of Jesse's service in the marines and to his heroism and decorations."

"*What?*" John's weary pose evaporated. "You can't be serious! That's some of the best stuff in the article."

"Nevertheless, I have to take it out."

"Why?" he snapped.

"Because I shouldn't have used it in the first place!" Cate sat very straight in her chair. "This was supposed to be about the hospital, not Jesse's war record. That stuff shouldn't be in the article at all." She paused, then added, "I'm taking it out, John."

He shook his head. "I can't let you do that."

"You can't stop me. Either I change the article or I withdraw it altogether."

"You already submitted it."

"I haven't signed anything." Her voice was calm, her face determined. "It's still mine to withdraw from submission, and that's what I'm doing, until I can rewrite it."

John held her gaze for several seconds, glaring at her, but she didn't back down. Finally he sighed, running a hand through the sparse strands atop his head. Cate felt the tension in her spine ease a little. She knew she'd won.

"You're a tough cookie, aren't you?"

She smiled and rose, walking over to his desk. "Only when I have to be. Can I have the article back?"

"Don't trust me?" He leaned back in his chair.

"I trust you. I just don't want it floating around." She waited, and after a moment he rose and went to a file cabinet in the corner. He searched, then pulled a folder from the top drawer.

"Here it is." He seemed to expect her to check the contents, and she did, unwilling to take chances. She had to be absolutely certain she had all the pictures as well as the text.

"It's all in there."

"I can see that." She relaxed and smiled at him. "It's very important that I not leave anything floating around, John."

"It must be. I hate to let you do this, you know." He walked with her to the door.

"I know you do," Cate said. "But if it's any comfort to you, you probably just saved the magazine from a lawsuit."

It was raining steadily when she reached the street level again, and she paused, dismayed. She'd gone out for her walk without her purse, only her keys and driver's license in her pocket. She had no money for a cab, or for an umbrella, and her jacket was meager protection against the rain. She patted her pockets another time, then turned them out, just to see...

A bus token. Cate stared at it for a moment, then zipped the manila folder inside her jacket and sprinted for the bus shelter on the corner, clutching the token tightly. The bus stopped directly in front of the hospital, so she was wet, but not saturated, when she got inside. A few minutes in the ladies' room with paper towels repaired the worst of the damage, though she still looked pretty damp.

Cate shrugged and turned away from the mirror. It didn't matter that she was wet as long as the article was dry. She hurried through the maze of hospital corridors, familiar with them now, searching for Jesse. It was late afternoon; he might still be making his rounds, or he might have finished already and gone home.

But he hadn't. She found him at the nurses' station on the fourth floor of the Peds pavilion, writing in a chart. He didn't see her approach.

"Jesse?" She stopped two steps behind him and spoke softly, but he wheeled around in his chair as if she'd shouted at him. He looked up, met her eyes and scowled. "What are you doing here?"

"I came to see you."

His face hardened to grimness. "I don't have time to talk now." He turned back to the chart.

"I can wait until you're done," she offered hesitantly.

Jesse threw down his pen and pushed himself sharply back from the desk. "I don't want to talk to you!" he snapped, his voice low and vehement. "Can't you understand that?"

"Yes, I can understand it, but I need to talk to you, Jesse. It's important!" She reached out, then saw his face. She dropped her hand before she touched him. "Please."

He sighed heavily. "All right." He bent over the chart again. "Wait for me in my office."

"Thank you," Cate whispered, but she didn't think he heard her.

She waited in his office, perching nervously on the lumpy chair with the cracked vinyl seat for nearly an hour. When she heard his steps in the hall, she straightened quickly and waited for him to come in.

He glanced at her as he swung the door closed and walked around to sit behind his desk. He took his stethoscope out of his pocket and shut it in a drawer, then folded his hands on the desktop and looked across at her.

"Well? What do you need to talk to me about?" he asked impatiently. His tone was no more forgiving than his expression.

Cate swallowed, her throat dry. "About this." She held out the folder, but Jesse didn't reach for it.

"What about it?"

"I had submitted it to the magazine, but I went over there today and got it back."

"I don't see what this has to do with anything." He pushed himself back from the desk and stood. "I've got a lot of work to do tonight, Cate. I need to get going."

"Jesse, wait!" She grabbed his arm to stop him. He looked pointedly at her hand, and she removed it from his arm. "I've got to explain this to you. I never meant to make you feel—"

"I'm not interested in your explanations. It's much too late for that." He yanked the door open. "I don't have anything else to say to you."

He held her eyes for a long moment, then walked out, closing the door very quietly, but very firmly, behind him.

It's much too late, it's much too late, it's much too late. Again and again that phrase echoed in Cate's head as she walked slowly along the corridors where she had hurried earlier. As long as she was at the hospital she ought to go see Melissa . . . as soon as she was sure she had her emotions under control.

She smiled when she peered into Melissa's room. "Hi there! How are you?"

"Hi, Cate!" Melissa cried, sitting up straight and grinning happily at her. The rag-doll Cate was sitting proudly on the pillow beside her. "I've got something for you!"

"Do you really?" Cate asked, smiling. It wasn't as hard this time. "What is it?"

"This!" With the flourish of a magician producing a rabbit from his hat, she pulled something small and shiny from under her pillow.

"What is it?" Cate walked over and perched on the edge of the bed.

"Hold out your hands and close your eyes," Melissa ordered.

Cate obeyed, closing her eyes tightly and extending her cupped hands. Something small and light dropped into her palm.

"You can look now," Melissa said with a giggle in her voice.

Cate opened her eyes, then opened her hands to reveal a small, rather lumpy circle of carefully molded tinfoil. Melissa watched her with sparkling eyes above the hands she had clamped over her mouth to stifle her giggles.

"It's a ring!" she announced. "And I made it for you!"

"Oh, Melissa, thank you!" Cate tried it on her fingers until she fitted it on the middle finger of her right hand. "It's really pretty, sweetheart." She leaned over and hugged Melissa tight, biting her lip against the tears that threatened. "Thank you so much!"

"Do you wanta know what kind of ring it is?"

"Of course I do." She loosened her arms so she could lean back and look into Melissa's pale, eager face. "What kind of ring is it?"

Melissa giggled behind her hand again, her eyes wide and bright with excitement. "It's a wedding ring!" she stage-whispered.

"A wedding ring!" Cate exclaimed. "Are you going to marry me, Melissa?"

"No! You're silly! I can't marry you, 'cause I'm a girl!" She leaned close, pulling Cate down so she could whisper in her ear. "It's for you to marry Dr. Jesse!"

Cate stiffened, then straightened slowly, forcing a smile, hoping Melissa wouldn't notice anything amiss.

"That's nice of you, honey, but you can't just tell two people go get married."

"Don't you like Dr. Jesse?"

"Oh, yes, I do, but we're friends. We aren't at the getting married stage."

"You're not gonna get married?"

"No, honey. Like I said, we're friends."

"Oh." Melissa scowled at the blanket. "I guess you don't want your ring, huh?"

"Yes, I do!" Cate asserted. "It's a beautiful ring, and you made it for me. Of course I want it! And you know what?" she asked conspiratorially.

"What?" Melissa began to smile tentatively again.

"Since you're my friend, this can be a friendship ring, all right?"

"Really?" she asked, wide-eyed.

"Sure." Cate grinned.

"You're really my friend?"

"Sure I am!" She reached out again to hug the little girl, and this time a tear trickled onto the fine, silky brown hair she smoothed with her hand.

Chapter Fifteen

Cate sniffed hard, swallowed the tears and sat up straight again, smiling mistily. "You are a sweet girl, Melissa Cotton, and your mommy and daddy should be very proud of you."

Melissa blushed with pleasure and ducked her head. "You're sweet, too, Cate," she whispered shyly.

Cate extended her hand, fingers spread to admire the ring. "I think my ring's really pretty, don't you?"

Melissa raised her head to look at the ring. The painstakingly molded tinfoil sparkled in the light. It *was* a pretty ring. The little girl's gap-toothed smile lit up the room. "Yeah. I think it looks pretty on your hand."

"What looks pretty?" Jesse asked from the doorway.

Cate's head jerked around at the sound of his voice. Her smile stiffened, and she slid off the bed. "Dr. Jesse's got to see you now, Melissa, so I'll come back some other time, okay?"

"Do you have to go?" Melissa pouted at her, but Cate was already moving toward the door.

"Yes, honey, I have to. I'll see you tomorrow." She slid past Jesse without looking him in the face. "Bye-bye!"

"Cate, wait!" He spoke softly, urgently. Reluctantly she stopped just outside Melissa's door.

"Yes?" She didn't quite meet his gaze.

"I thought you'd want to know. I got Melissa's latest pathology report." Cate's eyes opened wide, and she looked Jesse in the face for the first time.

"What is it?" she whispered.

"It's good." He half smiled, happy about the news, but unwilling, or unable, to share his happiness with Cate. "She'll have to have another week of chemo and then one more week in the hospital, but it looks like she'll be all right."

"Oh, Jesse!" Cate breathed, and lifted her hands to reach for him. He moved back, and she let her hands fall to her sides. No, she couldn't hug Jesse in her happiness. She closed her eyes against the pain and the gladness. "Oh, thank God," she whispered. She steadied herself and looked at him. "Thank you for telling me."

"Yeah." He turned his back and walked into Melissa's room. As she walked Cate could hear him asking again what was pretty. She prayed she could trust Melissa not to tell him what she'd made the ring for. It was too late even for jokes about love and marriage.

Too late. The grim words echoed in her brain as she worked to rewrite her article. She took the article apart and wrestled with the words, the ideas, until the pages blurred before her eyes and she could no longer decide how a point should be made.

It took her three exhausting days. When she'd finished she had subtly refocused the entire article on the hospital and the kids there. Jesse was still the pivot point, but he was no longer the sole character. She had tried to hint at the man Jesse was while concentrating on the work he was doing. She revealed nothing that he wished to keep private. She thought she had succeeded in writing an article Jesse would approve of. She desperately hoped she had.

She took it to the *Washington Month* offices herself and sat in John's office while he read it. She kept her left hand in her pocket, her fingers surreptitiously crossed. When he laid the last typewritten page aside John looked up at her with a gloomy scowl.

"I hate to say this." he paused for dramatic effect. Cate felt her pulse accelerate as she waited for the other shoe to drop. "I hate to say it, but I like this." He didn't look pleased; in fact, he looked dismayed, but Cate knew him by now.

"Better than the other one?" she asked carefully.

John thought about that, frowning at the pages and photos scattered across his desk. "I'm not sure why, but I think this is a better article." He shook his head, then looked across the desk at her. "What's different?"

"The focus." Cate shrugged. "I tried to keep Jesse as the centerpiece, but focus on the hospital and the kids, make it clear how badly the renovation is needed."

"That's it." John nodded. "There's a definite focus now, and the whole thing builds to a point, a conclusion. The first article was more of a fan letter to your doctor friend." He looked sidelong at her. "No offense, Cate, but I think it's more interesting this way."

"No offense taken." Cate let herself smile at last. She hadn't realized how tense she was until she relaxed, and noticed how wrung out she felt. "You don't know how badly I wanted to hear you say it's still a good article."

"Not just good, better." His lips twitched in the closest he ever got to a smile, and he rose. "I'll send you the proofs in a couple of days."

"Thank you, John." She let him walk her to the office door. "Could you do me a favor, though?"

"What's that?"

"Could you send me two sets of proofs? There's someone else who needs to see them."

"No problem," he said, shrugging.

"Thanks, John." He opened the door, and she paused beside him. "You're a sweetie." She kissed his cheek quickly, then walked out.

The proofs arrived by messenger late Friday afternoon. Cate snatched the package out of the poor man's hands, shoved his tip at him and tore the envelope open before he was halfway down the stairs.

It was even better than she'd hoped. She spread the long sheets out on the kitchen table and studied them, visualizing the impact the pictures would have when advertising had been inserted around them. It was good, really good. The pictures had been arranged to complement the text, and the message came through clearly. She stood back and nodded at the pages then went to get an envelope.

She had come up with a plan. This was her last chance to reach Jesse, and if it failed she wouldn't have anything else to try. She folded the papers neatly and paperclipped them together, then took out a sheet of stationery and sat down to write.

She poised the pen over the paper and hesitated. What could she say? What words could possibly communicate to Jesse that she understood now what she'd done, that she'd been wrong, she was sorry, she'd do anything, *anything* to make it right between them again?

Her hand moved, then stopped again. Words were so easy, too easy. Actions spoke louder than words, as the saying went. She thought a moment, then bent over the paper, writing carefully, as if she were going to get a grade on her penmanship.

"Dear Jesse," she wrote. "I was wrong, utterly wrong. I'm sorrier than I can say. I love you. Cate."

Quickly, before she could change hr mind, she clipped the note to the proofs, slid everything into the envelope, then added the smaller envelope that contained his clippings and medals. Whether he wanted them or not, they were his. The messenger service that had delivered the proofs to her was more than happy, for a substantial fee, to pick this envelope up at her door and take it to Jesse's office.

The messenger arrived fifteen minutes after Cate telephoned. She paid him, gave him the envelope and watched him pedal furiously away on his bicycle. Afterward she walked back into the living room and sat down. It was too late to change her mind; she was committed. She watched the clock, following in her mind the messenger's progress from Georgetown to the hospital. After twenty minutes she knew he would have arrived. Had Jesse gotten the envelope yet? Had he opened it? Read the article? Her note? Had she done the right thing?

All evening she waited, glaring at the phone, willing it to ring. Surely he must have gotten it by now. Surely he wouldn't throw it away unopened. He would read it, she promised herself, and then he would call her, and they would talk.

He would. He had to.

She fell asleep on the sofa sometime after midnight and woke, stiff and chilled, at three in the morning. The apartment was empty and echoing around her, and she shivered as she made her way to bed. Her bed was empty and cold; she was cold, frozen through to her bones. Her tears were slow and scalding, though, and they lasted a long time.

On Monday evening she had to admit defeat. Even if Jesse had been in Virginia over the weekend, he was home now; he must have gotten the envelope, must have read her note and her article. If he hadn't called her yet it was because he wasn't going to call her, wasn't going to forgive her.

She'd had a delicate treasure in her hands and broken it through her own self-centered insensitivity. She couldn't rail at fate or higher powers; she had no one to blame but herself, and the knowledge had a bitter taste.

Ten after ten, the kitchen clock said, and Jesse hadn't called. Face it, she told herself, he's not going to. She lifted the curtain and saw only the usual complement of late-night strollers on the street below. A few lazy snowflakes drifted past the glass. She dropped the curtain into place and turned away, hesitating.

She hadn't been outside in over three days, but there was no point in staying inside any longer. Jesse wasn't going to call her. She was sick of being cooped up, and she suddenly knew where she wanted to go. In a flurry she strode out of the room, pulled a coat from the closet and dragged it on as she trotted down the outside steps. She belted the camel-hair reefer close around her and turned up the collar against the frosty December evening, then stuffed her hands in her pockets and walked at a steady pace, threading her way through the flow of evening strollers.

She didn't see the bright lights, the people and the color all around her. She walked on, oblivious, intent on her goal.

It was quiet there, only a few people walking past the wall, looking for names, talking softly. Cate stood in the trees a little distance away, remembering her dream. She could almost see Brad there, calling to her from behind the black granite. What would he say, if she could talk to him again? What would he tell her?

She walked forward slowly out of the trees and across the grass to the wall. She touched his name lightly. He'd been only a boy, her husband, a boy and a husband and a soldier, so young. He was always cheerful, finding the best in everything, with no dark side to his personality. What would he have been like if he'd come back from that steaming jungle? Would he still have possessed that wonderful optimism, or would the jungle and the war have changed him?

She had loved him completely, with a girl's simple love, pure and uncomplicated. She was no longer capable of that kind of love; she had changed, grown. She'd been tried and tempered by sudden tragedy. Brad's death had pulled her from youth to maturity with a brutal jerk, and the pain had been so great that she'd hidden her emotions away for ten years rather than face that kind of loss again.

But then she met Jesse at this wall one morning, and she had begun to let herself feel again, let herself care and love again. And now she faced another loss, a loss she had brought on herself. Only she hadn't really lost Jesse; she'd driven him away.

Her intentions had been good, of course, but good intentions counted for very little when the result was so unremittingly bad. A tear slid down her cheek. Cate brushed it away impatiently and sniffed hard.

"I wish I could tell him, Brad," she said softly, gazing at his name on the wall. "I wish I could just talk to him for a few minutes and explain. I wish he would listen to me, but he hates me too much for that now."

She touched Brad's name, and a snowflake drifted onto her hand. More flakes were floating down around her as the snow began. A little breeze caught the snow and sent a ghostly eddy across the frozen grass.

"I know it's my fault. I know how badly I hurt him. I only wanted to help him, but I should have understood. More than anybody, I should have understood that I couldn't force him through the pain. I should have known what that would do to him. I did it, though, and now I have to live with the consequences." She sighed shakily, hopelessly. "I just wish I could talk to him," she whispered.

"And if you could talk to him," said a deep, male voice behind her, "what would you say?"

Cate whirled around, clutching her throat. Heart thumping frantically, she stared wide-eyed into the swirling snow. Jesse walked out of the darkness, stopped a yard away from her.

"What are you doing here?" she demanded in a thin, breathless voice she barely recognized as her own.

"I got your package this evening."

"This evening?" she asked idiotically. "I sent it on Friday. By messenger."

"I was out of town. I left for Virginia at noon on Friday." He took a step closer, watching her steadily, his face unreadable, his voice without emotion, neither angry nor warm. "What would you say?" he repeated, "if you could?"

Cate shook her head and looked down at the dusting of snow on the grass. "I don't know. I don't know if there's any point in saying anything now. It's probably too late...like you said."

"And if it's not? What would you say?" he insisted.

"I'd say—" Cate's throat was dry, and her voice cracked. She swallowed hard. "I'd say that I was wrong," she whispered. "I'd say that I was trying to help you, but I went far beyond my rights. I acted without thinking. I tried to force you to come face to face with the past. I thought it would help, but I had no right to try to force you that way. I'd say that I understand now what I did to you, and what it would have meant to have all of Washington reading those things in a magazine."

"But they won't read those things now, will they?" Jesse's voice was very quiet, as hushed as the snowy night. He stepped closer, reaching out to brush the snow off her shoulder. His touch was light, but she missed it when it was gone. "They won't read it, will they? Because the article is different now. You changed it."

"Yes. I made John give it back to me, and I rewrote it."

"Why did you do that? I thought you were proud of your work."

She shook her head gravely. "I was. It was a good article, but I was wrong to do it the way I did. I had to change it. I wanted to."

"Are you proud of the new article?" He watched her carefully as he waited for her reply.

"Yes," she told him without hesitation. "It's a better piece of work than the first one."

"Why do you say that? You liked the first version."

"I know I did. I liked it because it was about you. I enjoyed writing about you; it was easy for me to do. I worked a lot harder on the second version."

"Because you were changing it?"

"Because I was keeping the article focused." She shivered as the light, erratic wind gusted, rustling the leafless trees and swirling snow off the grass above the wall. Jesse frowned and pulled her collar closer under her chin, his fingers brushing her throat as he wrapped her muffler snugly around her neck. Cate felt a little glow of warmth inside her that had nothing to do with the muffler and everything to do with Jesse's touch.

"Focused on what?" he asked. "I don't understand."

"The first article didn't have a real focus. I didn't make a point because I was too busy concentrating on painting a glowing picture of you, and I just sort of loosely hung the rest of the article around that. The second time I made sure everything I wrote and every picture I used had a direct bearing on the hospital and the kids. It makes the point that the renovation is needed now. It didn't before."

"I'm glad you think it's better. I wouldn't want you to have to turn in something second-rate."

She lifted her chin proudly. "I wouldn't turn in something second-rate. If I hadn't been able to do a rewrite that was at least as good as the first article, I'd have pulled it from consideration."

"You could do that?" He was surprised.

"Yes. I hadn't signed anything or accepted money for the sale."

"Did the editor mind?"

"He wasn't happy about it at first. He thinks the rewrite is better, though."

Jesse nodded, then looked down for a moment. "When will it be published?"

"Probably in the February issue."

"Not until then?"

"They'll have to rush to get it in that soon. It wouldn't go in then except that they've been holding the space for it."

"But even though they were holding the space, you'd have pulled the article if you hadn't been able to rewrite it?"

She nodded.

"Would that have hurt your career?"

"It wouldn't have helped. Certainly I wouldn't have had a very good reputation with magazine editors."

"But you would have done it anyway." He looked into her eyes. "Why?"

Cate couldn't lie to him. "Because I love you."

If she'd hoped for some reaction, she was disappointed. "You said that in your note. You said it when you were trying to explain what you did, too. Why didn't you say it to me before?"

"Because I was afraid."

"Of what?" His voice was cool and only mildly interested. It took all Cate's courage to reply, but she knew this might be her only chance. She had to tell him the truth, whatever the cost.

"Of rejection, embarrassment, hurt pride." She swallowed hard and looked into his face. "I was afraid to be the first to say it. That was cowardly. I love you, Jesse."

His face didn't change. The little warm glow that had started inside her died away, and Cate felt the cold creeping into her soul. She had tried, and she had failed. She stepped back, turning away from him.

"It's late. You must have things you need to do," she said. "I'm sorry I took up your time." She didn't look back as she walked away.

After two steps he caught her arm. She looked up in surprise as he pulled her to a stop. "You weren't the only one who was afraid," he said. She stared mutely at him, afraid of what she was thinking. "I was scared, too. I love you, Cate."

"No!" She shook her head in quick denial. This wasn't true; it couldn't be. "I saw your face when you found out I'd taken your medals and things. You hate me! I saw your face!" She jerked free and began to run.

"Cate! Stop!" He caught her in only a few yards, grabbing her arm and swinging her around, stumbling and struggling, into his embrace. "Stop it, Cate! Please don't fight me! I love you! Can't you understand that? I love you!"

She was crying, sobbing bitterly, her fragile control shattered. She fought to get away from him, shaking her head in hysterical denial. Jesse tangled his hand in her hair, stilling her head long enough for him to find her mouth with his.

The kiss was hard and hot, shocking Cate into stillness. The stiffness left her body bit by bit, and Jesse pulled her closer, bending her back against the hard support of his arm, arching her body into the curve of his. He plundered her mouth, and Cate answered the demand of his kiss with her own desperate need, fed by grief and regret and despair. She slid her arms around his waist and clung to him, hardly able to believe that the nightmare was really ending.

An eternity passed before Jesse pulled his lips from hers. "I love you," he whispered against her throat. "I should have said it before. I love you."

Cate pulled her head back to look into his face. "I don't deserve your love, Jesse."

"Why not?" he demanded, frowning.

"Because of what I did. I hurt you so much." Cate forced herself to meet his gaze. "I tried to force you to deal with the memories by dredging them up. I brought out all the bad memories, and did it in a public way, even though I knew what it had done to you, what it's still doing to you." Tears stung her eyes, and she blinked them back. "I can't forgive myself for that, Jesse. I tried to force something that has to come slowly. I knew that, and I did it anyway. I'm sorry." Her voice wobbled. "That doesn't seem like enough, but I'm so sorry...."

She squeezed her eyes closed and buried her face in his chest, unable to go on.

"Oh, sweetheart." Jesse smoothed his hand over her hair, stroking, soothing, comforting. "Oh, Cate, I never meant to hurt you."

She shook her head against his coat. "No, Jesse, it's the other way around. I hurt you. I didn't mean to, I really didn't, but I was so sure I could make things happen the way I wanted just by forcing the issue." She was babbling, but she didn't seem to be able to stop. "I didn't think about how it would be, what it would do to you, bringing up all that stuff again." She jerked her head up, staring at him, her eyes wide and dark with self-condemnation. "I wanted it to make everything all right, so I told myself it would. I took too much on myself when I found that stuff buried in the drawer. I just took it and used it and never thought about the possibility that it would hurt you. I can't forgive myself for that, Jesse."

"You have to." He caught her chin when she would have lowered her head again. "You have to forgive yourself, because I already have." Cate opened her mouth to speak, but he laid his fingers across her lips. "I love you, and that's why I overreacted. I was hurt and angry, and I didn't stop to think that I'd never told you how I feel about the war. I just expected you to read my mind. You meant well, but I wouldn't listen to what you tried to say. I have no excuse for attacking you that way."

She pulled his hand away. "You don't need an excuse, Jesse. I gave you one."

"No. I didn't like what you'd done, but there was a better way to deal with it. I'm sorry I put you through all this."

"Don't be sorry, Jesse. Please don't." She laid her hands along his cheeks. "You were absolutely right, and I was utterly wrong."

"I don't agree. I think we were both a little bit wrong," he said gravely. "And I'm glad that it's over and done with. It's in the past. We can put it behind us, where it belongs."

"In the past?" she asked. "That past is always with us, Jesse." She glanced beyond him at the smooth black granite, at the columns of names looking out of the past at them. "You can't forget it."

"We don't have to forget," he said slowly. "What we have to do is remember, and learn from the memories." Holding Cate securely in his arms, he turned to look at the wall. "What would he say about this?"

"Brad?" Cate thought about him and smiled. "He'd congratulate us, and then he'd ask why on earth I'd waited all these years to start living again." She looked up at the man beside her, scarred by his past but still strong, looking forward to his future. "He loved me, Jesse. He wouldn't begrudge me my happiness."

"No, he wouldn't, would he?" Remembering, Jesse gazed at the wall for a moment. He nodded, a little salute to Brad, then turned with Cate tucked against his side and began to walk toward Constitution Avenue. "He'd be glad to know you're getting married again."

Cate stopped short. "What?"

"You're getting married again," Jesse repeated and pulled her along. "Come on, Cate. You're going to freeze to death, standing out here all night."

Stunned, she let him drag her down the sidewalk. "What do you mean, I'm getting married again?" she demanded. He didn't answer. *"Jesse!"*

He glanced down at her, his face patient. "You're getting married again. To me."

"Since when?"

"Since right now. I love you. You love me." He grinned. "It's simple; I'm making an honest woman of you."

"An honest—" She searched for words. "Jesse, that's Neanderthal!"

"Not in the least." He hauled her along the sidewalk, setting a brisk pace. "I just feel I ought to do the right thing by you," he added reasonably, "since I'm taking you home to make love to you all night long."

"Oh," she replied in a very small voice.

"We'll get married in Virginia," he informed her calmly. "There's no wait for a license there. I checked. In D.C. you have to wait till five days after the blood test."

Cate said nothing at all for half a block. When they stopped to wait for a traffic light to change she looked up at Jesse's face. He looked younger in the glow of the streetlights, like the Jesse she remembered from childhood. She laid her head on his shoulder.

"There's one problem," she said, and felt the movement as he looked down at her.

"Oh, yeah? What?"

"You haven't asked me to marry you." The traffic light changed, and she stepped off the curb, pulling Jesse with her.

"Will you marry me?" he asked in the middle of the street.

They crossed the street and stepped up onto the sidewalk again. "On one condition."

"What's that?"

"That we have Melissa for a flower girl, if she's well enough."

"She should be." He considered for a moment. "That sounds reasonable to me. After all, she told me I ought to marry you."

"She didn't!"

"She certainly did. She was really peeved with me for not doing it sooner." He chuckled.

"So this is all Melissa's idea?" Cate asked. "You didn't even think of it yourself?" She shook her head firmly. "In that case the deal's off, Jesse. I can't marry a man who didn't come up with the idea on his own."

"Not even if he loved you more than he thought it was possible to love a woman?" His voice was low and seductive. "Not even if he knows that he can't live without you?"

Cate shook her head, unable to speak for the emotion tightening her throat and stinging her eyes. Jesse pulled her into a darkened shop doorway and turned her into his arms.

"Not even," he murmured against her throat, "if he's going to take you home and make love to you until you can think of nothing but him?"

She looked into his face, loving it, loving him. She stroked his cheek with her fingertips. "You promise?" she whispered, and he gave a spurt of startled laughter.

He cupped her face in his hands and lifted it to his. "I promise," he swore to her, "for all our future, till death do us part."

And when Jesse kissed her, she knew the future was theirs, born out of the past, but unclouded by it, bright and shining. She wound her arms around his neck and gave him her love.

Silhouette Brings You:

Silhouette Christmas Stories

Four delightful, romantic stories celebrating the holiday season, written by four of your favorite Silhouette authors.

> **Nora Roberts**—*Home for Christmas*
> **Debbie Macomber**—*Let It Snow*
> **Tracy Sinclair**—*Under the Mistletoe*
> **Maura Seger**—*Starbright*

Each of these great authors has combined the wonder of falling in love with the magic of Christmas to bring you four unforgettable stories to touch your heart.

Indulge yourself during the holiday season...or give this book to a special friend for a heartwarming Christmas gift.

Available November 1986

XMAS-1

Silhouette Desire

**Available
October 1986**

California Copper

The second in an exciting new
Desire Trilogy by Joan Hohl.

If you fell in love with Thackery—the
laconic charmer of *Texas Gold*—you're
sure to feel the same about his twin
brother, Zackery.

In *California Copper*, Zackery meets the
beautiful Aubrey Mason on the windswept
Pacific coast. Tormented by memories,
Aubrey has only to trust...to embrace
Zack's flame...and he can ignite the fire in
her heart.

The trilogy continues when you
meet Kit Aimsley, the twins' half
sister, in *Nevada Silver*. Look for
Nevada Silver—coming soon from
Silhouette Books.

DT-B-1